PRESENT IMPERFECT

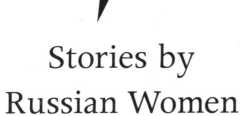

Stories by Russian Women

edited by

AYESHA KAGAL
AND NATASHA PEROVA

Introduction by

HELENA GOSCILO

WestviewPress
A Division of HarperCollinsPublishers

"A Marriage of Convenience" by Ksenia Klimova first appeared in *Stolitsa,* no. 52 (1992). "Witch's Tears" by Nina Sadur first appeared in *Ne pomnyashchaya zla* (Moscow: Moskovsky Rabochy, 1990). "The Three 'Loves' of Masha Peredreeva" by Galina Scherbakova first appeared in *Chistye prudy* (Moscow: Moskovsky Rabochy, 1990). "Cabiria from the Bypass" by Marina Palei first appeared in *Novyi mir,* no. 3 (1991).

Copyright © 1996 by Westview Press, Inc., A Division of HarperCollins Publishers, Inc.

Published in 1996 in the United States of America by Westview Press, Inc., 5500 Central Avenue, Boulder, Colorado, 80301-2877, and in the United Kingdom by Westview Press, 12 Hid's Copse Road, Cumnor Hill, Oxford OX2 9JJ. A slightly different version was first published as *Conscience Deluded* in India in 1994 by Kali for Women.

Library of Congress Cataloging-in-Publication Data
Present imperfect : stories by Russian women / edited by Ayesha Kagal
and Natasha Perova ; introduction by Helena Goscilo.
    p.   cm.
  "A slightly different version first published as 'Conscience
deluded' in India in 1994 by Kali for Women"--CIP pref.
  ISBN 0-8133-2675-3.—ISBN 0-8133-2676-1
  1. Short stories, Russian—Women authors—Translations into
English. 2. Russian fiction—20th century—Translations into
English. I. Kagal, Ayesha. II. Perova, Nataliia. III. Goscilo,
Helena, 1945– .
891.73'01089287—dc20   96-3383
                    1000720052   CIP

This book was typeset by Letra Libre, 1705 Fourteenth Street, Suite 391, Boulder, CO 80302.

The paper used in this publication meets the requirements of the American National Standard for Permanence of Paper for Printed Library Materials Z39-1984.

10   9   8   7   6   5   4   3   2   1

Present Imperfect

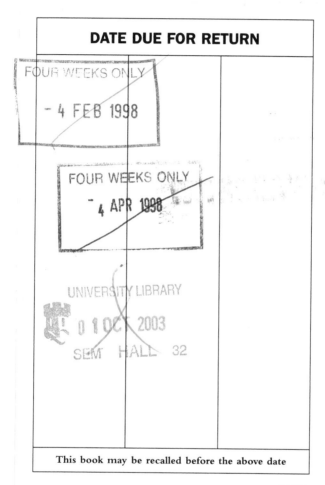

Contents

HELENA GOSCILO

INTRODUCTION

U NTIL THE 1980s, Russian women's fiction often lacked bite: It
tended to settle for politically safe themes, unmemorable character portrayal, plotlines that neither intrigued nor challenged the reader, and a
rather flaccid style of fatigued realism. With a few memorable exceptions,
such as Natalya Baranskaya's *A Day Like Any Other* (1969), I. Grekova's
"Ladies Hairdresser" (1963), Galina Scherbakova's "Wall" (1979), and
several mildly ironic stories by Viktoria Tokareva, that fiction coasted
along largely unnoticed. Its docility paralleled women's tacit accommoda-
tion with their unacknowledged status as second-class citizens in a society falsely advertising itself as gender-democratic.

Contrary to George Orwell's dire prediction, the eighties brought not
only perestroika but also several remarkable individual female talents in
addition to a post-Stalin generation of young women writers whose sense
of self and text clearly signaled a new sensibility. Tatyana Tolstaya made
her stunning debut in 1983 with "'On the Golden Porch ... ,'" and subsequently published a series of playfully profound stories unequaled in
their dense verbal texture, lushly poetic style, and tantalizing shifts in
viewpoint.[1] Ludmilla Petrushevskaya, whose first stories appeared in
1972, but whose later works were systematically rejected by countless
journals for a full decade, suddenly found acceptance and even popularity. Her psychologically freighted, deceptively laconic litanies of existential horror introduced readers to her unique authorial signature: the
obsessively garrulous narrator harboring ghastly secrets that surface

through a colloquial, often agrammatical language designed for defensive obfuscation.[2] The receptivity of Russian culture to physiology during and after glasnost (what Russians call *chernukha,* roughly translated as "grime and slime") assured Petrushevskaya's stark portrayal of life's underbelly a ready, if sometimes uncomfortable, audience. Toward the close of the decade, Ludmilla Ulitskaya finally broke into print with her marvelously insightful, fine-tuned portraits of small and adolescent girls, young, middle-aged, and old women, often projected against a background of historical turmoil or social oppression. Ulitskaya's clarity of vision and strong command of language sounded a genuinely fresh note in her affectionate depiction of Jewish life and frank but unsensationalist exploration of sexual impulses in all their manifestations. Although at first glance Ulitskaya's stories resemble Petrushevskaya's in their gynocentrism and taboo-breaking, on closer inspection, their unshakable faith in the significance and effectiveness of ethical behavior contrasts with Petrushevskaya's bleak conviction that people are fundamentally maimed and isolated in an alienated world.

As the Soviet Union crumbled, in an unprecedented publishing venture, Larisa Vaneeva and Svetlana Vasilenko compiled and saw through publication two anthologies of New Women's Writing: *The Woman Who Remembers No Evil* (1990) and *The New Amazons* (1991). Russian critics' shocked response to the contents, which included works by Vaneeva, Vasilenko, Nina Sadur, Irina Polyanskaya, Marina Palei, Valeria Narbikova, and Elena Tarasova, left no doubt that these narratives violated stale Soviet preconceptions of what is permissible or desirable in women's writing. Disapproval focused above all on what critics called the "unnecessary" explicitness of physical details and on the "unladylike" behavior of the female protagonists.[3] Indeed, both volumes not only enthusiastically embrace a "disobedient," transgressive concept of female creativity, but, for the first time in contemporary Russia, programmatically assert their status as specifically women's texts.

What apparently escaped affronted critics' notice was the thematic and stylistic diversity, vital imagination, and verbal boldness that mark many of the narratives. Not only do the selections bear the distinctive imprint of each author's voice but their aesthetic and emotional impact makes earlier women's fiction seem rather generic and timorously pallid by comparison. In that respect the entries in *Present Imperfect* both mirror and overlap with the two Russian anthologies, which also contain stories by Vasilenko, Palei, Polyanskaya, and Nina Sadur. As four of the most original practitioners of New Women's Prose—that is to say, narratives by the post-Stalinist generation that unhesitatingly transgress against Russia's inbred Victorianism about bodily matters—that quartet would inevitably be included by anyone assembling a volume of current Russian women's fiction. Together with the other authors here, they provide a reliable index of the range, depth, and richness of that segment of Russian cultural production today.

The late Lydia Ginzburg, like Ksenia Klimova, stands somewhat apart from the rest, both by virtue of her profession (she made her living as a critic) and the nature of her text. "Conscience Deluded" is characteristic of Ginzburg's manner in that its location on the border between fictional narrative and philosophical essay exemplifies the problem of categorizing her writing according to genre. In its meticulous dissection of multiple levels of moral psychology, this meditation on filial guilt, self-delusion, and the infinite complexity of our inner censoring mechanisms recalls Ginzburg's evocative recreations of the Leningrad blockade as well as some of her up-close cultural analyses.[4] As "Conscience Deluded" illustrates, it would be an exaggeration to claim that gender is even a peripheral issue for Ginzburg, whose concerns accord completely with High Culture masculinist preoccupations. Indeed, the figure of the remorseful but dithering son from the intelligentsia whose stunted sentiments retract almost completely in his father's hour of need stands at the heart of Andrey Bitov's fiction, with which Ginzburg's narrative has appreciably more in common than it has with the other selections in this volume. Thus the value of Ginzburg's narrative in this anthology is that of Otherness; notwithstanding her renowned mentoring of young Leningrad/Petersburg female poets, Ginzburg as author of "Conscience Deluded" represents, in a sense, what New Women's Prose both implicitly and explicitly defined itself *against*. Above all, the rigorous exclusion of all sensuality and sexuality in a text that deals with the gradual extinction of the human body underscores the peculiar sexlessness of Ginzburg's perspective on life, as if her public solution to her lesbianism demanded a denial or a radical marginalization of all libidinous appetite. "Conscience Deluded" may best be read, perhaps, as a contrast to the other selections in the anthology.

Known principally as a journalist, Klimova likewise straddles genres in her short pieces on the dispossessed and socially stigmatized, which implicitly argue for a more enlightened attitude toward the physically handicapped. Although physiology is a salient element in the poetics of Petrushevskaya, Palei, Ulitskaya, Vasilenko, Vaneeva, and Scherbakova, irreversible bodily affliction as a sociopsychological dilemma plays little part in their oeuvres.[5] Since Russians are more inclined to dwell on spiritual and emotional malaise, Klimova's emphasis on the partly incapacitated body—drawn in "Steps" without bathos—represents something rare in contemporary Russian prose.[6] By contrast, "A Marriage of Convenience" belongs to the sizable corpus of recent women's literature that demythologizes the institution of marriage, exposing it as a pragmatic arrangement untouched by the much-vaunted panacea of love. If formerly marriage and, above all, love tended to be the end-all and be-all of at least younger women, those lyric dreams of a heart-match have soured into nightmares. New Women's Prose spotlights the discrepancy between the promise of love and its disillusioning reality. Although individual men's drunkenness, violence, and terminal self-involvement frequently account for the replacement of breathless expectation with contemptuous resentment, in such stories as Nina Sadur's "Worm-Eaten Sonny," the essentialist assumption is that men are inherently incapable of generosity, tenderness, and affection.

Yet current Russian women's literature hardly whitewashes female psychology and conduct either, as evidenced by Galina Scherbakova's ironically titled "The Three 'Loves' of Masha Peredreeva." In Scherbakova's sardonic treatment, the materialistic protagonist, motivated exclusively by self-love, instances a new type of woman. This type is also at the center of Tokareva's novella *First Try* (1989)[7]: The insensitive, market-oriented self-seeker for whom men serve as stepping-stones to a more comfortable future and whose priorities clash with the preceding generation's. Although Masha's attempts to manipulate everyone in her orbit reveal simultaneously her moral and intellectual limitations and the gullibility or tough selfishness of contemporary Russian society, her petty machinations ultimately triumph.

Scherbakova vividly and economically captures the mores of "big city" life, of a small provincial town, and of the lethargic countryside, still mired in the torpor of preindustrialist rhythms. Eschewing all sentiment, she deftly conveys the spite and competitiveness of a loveless mother-daughter relationship, devoid of respect and sustained by the co-dependency that springs from the grim living conditions in Russia, which necessarily have transformed family relations into a support system fueled less by genuine attachment than contingency and an absence of alternatives. Strained, tense relationships between mothers and daughters figure prominently in contemporary Russian women's fiction (e.g., in Petrushevskaya, Nadezhda Kozhevnikova, Elena Makarova) and in film (e.g., Viacheslav Krishtofovich's *Adam's Rib* [1991]), often metonymically representing the conflicts between generations, the ruptures in Russian history that inform the novellas of Yury Trifonov and Vladimir Makanin.[8]

Generational incompatibility likewise plays a key role in Vasilenko's first-person narrative "Piggy," but serves as a prelude to anagnorisis that culminates in an affirmation of familial bonds. The frightened incomprehension of the heroine's son regarding her participation in what for him is the traumatic spectacle of slaughtering the family pig has its analogue in her alienated irritation with *her* mother, whose dowdy appearance and naive country habits elicit her daughter's pity and embarrassment. Since in Vasilenko's world—polluted by nuclear waste and human brutality—animals and children alone are the repositories of "uncontaminated" values, the combination of slain pig and her son's revulsion at the act effect the epiphany that brings about her reconciliation with both son and mother. As in Greek myth, the ritual of bloodletting restores harmony. Typical of Vasilenko, violence and physical realia that many would find offensive (the smell of sweat, urine, offal, and pig manure, the sight of spilled blood and evisceration) have a double-edged capacity to repel and wreak havoc, on the one hand, and to catalyze a self-confrontation that brings about a more profound moral awareness, on the other. Like most of Vasilenko's texts, "Piggy" makes a strong appeal to the senses through the heroine's sensual pleasure in the world refracted through her vision: We are invited to luxuriate with her in the aroma of grass, dill, and over-ripe apples, the texture of the ground under her feet, the tar on the shed, and so forth.

Whereas Vasilenko's authorial manner shares many features with that of Vaneeva and, to a lesser extent, Ulitskaya and others, she resorts to a modernist technique not often invoked in contemporary Russian women's fiction: the suspension of plot narrative through an apostrophe to the reader that refers directly to the act of authoring and thus fractures the "realist" illusion. That device, which in her prizewinning story "Going After Goat-Antelopes" (1989)[9] combines with the equally uncommon ploy of providing more than one possible ending, implies that everything in life is susceptible to narration. As soon as we attempt a narrative, we "tell stories" from an inescapably limited, subjective perspective. In a sense, this break in the regular tempo of verisimilar narrative is the equivalent of Petrushevskaya's loaded omissions, her telling silence.

Whereas Scherbakova perceives little that is redemptive or even desirable in the biological accident of family, and whereas for Vasilenko the family may provide sanctuary from existential terrors, Ulitskaya conceives of successive generations as an image and guarantor of continuity.

In "March 1953," as in "Gulia,"[10] "Barley Soup,"[11] and the novella *Sonech-ka* (1992), families transmit the legacy of humanistic values that ensure decency—a paramount imperative in her fictional world. The conclusion of "March 1953" synchronizes three separate fates, two of them entangled in the plotline elaborated in the story, the third occurring behind the scenes, in Russian history. Reminiscent of Tolstaya's "Rendezvous with the Bird," they all register a rite of passage: a young Jewish girl's entry into womanhood and her great grandfather's and Stalin's "transition" to the next world. The intersection of deaths is critical to Ulitskaya's themes of continuity and moral responsibility: The old Jewish shoemaker Aaron dies peacefully, having passed on his tolerant wisdom to the courageous Lily, a heritage that contrasts pointedly with Stalin's bloody legacy of suspicion, betrayal, and wholesale murder. Without commentary, Ulitskaya eloquently juxtaposes, on the one hand, the results of Aaron's philosophy of life—moral and physical resistance to injustice, in the form of Lily's victorious battle with Bodrik, the anti-Semitic bully—with the consequences of Stalin's, on the other—the camps, in which her Stalinist father ("the son of decent parents") works for the KGB. Thus the biological change that signals the girl's new capacity to create life and perpetuate her family line (the flow of menstrual blood) temporally coincides with the biological change (Stalin's death) that will prevent others' blood from flowing needlessly in loss of life.

In her low-key acceptance of the body, its drives and functions, Ulitskaya unproblematically refers to the groin, to pubic hair, to menstruation and vomiting, and to sexual attraction at puberty. Just as matter-of-factly she documents the anti-Semitism that persisted throughout the Soviet regime and reached its apogee during the hysterical witch-hunts under Stalin. Ulitskaya's admirable sense of balance, her capacity to understand both sides of an issue, to identify mitigating circumstances for questionable actions infuse her stories with an aura of warmth that might, but should not, be confused with sentimental reassurance.

Like Ulitskaya, but in more concentrated form and in greater detail, Marina Palei acknowledges the physical dimension in life. Her early training in medicine doubtless accounts in part for her emphasis on the body—an emphasis that runs counter to decades of Soviet puritanism and that leaps from the pages of such stories as "The Day of the Poplar Down," "The Losers' Division," and "Rendezvous."[12] Her novella *Cabiria from the Bypass*, the first third of which is extracted here, similarly flouts Soviet conventions of propriety in portraying, with humor and zest, the epic-scale sexual adventures of its insatiable heroine. Analogized through her name with the ancient gods of fertility and the idealistic prostitute from Fellini's film *The Nights of Cabiria* (1956), Cabiria devotes her energies singlemindedly to intercourse with any willing and available man. The novella has much in common with Tolstaya's "Fire and Dust," but above all it revives the tradition of Henry Fielding's *Tom Jones*, with its rollicking series of sexual encounters and its unhesitating preference for honest lust over pious repression. Presented through her female cousin's sardonic eyes—not judgmentally, but with reluctant admiration and awe—Cabiria ultimately emerges as the irrepressible, self-regenerative life force. That uncontainable robustness communicates itself on the authorial level too, for Palei mimics her protagonist's exuberance through vigorous narrative momentum and colorful verbal pyrotechnics.

Equally impressive not only in its display of the powers of language, but also in its self-assured creation of an animistic universe is Nina Sadur's story cycle *Percipient,* to which the three selections in this volume belong. With the aid of folklore, Sadur materializes a world of enigmatic, uncontrollable forces to which human volition seems irrelevant. Populated by witches, cats, and pseudohuman creatures, full of totemic objects invested with magic powers (e.g., rings, seeds, pieces of cloth, hair), this environment vibrates with emanations that point to the irrationality (or inexplicability) of its most significant phenomena. As in fairy tales and E.T.A. Hoffmann's works, beings and objects undergo transformations, people lapse into hypnotic-like states, cast spells, and experience visions and dreams that suggest contacts with an unknowable realm. That realm, ultimately, consists of the subconscious and unconscious layers of the psyche, or, in spiritual terms, the soul.

Sadur's paramount interest lies not in social, but in psychological and metaphysical issues. Hence the deaths, "births," "supernatural" communications, symbol-laden dreams and "prophesies" that reticulate throughout her narratives. Taking the traditional situation of a romance as her starting point, Sadur proceeds to encode violence, hatred, jealousy ("Witch's Tears"), awakened sexuality ("Rings"), sexual fears ("Dear Little Redhead"), and guilt in a maximally condensed, elliptic form that scrupulously omits any and all clarification. Her stories of love, female friendship, motherhood, and failed relations may be called psychic dramas, with passionate impulses and emotions (the submerged portion of the iceberg) concretized in ambiguous but tangible matter (the visible tip).

Sadur's daughter Yekaterina, a youthful newcomer to literature, clearly owes a debt to her mother, to the fin-de-siècle strand in Russian Symbolism, and to E.T.A Hoffmann's *Kunstlernovelle*. "Kozlov's Nights," in fact, reads like a recasting of Hoffmann's "The Golden Pot" in the spirit of Fyodor Sologub, who also yoked polarities—spirit and matter, good and evil, life and death, love and hatred—and explored "abnormal" psychological states (e.g., Kozlov's tormenting languor), "supernatural" powers (Alyonka), and occurrences that defy logical explanation. Sadur resorts to folklore *topoi* (e.g., magical metamorphoses, appearances and disappearances, and the seductive but deadly *rusalka* [mermaid]) to orchestrate the atmosphere of a sensual, fantastic borderline state of near-trance in which the artist Kozlov yearns and languishes. At the same time, she creates a palpable everyday world through minutely particularized descriptions that transmit the look, smell, or feel of a locale or item. For the artist Kozlov, who molds wax figures that appear to take on life, the dividing lines between tangible and imagined, alive and dead, fatal and salvatory blur and lose significance. Caught, like Hoffmann's Anselmus, between the safe love of the meek, predictable Asya (Hoffmann's Veronika) and the bewitching allure of the reputedly lethal Alyonka (Hoffmann's Serpentina), Kozlov thrashes about, awaiting his fate, which, at story's end, remains undecided. As does Nina Sadur's cycle, "Kozlov's Nights" conjures up dark forces that swallow up human will. And, just as in *Percipient,* the helpless individual remains ultimately isolated, unknowable not only to others, but also to himself.

If the Sadurs perceive the self as impenetrable, Irina Polyanskaya's "The Game" posits the transparency of others. The entire story, in fact, consists of a psychological reading by an adult woman of a girl in whom she perceives her former, immature self. Projection, identification, and semiotic skills—as key components in interpreting "the human text"—converge in this first-person record of several near-wordless chance encounters with an adolescent that trigger the act of analysis. However discerning, the narrator's dispassionate explication of the girl's naive self-presentation both finalizes the object of her ironic dissection and reveals the rigorously guarded limits of the narrator's understanding. That self-congratulatory comprehension never translates into active empathy, which would require an *emotional* output in addition to the safely intellectual observation that preserves distance. When the narrator finds her status of self-positing subject imperiled by the girl's demanding gaze, she flees from the threat of becoming an object, from losing her precarious power of detached observer, and achieves a dubious victory in the "game" by diagnosing her "opponent" as "mad." Polyanskaya's story performs the task, unusual in the Russian context, of showing woman as disengaged and aloof, unwilling to assume the role of surrogate mother—a withdrawal that belies the reassuring Russian myth of women's eternal readiness to nurture the needy and to bandage wounded psyches. Likewise, the coolly sardonic tone of Polyanskaya's narrative militates against the popular notion of women's emotional, intuitive apprehension of the world and its inhabitants.

Current women's prose in Russia, then, has extended the boundaries as well as multiplied and intensified the hues of fictionalized womanhood. In the process of doing so, it has relegated manhood and its inscription to the periphery. Of the selections in this volume, only the narratives by Ginzburg and Yekaterina Sadur proceed from a male viewpoint; Vasilenko and Polyanskaya depict an almost exclusively female universe; and in the remaining stories, men play decidedly secondary roles. Such perennial issues as ethical choice, the inviolability of the self, generational clashes, family relations, and sexuality are elaborated through women-centered plots. Resolutions hinge on decisions and actions undertaken by females of will, appetite, and energy, whether they be Ulitskaya's gutsy Lily, Scherbakova's vulgar Masha, or Palei's liberated, lascivious Cabiria.

Stylistically, too, New Women's Prose has broken fresh ground, drawing creatively on folklore and myth, engaging in wordplay, and exploiting the destabilizing potential of irony. In contrast to the wordy near-journalese of Russian women's fiction of the 1970s, today's female authors challenge and pleasure their readers through texts that engage, puzzle, and intrigue as much by the complexity of their manner as by the originality of their perspectives on reality.

Notes

1. All but one of Tolstaya's stories have appeared in English translation: *On the Golden Porch* (New York: Alfred A. Knopf, 1989) and *Sleepwalker in a Fog* (New York: Alfred A. Knopf, 1991).

2. Petrushevskaya's longest and most complex work to date is the superb, dark novella *The Time: Night* (London: Virago Press, 1994), which was shortlisted for the first Russian Booker Prize in 1992. A collection of her stories, titled *Immortal Love*, appeared in 1994, likewise published by Virago Press.

3. For samples of these reactions, see the volume of annotated translations titled *Skirted Issues: The Discreteness and Indiscretions of Russian Women's Prose*,

ed. Helena Goscilo, *Russian Studies in Literature*, vol. 28, no. 2 (Armonk: M.E. Sharpe, Spring 1992).

4. For a translation of an excerpt from her "documentary novella," as she called it, see Lydia Ginzburg, "The Siege of Leningrad: Notes of a Survivor," *Soviet Women Writing*, ed. Jacqueline Decter (New York: Abbeville Press, 1990), 23–49. For a British version of the entire text, see Lydia Ginzburg, *Blockade Diary*, trans. Alan Myers (London: Harvill Press, 1995).

5. Ulitskaya's "A Chosen People," however, is a notable exception, insofar as it offers a mystical reading of three women's physical infirmities. That story and others by authors included in this collection appear in *Lives in Transit: Recent Russian Women's Writing*, ed. Helena Goscilo (Ann Arbor, Mich.: Ardis, 1995).

6. Another example of this unusual focus is Elena Tarasova's story "The Woman Who Remembers No Evil," translated as "She Who Bears No Ill" in *Half a Revolution*, ed. Masha Gessen (Pittsburgh: Cleis Press, 1995), 96–126.

7. See *Lives in Transit* 11–36.

8. Makanin won the Russian Booker Prize in 1994. For a sample of his work, see his novella *Left Behind* in *Glasnost: An Anthology of Russian Literature Under Gorbachev*, eds. Helena Goscilo and Byron Lindsey (Ann Arbor, Mich.: Ardis, 1990).

9. See *Lives in Transit* 46–68.

10. See *Lives in Transit* 3–10.

11. See *Glas*, no. 6 (1993): 65–72.

12. See, respectively, *Half a Revolution* 62–69; *Lives in Transit* 191–202, 108–110.

LUDMILLA ULITSKAYA

MARCH 1953

It was an utterly dreadful winter, with the frosty air raw and suffocating, the clouds an especially dirty quilt that had slipped down on the hunched shoulders of a sunken sky. Great-grandfather Aaron had been bedridden since the previous autumn and was slowly dying on the narrow carpet-covered couch, looking around affectionately with sunken gray-yellow eyes and never unstrapping the phylactery with its scriptural texts from his left arm. With his right hand he held to his stomach a flat electric bed warmer enveloped in worn gray serge, the acme of technological progress at the turn of the century, which his son Alexander had brought from Vienna just before the Great War, when he had come back home as a young professor of medicine after eight years of studying abroad.

The bed warmer really ought not to have been allowed, but the mild mechanical heat alleviated Great-grandfather's pain and his oncologist son finally yielded to the old man's request. His son had no illusions regarding the size of the tumor, the extent to which it had metastasized, or the inoperability of the condition, and deferred to the quiet courage of a father who in all his ninety years had never been known to feel sorry for himself.

Little Lily, Aaron's great-granddaughter, his favorite, with her shining brown eyes and her matte black hair, would come home in her brown school tunic, covered in chalk and violet ink stains, pink and loving, and would edge over onto the couch, on his sore side. All elbows and plump knees, she would pull the tartan rug over onto herself and whisper into his scrawny, hairy ear, "Go on, Granddad ... tell me a story."

And Aaron would tell her of Daniel, or Gideon, of legendary heroes of the past and fair virgins, of wise men and czars with obscure names, all of them long-dead members of their tribe, until Lily was firmly persuaded that her great-grandfather, himself so ancient, must have known and personally remembered some of them at least.

It was a dreadful winter for Lily too. She too felt the special heaviness of the sky, the demoralization at home, the whiff of hostility in the streets. She was eleven years old. Her armpits ached and her nipples itched incessantly. From time to time a wave of disgust would break over her at all the little changes taking place in her body, the swellings and the coarse dark hairs, the pustules on her forehead; her very soul protested blindly at all these disagreeable, impure things. Absolutely everything seemed revolting and reminded her of the greasy, carroty-yellow film on the top of mushroom soup: dispiriting Gedike, whom she murdered daily on the cold piano; the scratchy woolen leggings she pulled on every morning; and the morbid violet covers of her exercise books. Only by snuggling up to her great-grandfather, who smelled of camphor and old paper, could she be delivered from the malaise that tormented her.

Lily's grandmother Bela Zinovievna was a skin specialist, and she too was a professor. She and Alexander were a sturdy pair, who between them pulled no small load. He was a tall, bony man with large ears, given to cracking rather witless jokes, but with all his wits about him when performing in the operating theater. He liked to say that all his life he had been devoted to two ladies, Bela and medicine. Bela was plump and short, with penciled eyebrows and lips painted red; her hair was a dazzling white, and she didn't give a thought to the competition's chances.

Both of them were curiously moved when they would come home from work to find the old man and the young girl lost in a world all their own. They would exchange a glance, and Bela would brush a tear from the corner of her eye, smudging the eyeliner. Her husband would drum his fingers on the table in warning and Bela would raise an open hand, as if they communicated in sign language. They had any number of such gestures, secret communications that left them with little need for words, divining everything as they did from the shared currents of their hearts.

This very alive couple recognized that their aged father was taking his leave of life, and tarrying on the threshold of death, he was passing on some rather questionable wisdom to his posterity, a young girl, herself on the threshold of puberty. The highly educated professors regarded these aeons-old legends of an ancient people as a homespun garment that human thought had outgrown, unlike their own thinking, of course, disciplined and honed by the school of European positivism in Vienna and Zurich, and trained to a scholarly athleticism. Worshiping only the cardboard god of nimble-footed scientific fact, they courageously lived their lives in comfortless but honest atheism. For all that, both of them felt that here on the threadbare couch, in the very presence of Death, who deigned to bide his time, a unique oasis was in bloom. Here there was no Jewish doctors' plot to poison the Politburo, and here the superstitious hysteria at the wickedness of the poisoners, which had possessed millions of people, had no dominion. Only here did the real poison—the fear, servility, and devil worship—retreat. Demoralized, living every day in the expectation of arrest, exile, or worse, the highly educated professors were reluctant to leave that dining room, a room shared by all in the house, where the old man lay ill, to pursue their scholarly routine. Instead they sat themselves in the armchairs beside that greatest, at the time, of all rarities, a television set (which was not, however, switched on), and listened, entranced, to the old man's cooing singsong. He was telling the tale of Mordecai and Haman.

Their smiles to each other reflected the anguish of their spirits, but they made no mention of the lunacy into which they plunged each day on leaving home.

They had lived through a great war, had lost brothers, nephews, and numerous relatives, but they had not lost each other, their little family, or the full measure of their trust, friendship, and tenderness for each other. They had achieved a solidly based and unshowy success and should, it seemed, have been able to count on a good ten years more, while health, strength, and worldly wisdom were in a happy equilibrium, to live as they had always wanted, working through an all too busy week, going away on the weekends to their newly completed dacha to play Schubert duets on the rather indifferent piano they had there, to bathe after dinner among the water lilies in the dark river, drink tea from the samovar on the wooden veranda in the slanting rays of the setting sun, and in the evening read Dickens or Mérimée and fall into sleep together in an embrace, which in forty some years had become so habitual that it was impossible to tell whether its evident comfort came from an interlocking of their convexities and concavities however they lay, or whether over the years their nocturnal embrace had reshaped their bodies into the present unity.

They already had more than their fair share of distress from the long-standing conflict with their son, who had chosen of his own free will to work in an area into which no normal human being would have been lured at any price. He occupied an exalted but vague position and lived in the frozen northeast beyond the Arctic Circle with his bear-like wife, Shura, and their young son, Alexander. The gods seemed to be mocking them by the fact that the two members of the family furthest from each other should bear the same name.

In 1943 their son had brought his older child, Lily, to the military hospital in Viatka where his parents were working twelve hours a day at the operating table. The little girl was five months old, weighed seven pounds, and looked like a shriveled doll. From that day right through to the end of the war they worked different hours, Alexander Aaronovich usually taking the night shift. Lily, restored to health and proper plumpness by Bela Zinovievna, stayed on with her grandmother and grandfather, reborn to the happy destiny of being the granddaughter of two professors. Knowing how ready her natural mother was to take offense, and Shura did on occasion come to see her, Lily's foster parents had her call them Bela and Alex. Great-grandfather she called Granddad.

Bela and Alex were sitting now in the old soft armchairs with their no-nonsense loose covers, half-turned away from the couch, pretending they were not listening to what the old man and his great-granddaughter were whispering about.

"Oh, Granddad," Lily exclaimed in horror. "You mean to say they hanged absolutely all the enemies from a gallows?"

"I'm not saying one thing was good and another bad. I'm just telling you what happened," Great-grandfather answered, with a suggestion of regret in his voice.

"Other people will come to get even, and kill Mordecai," the little girl said anxiously.

"Yes, of course," he said, cheering up for some reason. "Quite right. That's just what did happen. Other people came and killed those people, and then all over again. ... Let me tell you this, though. Israel lives not through victories: Israel lives because of ..." He put his left hand with the phylactery strap to his forehead and extended the fingers upward. "Do you understand?"

"Because of God?" the girl asked.

"There now, I said you were a clever girl." Great-grandfather Aaron smiled his toothless, baby smile.

"Did you hear what he's filling the child's head with?" Bela asked her husband in vexation when they were alone in their bedroom, lying on what Alex laughingly called their double writing desk.

"Bela, my sweet, he's a simple shoemaker, my father, but it's not for me to lecture him. To tell the truth, I sometimes think I would have been better off a shoemaker myself," Alex said darkly.

"What way is that to talk? You don't get to regress!" dear, clever Bela responded testily.

"Then don't you go upsetting yourself on Lily's behalf." He smiled wickedly.

"Oh, you!" Bela dismissed him. She was a practical person, not given to ethereal speculation. "That doesn't worry me in the slightest. What does worry me, though, is that she will blurt something out at school."

Alex shrugged. "My own dear Bela! That really doesn't matter any longer in the slightest."

*   *   *

Bela Zinovievna's fears were groundless. Lily had no chance to blurt anything out at school. Since last autumn nobody in her class would talk to her. Nobody except Ninka Kniazeva, whom the authorities kept meaning to send away to a school for mental defectives, only they could never get all the paperwork together. Large and pretty, Ninka had developed earlier than most girls from the north. She was the one girl in the class who, because she was feebleminded, was prepared not only to say hello to Lily but actually to be her partner when they marched in pairs loud and shrieking to some museum, which, invariably, had been awarded the Order of the Red Banner.

The times had generated their own rigid conventions: Tatars made friends with other Tatars, dunces befriended others similarly afflicted, the children of doctors played with the children of other doctors, and this was especially true of the children of Jewish doctors. Never in ancient India had the caste system been so risible and petty. Lily had been friendless since her neighbor and classmate Tania Kogan had been packed off by her parents to relatives in Riga before the New Year, with the result that the last two months had been insufferable.

Lily assumed every outburst of laughter or unwonted liveliness, every whisper was directed against her. Everywhere she went she heard them sneering and spitting out "Jew-girl" at her, and most hurtful of all was the fact that she began to associate this gluey, resinous word with their surname, with Great-grandfather Aaron and his pungent leather books, the honeyed, cinnamon smell of the Orient and the viscous golden light that always surrounded him and filled the whole of the left-hand side of the room where he lay.

To make matters worse, in some incomprehensible way the two things enfolded each other and would do so for all time, the golden light that il-luminated her home, and that sticky, sneering spit-word in the street.

        *   *   *

Barely had the hoarse bell of freedom rattled out its long-awaited mes-sage before Lily had whisked her exemplary notebooks into her briefcase and was rushing on clumsy legs to the cloakroom in order to burst out into the fresh air as soon as could be, without time even to do up the but-tons on her coat and the wretched hook at the neck. Then it was away over the lumpy, snow-gray, icy slush, through the puddles with their broken ice, her flipping and flopping galoshes splashing her stockings and the hem of her coat, one more courtyard to go, and into the stairwell of her block of apartments with its reassuring smell of damp whitewash, then up the stairs to the first floor, which didn't have a landing but only a smooth sweep of the stairs to the tall black door on which the welcoming brass plate with their awful, ridiculous, shaming surname, Yizhmorsky, was affixed.

Recently she had been contending with a further trial. As she came out of the playground Victor Bodrov would be swinging on the large, rusty gate, waiting for her. Everybody was afraid of him, and he was known in their neighborhood as Bodrik. He had blue, tinplate eyes and a nonde-script face. The game was simple enough. There was only one way out of the playground: through Bodrik's gate. As Lily approached it, trying to burrow her way as deeply as possible into the crowd, her classmates, aware of what was to come, would either draw back a little or run on ahead. When she entered the danger zone Bodrik would let her go for-ward a little before launching the gate with his foot. It would give a loathsome creak before crashing into her back. It did not hurt much, but it was humiliating. Each day the game acquired some new twist. One time Lily turned around to face the gate rather than be thumped in the back by it. She grabbed its iron rails and hung on.

Another time she stopped and waited a short way from the gate for a long time, pretending that going home was the last thing on her mind, but Bodrik was short of neither patience nor spare time, and having kept her at bay for half an hour he watched with satisfaction as she tried and failed to squeeze through the railings of the school fence. Even a skinny girl would have found it a tight fit, and Lily was further encumbered by her thick coat.

She scored a point on just one occasion by managing to skip through immediately in front of one of the teachers, elderly Antonina Vladimirov-na, whose East Siberian face registered utter amazement at such bad manners.

The sport improved daily and attracted an ever-increasing crowd of spectators with time on their hands. Only yesterday they had been rewarded with the truly remarkable spectacle of Lily's desperate and almost successful attempt to climb over the flat, spear-like tops of the school's cast-iron railings. She first wedged her briefcase between two of the railings, then stepped in a place she had spotted earlier where some of the bars were bent. She had climbed right to the top, thrown one foot over, then the other, only to realize her mistake in not having turned to face the fence. Rigid with fear, she maneuvered herself around and slithered slowly down, pressing her face against the rusty iron.

The hem of her coat caught on one of the spears. When she finally realized what was holding her back she gave it a good tug. The sturdy material of what had been a professor's overcoat before being born again to made-over life covering her plump young body, stretched to its utmost, resisting with all its well-twilled fibers.

The observers hooted ecstatically. Lily flapped again like a great fat bird and, with a low ripping sound, the coat released her. When she reached the ground Bodrik was waiting, her muddied briefcase in his hands and a genial smile on his face. "Good for you, Lily-girl. What a gymnast! Want to do it again?"

And with the practiced hand of a marksman tossing a clay pigeon he threw her briefcase up in the air, seemingly without effort, but in fact he flicked his wrist with the precision of an aborigine throwing a boomerang. The briefcase sailed upward, its sides bulging, turned over in midair, and fell back to the ground on the far side of the fence. Everybody laughed.

Lily picked up her wooly hat with its two idiotic bobbles and, without a backward glance, using all her strength not to run, went home.

Nobody chased after her. Half an hour later her devoted Ninka brought her the briefcase, which she had wiped with a handkerchief, and pushed it through the door to her. In the morning Lily tried hard to be ill, complaining of a sore throat. Bela Zinovievna took a quick look in her mouth, popped a thermometer under her arm, glanced at the elusive column of mercury, and darkly pronounced sentence. "Up you get, young lady. You've got work to do. We all have."

That was her religion, and she would not countenance the sacrilege of idleness. Lily crept unwillingly to school and sat out three class periods, oppressed by the prospect of her ineluctable passage through the gates of Hell. During the fourth period, however, something happened.

The date was March 2, and the wheel of the unsinkable ship of the Soviet state had not yet slipped from the grasp of its Great Helmsman. Alexander Aaronovich and Bela Zinovievna, had they heard from their secretive granddaughter of this incredible act of courage, would have been very heartened.

Toward the end of Lily's fourth class Antonina Vladimirovna, with a glint from the most animate part of her face, her steel teeth, locked in perpetual metallic dialogue with a silver figure-eight brooch that she wore at her collar (and that looked like a pile of doggy-do), took the polished one-and-a-half-yard pointer in her hand and headed purposefully toward a dusty, color-printed poster hanging to one side of the classroom. Holding the pointer like a rapier, she thrust its end into the unyielding word "International."

"Look over here, children," she said. "Children" was how she referred to her charges, taking exception to both the old school's "girls" and the faceless modernity of "kids." "We have here pictures of representatives of all the peoples of our great multinational motherland. Look, here are Russians and Ukrainians and Georgians and ..."—Lily sat back, half looking away in mute horror. Was she really going to say it, making the whole class turn to stare at her?—"... and Tatars," the teacher continued. Everybody turned to stare instead at Raia Akhmetova, whose face flushed darkly. But Antonina Vladimirovna continued her headlong progress down the same dangerous path, "and Armenians and Azerbizhanis ..." (she actually said that, rather than "Azerbaijanis"). She's not going to, she's not going to, ohmigod! "... and Jews!"

Lily froze. The entire class turned to stare at her.

Antonina Vladimirovna was a holy fool, a thoroughbred plebeian descended from a sacristan grandfather and a mother who took in washing. She was a spinster with a note on her medical file, "virgina intacta," and had adopted an orphan, squint-eyed, ill-natured Zoika, during the war. She was an admirer of Chernyshevsky with all his nineteenth-century didacticism, and worshiped, a feminist before her time, at the shrine of the women of social democracy, Klara Zetkin, Rosa Luxemburg, and Nadezhda Krupskaia. She believed in "the primacy of matter" as fervently as her grandfather the sacristan had believed in the Immaculate Conception, was as transparently honest as a pane of glass, and knew for a fact that although enemies no doubt were enemies, Jews were nevertheless simply Jews.

Lily failed to register the magnanimity of her gesture, conscious only of being stuck to the varnished schoolbench by the strip of bare leg between her too-short stockings and the tight elastic of her hated, itchy blue Chinese flannel panties. "And all our peoples are equal," Antonina Vladimirovna continued her sacred pedagogic duty. "There is no such thing as a bad people. Every people has its heroes and its criminals, and even enemies of the people ..."

She rambled on and got off the point, but Lily was no longer listening. She could feel a little vein throbbing beside her nose and touched the place, trying to decide whether Svetka Bagaturiia, who sat across the aisle from her, would be able to see it pulsing.

*   *   *

As she neared the school gate Lily discovered she was in luck: Bodrik wasn't there. She went skipping home with a sense of complete liberation, never stopping to think that he might be back tomorrow. The door to their apartment building, usually held tightly closed by a strong spring, was slightly ajar today, but Lily dismissed the fact. She threw the door open and, stepping from light into darkness, was able to make out only the dark silhouette of a man standing by the inner door. It was Bodrik. He had been holding the door slightly open with his foot so as to see her as she came in.

Two yards of pitch darkness separated them, but she could see that for some reason he was standing with his back pressed against the inner door, his arms spread out in a cross and his head with its thick blond hair inclined to one side. He was an actor, was Bodrik, and now he was playing a great and terrible role, which he thought was Christ when in fact it was that of a sad, brazen little thug. Opposite him stood a girl with a dolorous Semitic face, a delicate, high-bridged nose, eyes that slanted down at the corners, a caring, full-lipped mouth—the incarnation of Joseph's Mary.

"What did you Jews want to go crucifying our Christ for, then?" he asked sarcastically. From his tone you would have thought Jesus had been crucified by the Jews specifically so that he, Bodrik, would have a God-given right to wallop Lily's backside with a rusty iron gate.

She froze in anticipation, as if forgetting that she could still get back out into the courtyard and run away. The main entrance door was just behind her, but for some reason she stood transfixed.

Bodrik lunged forward, put his arms tightly round her and slid his hands down. He pulled up her coat, which was unbuttoned, and pawed that same strip of bare leg between her stocking and where the elastic of her panties was pulled up right into her groin.

She wriggled free, rushed over to one corner, and rammed her briefcase into Bodrik's soft groin. He gasped. In the total darkness she easily found the door handle and ran outside. A vivid pink flame flared in her head, the air burst into flames around her, and such crimson rage suffused everything around that she shook violently, barely able to contain the immensity of an emotion that she could not name but that knew no bounds.

The door slowly opened and, shoulder first, slightly off balance, Bodrik emerged. She hurled herself at him, seized him by the shoulders, and with a shriek smashed him back against the door as hard as she could. The surprise of the attack completely bewildered him. The feelings he had long felt toward her, a mixture of attraction, spite, and an unacknowledged envy of her clean, well-fed life, were no match for the strength and inner conviction of the unadulterated rage that was seething in her soul.

He tried to break away and shake her off, but couldn't. He couldn't even get a good enough swing to punch her. He only succeeded in maneuvering himself around the corner from the entrance door into an alcove in the wall where at least they were not in full view of people walking through the courtyard. Even this was not to his advantage. She shook him by the shoulders and now beat his head against the rough gray stone. His teeth began chattering and he succeeded only in freeing one hand and drawing it twice down her sweating red face, not even like a man with his fist clenched, but open, leaving four shameful dirty scratch marks. She did not even feel it. She kept hurling him back against the wall, until suddenly the rage broke free from her like an inflated red balloon and drifted away. Then she let him go, turned an undefended back, and without crediting him with the initiative to attack her from behind, tromped back unhindered to the entryway.

How she had fancied him last summer. She had stood behind grandmother's net curtains watching him for hours as he waved his long pole with the cloth flapping on the end of it, his doves rising lazily, circling above the dovecote like a disorderly crowd before forming up, making great, smooth circles that grew wider and wider, and then flying away into the fresh, washed summer sky. She would slow down deliberately as she walked past the place where the Bodrovs lived, a shack with only two windows that had the dovecote, a shed for the rabbits, and a chicken coop attached to it. She would eye the fascinating intimate details of somebody else's private life, the iron kegs, the workbench at which the elder Bodrov busied himself, having recently emerged to a no doubt short-lived spell of freedom from his more traditional state of incarceration, the rusty water heater left lying outside ...

At the end of the summer Bela Zinovievna, who relentlessly observed anachronistic obligations of the rich toward the poor that only she remembered, sent Lily to the yardkeeper's house with a starchily ironed and neatly folded pile of the clothes that Lily had rapidly outgrown that year. The Bodrov girls, Nina and Niusha, divided up Lily's goodies with much shrieking and whooping. Tonia the yardkeeper thanked Lily and pressed a small green cucumber into her hand, but Bodrik, who had seen her coming in the distance, took himself off to his doves and rabbits and chickens. The whole time she was in their little territory fenced off from the rest of the courtyard he never showed himself. Lily kept looking over to see whether perhaps he was going to come out.

Only now, as she stood in the entrance to her own stylish apartment building, did she realize that her handout had been a most humiliating thing for him.

Old Nastia, who had lived with them some twenty years, was not home. Lily had been going to climb into bed with her great-grandfather, but he was sound asleep, snoring occasionally, manifestly indifferent to her plight. She ran through to Grandmother's room, to the "divan of woe" as Bela Zinovievna called the chaise longue, the only item not duplicated in her realm of doubles where everything came in twos, as if the room were divided by an invisible mirror. There were two proud beds ornamented with bronze, two bedside tables, and two marginally different pictures in identical frames. On this divan of woe Lily would sleep if she was ill, when Grandmother would take her into her own room, and she would come to cry on it when something happened in her young life to upset her.

Now she was feverish. She had an ache somewhere below her stomach, and she rolled up on the divan, drawing over her head the heavy check dressing gown with its twined and fraying purple cord. She just wanted to sleep, and sleep she did, instantly, still remembering, even in sleep, how much she wanted to sleep.

She slept for a long time, but through it all there ran a nagging sense of pain and utter revulsion. Revulsion at the coarseness of the divan's pillow, revulsion at the soapy smell of "Red Moscow," Grandmother's favorite perfume, with its indecent suggestion of underwear. Overlaying it all was a boundless longing to escape into a warm, round hiding place she had always known was there, where she could sink into a deeper sleep, and where there would be neither perfume nor pain nor this unsettling sense of shame that she could not understand, a place where there would be nothing, just nothing.

She did not hear the muffled activity around her grandfather through the wall, Nastia's sobs, the quiet clink of a hypodermic needle. Great-grandfather Aaron was in a bad way.

At eight o'clock in the evening, she was awakened by her grandmother and she must have succeeded in escaping far, far away, because when she woke she could not at once tell where she was, so distant was the place from which she had to return to the paired symmetry and orderly world of Grandmother's room. She was startled by the bright face above her, which seemed unrecognizable and jumbled, as if the recesses of sleep where she had dwelt were so singular as to exclude any possibility of pairing or symmetry.

Bela Zinovievna, for her part, was examining with undisguised amazement four fresh scratch marks that ran from Lily's forehead, across her cheeks, and down to her chin.

"Good Lord, Lily. What has happened to your face?" she asked.

Lily had to think for a moment, so completely had she forgotten the events of the day. Then, all at once, everything came back to her, what had happened that day, and the week before, and last summer, but it was wholly altered, unrecognizable, and—completely unimportant. It was all just silly nonsense that had taken place a long time ago and that was already half forgotten.

"Oh, it's nothing. I had a little fight with Bodrik," Lily answered nonchalantly, a smile on her sleepy face.

"What do you mean, a little fight?" Bela Zinovievna demanded.

"Some drivel about why we crucified Christ," Lily said with a smile.

"What?" Bela Zinovievna exclaimed, knitting her black brows, and without waiting for a reply she told Lily to get dressed immediately.

An afterglow of the anger that had swept over Lily by the entrance door now suffused her grandmother.

"How low. What rank ingratitude!" Bela Zinovievna raged, dragging the reluctant Lily to the Bodrovs' shack. It wasn't just the neat thirty-ruble notes that Bela Zinovievna unfailingly gave each holiday to this unfortunate drink-sodden mother who had fallen so low, nor the piles of her Lily's still perfectly presentable hand-me-downs. What offended her symmetrical ideas of fairness was the very idea of Tonia's son raising his hand to her pure, unsullied little girl, profaning her with his dirty touch, inflicting these horrible scratches on her young dusky pink face. (She would have to remember to bathe them with permanganate.)

Bela Zinovievna knocked, then flung the rickety door open without waiting. It was impossible to tell immediately what and who was where in the room, with its large stove and lines laden with damp wash. The stench of the poverty was dreadful, a blend of urine, mold, fungus, and seaweed. Worse even than Red Moscow.

"Tonia!" Bela Zinovievna called imperiously. Something rustled behind the stove.

Lily looked around at both sides. What struck her most was the floor. It was earthen, with an intermittent covering of uneven boards. In a corner, on a broad iron bed with rusty bars exactly like those of the school railings, Bodrik was lying on a colored blanket. At his feet sat Nina and Niusha, winding broad crumpled ribbons onto the bedstead, painstakingly spitting on them before each wind. On the floor beside the bed stood a dented basin that had once been round.

Stocky little Tonia emerged rather unsteadily from behind the stove, straightening her skirt as she came. "Here I am, Belzinovna!" she smiled, and on each cheek of her broad, flat face there appeared a large dimple, as round as a belly button.

"Just you look what your Victor has done to my little girl!" Bela Zinovievna said severely, while Tonia strained her whitish eyes, still unable to make out what that was. In the dim light the scratches that had so incensed Bela Zinovievna really were barely visible. Lily retreated toward the door, embarrassed. Bodrik rolled his head, leaned over from the bed and quietly vomited into the basin.

"Oh, you shit!" Tonia shouted, turning on her son. "Get up, will you? What are you sprawling about there for?"

*   *   *

Neither of them spoke as they crossed the courtyard. Lily again trailed behind, and again felt as bad as she had earlier before falling asleep. When she got back home she went to the toilet, locked the door, and sat, clutching her aching belly. Never before had she felt so ill. She looked down at her panties and saw a tulip-shaped bloodstain on the sky-blue material.

I am dying, she guessed. What a dreadful, shameful way to go.

At that moment she forgot everything her grandmother had warned her would happen. She pulled her soiled underpants off in disgust and shoved them under the upturned bucket used for washing the floors. She hid her scratched face in her cold hands and waited for death as her heart turned to glass.

Goaded by her expectation, Death came to the house at last. On his carpet-covered divan old Aaron the shoemaker was drawing his final infrequent breaths. He was unconscious. His eyelids, which had long since lost their eyelashes, were not completely shut, but his eyes were not visible, only a cloudy, whitish film. His withered hands lay above the quilt and the worn-out leather straps were still wound around his left arm. As his custom dictated, he had not removed them for a month. His children, the professors, burdened with much useless medical knowledge, stood by his bedside.

In the yardkeeper's house, on his iron bed, lay Bodrik, suffering from mild concussion.

On his narrow couch in a house in the countryside near Moscow, half covered by an old army blanket, another man lay dead.

But it was still only March 2, and several long days would pass before Lily's father, the son of decent parents, would step out onto wooden boards, his face puffy, his heart black with grief, his epaulets an innocent light blue, to announce to a gray rectangle of many thousands of men, one part of a great people that had been lost in a distant place, not registered by the botched color printing on the garish poster on the wall of Lily's classroom, that Comrade Stalin was dead.

That night, however, everybody forgot about a little girl who had locked herself in the toilet.

Translated by Arch Tait

SVETLANA   VASILENKO

PIGGY

I HATED THE PIG from the very first day. I already hated it at the station, when I hugged and kissed my mother. Her faded cotton dress gave off a sharp, unpleasant smell that made me wince.

"Haven't you slaughtered it yet?" I asked.

"No. Why, do I smell?" My mother began to sniff in fright at her shoulders, turning her head from side to side, putting her nose to the cloth and taking several quick, short sniffs.

"I don't notice it," she said in guilty embarrassment. "I've got used to it." And she stood stock-still for a moment.

She often used to freeze like that, like a bird: She stood there—tall, bony, and plain, with her sunburned collarbones protruding (she liked dresses with a wide neck), ungainly, with bird-like eyelids that made her small eyes look closed—she froze motionless, as though she had forgotten where she was and who she was, and then yawned affectedly (after one of these affected yawns she usually said something that was important to her, something she didn't want to say, but she overcame her hesitation and said it anyway, after a yawn, as if it was nothing special, and I disliked this little trick of hers, because I knew that it was something important to her). "That's what the girls at work keep saying, slaughter it. What's it good for, they say. You smell of that pig of yours, they say. I never seem to do anything but wash, wash, wash."

She gave me a frightened glance, and once again I was overcome by a wave of shame and pity. I know these "girls" she works with: fat, and

25

proud of it, white-skinned, self-satisfied, with the sing-song hypocritical voices of the wives of bosses—directors of shops and cafes, warehouse managers. I remember very well how we bought her a pair of gold-plated earrings for ten rubles, because they were exactly the same as Ifteeva's gold ones that cost two hundred—they had exactly the same little lilac stones set in them as the ones that belonged to Ifteeva, the wife of the city gas supply manager. I remember very well how happy she was and how long it was before they noticed her new earrings, and mother sat there tense and straight, stock-still, and her ears, which had been specially pierced for the first time in her life—at fifty-four—turned bright red and looked as though they were stretching with the weight of the earrings, as though the earrings weighed a kilogram apiece. And then they noticed! They cackled in joy and fluttered their plump hands, with the fingers that stuck out and couldn't come together because of the huge rings on them, the rings with stones and the plain bands, but the expression in their eyes was cold, hostile, and cautious. "Masha? Where would she get them? Our Masha?" And mother's face thawed, thawed the way icicles do, and her lips stretched out into a smile of inane happiness, and she was so happy sitting there. ... And they touched mother's ears with their short, fat fingers, and it hurt, but mother didn't show it; they took off her earrings as though to admire them, but they started avidly searching for the hallmark—and when they didn't find one, they glanced at each other in triumph, and now their eyes were as glad as the expression on their faces and their triumphant voices. "Well now, Maria Stepanovna, you nearly fooled us, for a moment we actually thought ..." They weren't being hypocritical now, they were genuinely glad as they forgave Maria Stepanovna her little trick. But mother tried to convince them, in an unnaturally high voice, that the earrings were silver. "They put a hallmark on silver, too, Maria Stepanovna, but there's nothing on these." Ifteeva herself fastened the earrings back on mother's ears with her very own gold-laden hands. And mother gradually hunched over, and then froze motionless, and her face froze, and from the small eyes that looked as though they were closed, the tears flowed down over her face and onto the lips that were set in a broad, pitiful smile.

"Let's go then, shall we?" Somehow my words came out a bit harsh.

"Why don't we take the bus?" mother asked.

I had a sudden vision of people wrinkling up their noses and turning away from my mother, who smells of pig manure—the men who smell of wine and eau de cologne, and their sweet-scented wives, and their children who smell of oranges—and I winced momentarily in pain, as though it had actually happened. I wouldn't let anyone, not anyone, turn their backs on my mother!

"We can walk. We're not that old yet!" I quickly bent down over the suitcases so that mother wouldn't notice my grimace.

It was as though I was running away from her with the two heavy suitcases (don't help me, I can manage, it's balanced like this). And the heavier the suitcases got, and the more cramped my fingers were, the faster I ran, with short little steps, my feet and the suitcases raising dust from the goosefoot and heather that half-covered the narrow asphalted pavement; almost nobody ever walked along it. I could hear mother's rapid breaths growing shorter and jerkier, and for an instant I had the unpleasant feeling that it was a dog chasing me, and I began to run still faster, without looking where I put my feet and expecting to stumble and fall at any moment.

"Daughter," I heard my mother's call and stopped in surprise. Nobody had called me that for a whole year. "Let's have a rest."

I put down the suitcase, which fell over and bounced gently on the heather. I turned around. Mother was running toward me, her red face empty of all expression except the single desire to catch up with me; her hair was tousled and her dress had crept up above her knees from running, her legs were a dead white.

That's my mother, I suddenly thought, and once again there was that wave of pity for her—for my mother—and resentment for what someone had done to her, and despair that I couldn't change anything or punish anyone for the fact that my beautiful mother had become this woman. But when she ran up, breathing fast and jerkily, the same sharp, unpleasant smell stung my nose, even sharper now, mixed with a smell of sweat that made it quite intolerable.

"You!" I cried, and I realized that I had only run so fast in order to shout out the word, in order to run as far away from other people as possible and yell out what I felt, in order to run away from this pity and shame and despair and love for her, in order to be free of her by crying out, "You! You're an engineer, and just look at yourself! I'm ashamed to look at you, I'm ashamed to be seen with you! You keep a pig! You smell of pig! I'm going to slaughter that pig of yours! You farm laborer! Are you short of money? Then I'll go to work, do you hear? You go around the garbage dumps collecting scraps for swill!"

(While my heroine carries on shouting, I'll explain why she's doing it, why she's in such a furious rage. She has come to spend her college holidays in a garrison town. The civilian population here lives in small

Finnish-style houses, and the others live in five-story blocks. The town, which is the real thing, with squares, monuments and parks, has its own laws. In this town it is forbidden to keep chickens, rabbits, and other filthy beasts. But the civilians in the Finnish houses keep them anyway. From time to time the population is fined for such unsanitary habits, and the chickens and the rabbits are temporarily evacuated from the town. And then people start keeping them again. And my heroine's mother has begun to keep a pig. Now do you understand?

What is this then, some kind of revolt? It's simply that my heroine's mother is poor. All on her own, without a husband, she has to clothe her daughter and pay for her education as an engineer: The town despises people without a higher education. The town has its own laws. And the daughter knows them well. Her mother has to feed and clothe a grandson, who will appear in the story later. The town despises those who have a child without a husband. The daughter knows this, but the child is there to be cared for, and without a husband. These things happen.

My heroine's mother is poor. But poor with a special kind of poverty. Alongside the wives of officers, the children of officers, the grandchildren of officers, where there is no place to hide yourself and your poverty. In this town you and your poverty are like a gaping hole in an officer's overcoat, you can be spotted for miles around. In her internal monologue my heroine will even use the words "majors' and colonels' wives." She is afraid to actually say it, she is afraid of betraying some military secret. She will never say how she entered this town, but she will enter it through the checkpoint, her mother will get a pass for her. She won't dare talk about it. She is a daughter of this taciturn town, and she honors its laws and secrets. She is prepared to be poor, as long as her poverty is proud and pure. Her mother has taken in a pig, and her poverty has become shameful. I won't interfere from now on, I won't say any more. I am also a daughter of this town.)

I went on shouting for a long time, repeating the same things over and over again, it was all the same to me what I shouted, as long as I shouted it at her, at this pitiful woman in the patched shoes, at this hateful woman in the faded dress, at my stupid mother, whom I loved more than anyone else on earth, with a broken, pitiful, stupid love. I saw her grow upset, hunch over, draw her head into her shoulders, as though I was beating her about the head, and then suddenly straighten up, her face taking on a bored expression, and she froze stock-still, with a bored face, and she seemed to close her eyes, as though she wasn't listening to me. She was asleep and having a boring dream.

I stopped shouting, because I didn't understand what was wrong with her. And when I stopped, she gave an affected yawn and said in a bored voice, "You're only shouting because you don't understand a thing. Me and Vaska had to get through the winter, and you know what kind of a winter it was. And as for the scraps that I collected from the garbage, only me and Vaska know about that. And I kept him warm by the stove, he was only a piglet. But you should see him now. And it's only scraps. ... I couldn't slaughter him now, not after we lived through the winter together. I feel sorry for him."

She stopped speaking. She looked at me with offended pride.

"But what are you keeping him for?" I asked in astonishment. "If you're not going to slaughter him? Are you training him or something?"

"I will slaughter him, when it's the right time for pigs to be slaughtered, in November. He's no worse than any other pig, is he? It's not the right time now, is it?" asked my mother, as if amazed that I didn't know such a simple thing.

"No, it isn't," I said.

"There you are then," said my mother, and she drew herself up straight and proud as could be.

Caught out by her idiotic logic, I whispered, "You're crazy"—and immediately realized that she wasn't crazy, and her logic wasn't idiotic, and I couldn't accuse her, judge her, or even forgive her, because I hadn't lived with her for a long time, and she lived with Vaska the pig and the rabbits and the dog, Fenya, with a chicken who didn't lay, with the cherry trees, the apple trees, and the currant bushes—and they had their own special logic, and they understood each other completely, and Vaska meant more to her than all the girls at work, and this Vaska that she looked after and fed even meant more to her now than I did, because all this was her life now. I understood it all. And from that moment I hated Vaska.

We turned into our street and it was as though someone had opened the oven door in a stove: at the end of the street the sun was burning down. It blazed orange, like glowing anthracite, not sinking behind the horizon the way it is supposed to, but flaking into burning lumps and lying there on its own blazing fragments, slowly disintegrating, as though it had been stirred with a poker. This was my sun, this was my sunset, so unlike the pink, modest northern sunsets, this was my street, where everything was familiar and dear to me—the old silver-torsoed poplars bearing aloft their thick, dense-green foliage, and the young cherry trees with their branches almost bare (it had been a good harvest),that were planted here instead of the white and pink acacias that the frost had killed off in a cold year, and the potatoes, with their simple little white florets, growing in front of every one of the Finnish houses, outside the yard, between the pavement and the asphalted roadway, instead of the heather, which had been painstakingly scythed down one summer when there was cholera around by the neighbors we now met, whose names I had learned to pronounce with my very first words, the neighbors who never went away anywhere or grew old (only the children changed, they shot up at a tremendous rate like poplars, and the ones that were riding about on tricycles last year were fixing motors to their bicycles this year and roaring off on their improvised mopeds as far as the withered maple, which was as far as they were allowed to go: the place where since the beginning of time they played hopscotch and the little kids rode around on the hopscotch squares on their tricycles). The sunset, the street, and the people seemed eternal. I knew what the neighbors would ask and what I would answer. I recognized the nasty, evasive look in their eyes when they spoke about the other neighbors. I seemed to know everything in advance, and I greeted the most startling pieces of news—that Uncle Volodya had died of cancer a month after his wife's death, that Uncle Grisha had hung himself, and Aunty Raya had left Uncle Victor after living with him for thirteen years—with a counterfeit astonishment and a counterfeit sorrow to match their own, as though it was old familiar news that wouldn't affect the life of our street, just as it hadn't been affected by the cold winter, or the cholera that summer.

Step by step, meeting by meeting, I worked my way into our street, the way a screw threads its way in, glad to feel the familiar captivity tighten at every turn.

And when I saw my neighbor Ira running down the other side of the street with an empty milk can, I shouted to her in my pleasure at the fact that everyone here knew me and I could shout out loud for all the street to hear. "Ira, save a place for me in the milk line!" And she waved her hand in greeting as she ran and shouted, "Right!" She shouted it as simply as if I had lived there for the last hundred years without ever going away.

And there was my three-year-old son zig-zagging toward us at a run, his arms thrust out in imitation of an airplane, the way children run to their mothers who have just come home from work.

I went into my very own yard and smiled at the sweetish smell of my son's urine by the doorway, I dodged Fenka's long, heavy tail as he wagged it in greeting, I grabbed him by the mane and said, "So you know me, you crocodile!" and he gently took my hands into his jaws. I took off my shoes and went into the garden, and through the grass my heels could feel the cinders that my mother had scattered on the path in the winter. Next came the boards that the rain had turned gray, and without looking down I instinctively stepped over the place where the point of a nail had always stuck up. I turned around to look: The nail was still sticking up. I stood silently in front of the apple tree withered from old age and remembered the word *damn*.

"Damn," my mother had written in one of her letters. "Our best apple tree has withered. But we'll wait a bit yet."

A young cherry tree had withered too, the one that had competed with the poplars, shooting way up above the television aerial. At first the blossoms had withered—it had blossomed for the first time in five years—they had been caught by the frost at that height and withered, and then no leaves had appeared for a long time. And now, in July, it was obvious that the cherry tree had withered altogether.

"It's your own fault," I reproached it, "you lanky brute!"

I was caught by a breath of wind and enveloped in a sharp, unpleasant smell, and I froze, as though while I stood there, in my own garden, I had been sluiced down with slops from the windows of my own house. And the slops kept pouring down. The wind had no intention of changing its direction, the stench grew thicker, and I felt an intense fury welling up inside me. My orchard!—where I knew everything, where every nail and every smell was fixed in my memory, and now everything (even my mother!) was polluted with this vile alien stench that had killed the delicate flowers of the cherry tree that had blossomed for the first time in five years. I was sure now that it wasn't the cold that had killed it. It had spent five years growing before it blossomed, and then because of this. ...

I went over to it with my head lowered, cutting through the dense wave of the stench with my head, and breathing it in deeply, in order to hate this pig even more, in case it should turn out to be likable and good-natured. I breathed in the smell in the naive hope that the air would pass through my lungs as through a filter and once again begin to smell of overripe apples and dill, to smell the way the grass does in the evening, or the tar and dusty boards of the shed after the sun has been warming them all day long. Yes, better if it smelled of dust. It stood there up to its belly in mud, looking at me. One eye was brown, with a fixed, malicious stare, the other was blue and half-covered by short white eyelashes: This pig seemed to be winking at me! Its snout was long and predatory, somehow not like a pig's, without any fat cheeks, and caked in mud. The whole of its long thin body had a hungry and predatory look. It began to urinate as it stood there, and the taut, transparent stream seemed to flow for an unnaturally long time. I knew that the pig was being raised to be shared—half for mother and half for Aunty Galya, who brought a bucket of slops each day—and I mentally chopped the pig's head in two halves, one with the blue, winking eye, and one with the malicious, intelligent one.

"That's the way," I said.

And suddenly the pig put its forefeet into the wooden trough filled with filthy swill and growled. It actually growled, but the threat was helpless, like the growling of a wild beast held in a cage when someone approaches it. The eyelid with the short lashes over the blue left eye lifted, and the red pupil glared balefully at me. Then it began to chew the trough in hopeless fury, and its fangs were the same rich yellow as the timber they exposed.

"He's hungry," I heard my mother say. "Hang on, Vaska, I'll feed you in a moment."

Mother began to drive the pig out of the trough with a branch and it screwed up its eyes and made stupid attempts to dodge the blows, then it staggered awkwardly and the trough tipped over, mother leaned over the fencing and righted the trough with the round wooden lid of a barrel, flung the lid under the pig's feet, and poured a bucketful of slops into the trough. The pig immediately stood in it again, stuck its long snout into the slops up to its eyes, and breathed out in the water with a gurgling sound, the slops heaved and bubbled, the pig raised its snout with a pale-green strip of boiled onion dangling from it like a strand of spittle. It chewed the melon skins crookedly, chomping wetly as though it had no teeth. It sucked in the air with noisy relish, as though it was something edible, and plunged back into the slops. Its hind legs slipped and skidded around on the circle of wood, it tensed its leg muscles in an effort to hold them steady, and its back trembled slightly from the tension.

Somebody nudged me in the side, and I turned around. My son was clambering up the fence to look at the pig. He suddenly leaned sharply forward and, afraid that he would fall headfirst, I swept him off the fence with my arm, and then, even more alarmed, I grabbed him and showered kisses on his wailing mouth, which was stretched so wide that I could see his moist pink throat. I kissed his wet eyes and his arms, as though I was checking with my lips to make sure that they were not broken, and over his choking sobs I shouted at my mother, "Pigs like that eat children! It's got to be slaughtered!" And I grabbed up my son and ran into the house, carrying him off the way some female animal would carry off her cub, kissing him constantly as though I was licking him clean—carrying him well away from danger.

And as I ran along the wooden boards, the nail stuck into my foot, right through to the bone, and blinded by the pain I yelled, "Slaughter it!"

*   *   *

Vaska was slaughtered a month later. Four people joined in—mother, Aunty Galya—a small, rotund woman who chattered ceaselessly, like a dry poppyhead rattling in the wind—me, and Uncle Kolya. Uncle Kolya killed all the animals on our street. He punched rabbits in the forehead, he beheaded chickens and cocks, he shot sick or thieving dogs. There was only one pig on the street, the first pig Uncle Kolya ever had to kill. He was dressed up in the gear he always wore for this kind of work. The check shirt stained all over with blood, which he never washed, was unbuttoned to reveal his smooth chest, sunburned almost brown. His skinny white legs in the galoshes protruded from crumpled, faded jeans rolled up to his knees, and the mud caked on them made them look as though they were made of clay. He tested a long, gleaming knife on his forelock, which was coarse and white as a pig's bristles, and gave a nervous laugh.

"Have you got the rope ready, Maria Stepanovna?" he asked.

"Rope, what rope? Oh, yes, the rope." Mother fussed, without moving her feet from the spot. Then she ran over to the withered apple tree to take down the clothesline. Uncle Kolya wound it several times around his palms, tugged on it sharply a few times, and it snapped without even stretching. "Rotten." Uncle Kolya spat, and the gob of spittle landed exactly on the end of the snapped rope. "I told you, Masha!" Mother began to fuss again, plunged into the shed, and rummaged around confusedly in there, stumbling over ringing metal basins, and when there was the clanking sound of bottles spilling across the floor, Uncle Kolya spat again, "Crazy damned woman! And she's going to slaughter it!"

Mother halted uncertainly in the door of the shed, holding out a piece of wire with a guilty look, as though she was afraid that it would be rejected too, and she asked in a frightened voice, "Will that do, Kolya?"

He twisted up his mouth disdainfully, looked at the wire and nodded his head curtly. "It'll do. Hold it!" And he hacked at the wire as hard as he could with the knife. There was a sound of scraping metal, the knife slipped, Uncle Kolya was unable to contain himself any longer and he yelled, "Hold it tighter, can't you? You'll damage the knife! You and your pigs!" And without finishing what he was saying, he struck viciously at the wire again with his knife, and spat in satisfaction. "That's it."

We decided to drive the pig out from behind the fencing and get it down where the ground was clean. But Vaska wouldn't come out of his little wooden sty. He retreated into a corner and growled menacingly. He didn't even come out when mother poured him some slops.

"He can feel it," said mother happily. "Maybe we should wash him, Kolya?"

"We'll wash him alright," chuckled Uncle Kolya. "With fire."

He handed mother the knife, moved aside the fencing and began wading, up to his knees in foul-smelling wash, toward the sty. Pulling his feet out with a loud squelching sound, he muttered angrily, "You need waders in this bog, some slaughterers."

Uncle Kolya beat the pig's growling snout until it turned its hindquarters toward him, and then he quickly tied a knot on its leg and began to tug at the wire. The pig shifted its feet, but it didn't move. He tugged harder. The pig hopped awkwardly and began to edge backward slowly, then it turned around and stopped, gazing at us dully. Its brown eye, usually lively and intelligently malicious, had a sleepy, doomed look. It growled again, but briefly, as if only half awake.

Uncle Kolya beat it on the sides, on the hindquarters, between the eyes, but all it did was to shudder where it was beaten, grunting after each blow without moving, bracing its front legs with all its might against the wooden barrel lid, which sank deeper and deeper into the mud. There was a gleam of hopeless despair in its red eye, and the redness in it swelled and expanded, covering the blue, until it stared with a senseless, bloody look.

Suddenly the pig made a dash toward us, and we started back in surprise. It got about three yards, the length of the wire, until Uncle Kolya pulled it up with a hand that had turned blue, and it fell over on its side, squealing in pain and terror in a way that set our ears ringing.

We all set on it at once, bracing our legs against the ground. Holding a basin to collect the blood, I crept along its body to the throat, feeling the rippling of its tensed muscles, and the desire of its every cell to live, and the squealing ringing inside its body. A few times it gathered its final strength and almost threw us off, and Uncle Kolya yelled above its squealing in a terrible voice, "Where's the knife? Where's the knife?" And

mother waved the long knife in front of us stupidly; she was also struggling to hold the pig and she didn't notice the knife in her own hand.

"Mother! The knife!" I shouted, and I couldn't hear my voice over the
squealing. But Uncle Kolya read what I was shouting on my lips and he
turned around, lifting one shoulder and pressing the pig down to the
ground even more heavily with the other, grabbed the knife from my
panic-stricken mother's hand, stuck it into the pig's neck, and twisted it.
The piercing squeal turned into a squelching and gurgling, the flesh parted gently under the knife, forming a semicircle that looked like a smile on
the throat, and the dark-red blood flowed out of it, steaming, into the
basin I had set in place. The pig's eyes, at first wide open, closed very
gently, and I comforted the pig, "There now, that's all, see how quick it
is. It's almost over."

Its body shuddered occasionally. In twenty seconds it was all over. I
poured the blood, which was already curdling, into a clean jar and closed
it with a plastic lid.

Vaska lay there quite different from the pig I had grown used to seeing.
No maliciously intelligent right eye, nor screwed up left eye; its eyes were
calmly closed.

I looked at it for a long time. But there were things to be done.

Uncle Kolya scorched the pig's side with a blowtorch. The mud and the
bristles curled up into black shavings, and we scraped them off with
knives to expose the white skin. The blowtorch went back over the same
place, and the white skin turned a glossy yellow, darkened, and began to
bake a red color. We turned the pig over on its side and its belly was so
dirty that mother decided to wipe it down with a rag. And when the
dirty water ran off down its sides, we suddenly saw defenseless pink nipples protruding in pitiful naïveté from the soft, white belly. It was a she
and not a Vaska at all, I'd never even thought of it—it was always just
Vaska. She had thirteen nipples, seven on one side and six on the other.
All the nipples were paired off opposite each other, and the odd one out
was covered by the bristles on her breast. We scorched the belly and
scraped the skin clumsily, and the nipples bled. Then we scorched the
head, and it became like thousands of others that are sold in markets and
shops—an appetizingly stupid head.

My son was standing beside Uncle Kolya. He'd been hanging around
for a long time, since the very beginning, but I'd had no chance to send
him away. And there was the vague idea, not even an idea, but a feeling,
that my son must not be like my effeminate contemporaries, who felt sick
at the sight of a severed cock's head. He must be a man who could slaugh-

ter a pig himself, or shoot a sick dog and punch a rabbit in the forehead, like Uncle Kolya. So I didn't send him away.

We slit open the belly. And my son froze as he watched the pearly intestines tumbling out of the cavity, the dark-red, trembling liver, the white stomach, slippery and taut, with its lilac-colored veins, and he kept repeating calmly, or so I thought, "They've killed piggy, they've killed piggy. ..." (How was I to know then that he would remember this for a whole year, repeating perplexedly, "They've killed piggy," that he would dream of this slaughtered pig for the whole year, maybe all his life?)

I was irritated that he was so calm. I was irritated that I was so calm. And when I saw the trough filled to the brim with the innards, I had the sudden thought that these innards probably weighed more than the meat, and we would have been better off to sell the pig for live weight to the slaughterhouse than go to all this trouble. The fact that I could have such a thought at such a moment horrified me, and my calmness, a certain spiritual inertia, began to depress me. I could recall very well how my godfather, a veterinary surgeon, had slaughtered a pig on a farm, on a pig farm, how it had squealed, hanging on the rope on the pillar with the cross beam, how I had squealed with it, how they had slit its throat, and the blood had gushed out, flowing over its belly, how it had gone limp and hung there as though it had been crucified. I remembered its bloody head with the flayed skin, with the white eyeballs that had tumbled out, and which had turned lilac when we got home. After that I had begun to hate my godfather.

So why was I so calm now?

I saw them hack Vaska in half. They chopped the head in two. I wrangled with the female neighbors who had come running to buy the meat and sold pieces for four rubles a kilogram, and not for three-fifty as they wanted—it was freshly killed meat after all!

I came to an agreement with one of the neighbors. For washing the intestines, we would give her half of them.

I gave the rabbits their feed, they were usually gluttonous, but for some reason, they wouldn't come out today. I glanced in at them. They were sitting three-deep against the back wall, panting and shuddering. Even they had sensed death!

I did everything I had to, but my calmness nagged at me and stopped me doing what I had to do calmly.

I sat down beside what was once Vaska. The jar of blood stood on the rabbit hutch, and the blood had already completely coagulated and gleamed like dark red jelly in the sun.

Large green bluebottles hung like clusters of poisonous berries on the blood-spattered goosefoot. In the trough the dark red liver trembled as though it were alive.

And suddenly I saw the pig again, with a smile that seemed to be asking me forgiveness for some offense that I had actually committed against it.

A sharp, unpleasant smell reached me. It was the wind blowing from Vaska's pen, and it was as though Vaska were still alive. Vaska was dead, but the smell would live on for a long time yet.

I felt someone watching me, following my every glance, my every movement. Perhaps that was why my calmness irritated me so much—someone else could see it too. I raised my head and saw my son. He was standing by the shed. He was examining me, his brow wrinkled, struggling painfully to understand something. His gaze was entirely adult and unfamiliar. His blue eyes watched me with intent malice.

"Come here," I said to him.

He didn't move. I stood up. He began to back away. His eyes were filled with terror. His back was pressing against the wall of the shed, but he went on trying to back away, squeezing himself against the gray planks, on his tiptoes. I wanted to take a step toward him but I was afraid to. I took a step. He began to move away from me sideways, his back rubbing against the gray boards. He had no shirt on, just his shorts, and I dashed toward him, afraid that he would get splinters in his back. The planks came to an end and with nothing to support him, he leaned helplessly backwards, but he kept his footing, turned around and ran, constantly glancing around behind him (and looking at me with that same hunted look).

I called his name. He ran away. And still not knowing why, I ran after him.

We ran along the broad asphalted road, along our street at first. I almost caught up with him, but I was out of breath. My breathing was short and fast as I ran behind him, he must have heard it, and it almost certainly startled him. At first I saw astonishment in his eyes when he glanced around, but then something in their expression changed—ever so slightly—and now he was looking at me the way people look at a mad dog—and he ran even faster.

He turned into another street. I was falling behind. A car could shoot around the corner at any moment.

"Wait!" I shouted, I was short of breath and it came out hoarse and weak. He kept running.

"Son!" I called, gasping for breath. "Son!" I implored him.

He stopped. He turned around and waited for me. My hair was all tousled, a coarse strand of it was prickling my lips, and I bit it between my teeth; my face was sweaty, and I had only one thought pounding in my head, to get to him quickly. My mother's old boots—the wrong size—were cutting into my skin, the dung-wash was slopping about inside them; my mother's cotton dress had ridden up and got tangled between my legs.

And when there was no more than two steps to go, I stopped, I was halted by his gaze—the cold, hateful gaze of my son. His blue eyes had paled from hatred and seemed like a complete stranger's. I stood there, breathing heavily, not daring to approach him. I smelled of a sharp, unpleasant mixture of sweat and pig manure.

"You!" said my son, and I could tell that his throat was dry from hatred. "You killed piggy!" His dry lips twisted convulsively in anger. Then the corners of his lips slowly crept downward, very slowly, as though it was very painful, and he gasped out, "Mommy!"

And we rushed toward each other.

"Mommy!" he cried desperately, sobbing, "don't kill piggy."

And I silently pressed his struggling body closer to my own, and I could feel my heart's blood rising through my throat and scalding it so that I couldn't breathe out, until it gushed in hot streams into my head, melting my brain, transforming it into molten lava.

"Don't kill piggy!"

"The truth, the truth ... you mustn't spare him ... he has to know the truth"—this idea of mine seemed to be written in large crooked letters on a piece of paper there in my head, it was still there among the molten lava, it was all I could read, and in a dry, hot voice, because my throat had been scorched, I said to my son, "We have to, we have to kill him, that's the way life is!"

And he began to struggle again ("Don't kill him, don't"), but now it was as though a stranger's body was struggling in my arms, wriggling in an attempt to slip free, and it was pointless my squeezing it tighter and tighter—it belonged to a stranger. And suddenly I saw that the lava in my head had reached the sheet of paper—"The truth, nothing but the truth, don't spare him."—and it burst into flames and was transformed into a big black sheet of ash, which rustled gently as it crumbled, and I understood, with all my body I understood, that my son was right, we mustn't, we mustn't! I saw that someone irrefutably logical, someone immeasurably more intelligent than all of us put together, who knew all the causes and the consequences, the beginnings and the ends of things, who controlled life and death and was therefore callous, merciless, and unjust, not good or evil, but simply a bookkeeper indifferent to everything, with blank eyes and a gray face, was drawing up his balance, and to make up some credits or some debits this faceless person was taking away my son, my mother, and me and sadly repeating the standard truth: "We have to, that's the way life is," and together with my son I shouted, "Don't! Don't"—and I felt that as long as I kept on shouting that—and I would keep on shouting all my life—then nothing would happen to my son or my mother. That person wouldn't dare to take them away from me, they wouldn't die, as long as I kept on shouting.

We held each other tight and cried. I got blood on my son's forehead (my hands were bloody) and tried to rub it off with spittle and only smeared more on him, and I kissed his forehead, and my lips became salty. I felt my heart pounding and my son's heart beating along with it. I saw his moist eyes, and his eyes loved me, and I loved them, and I knew that we would never be so happy again. And I held his heart, which was choking and longing to dash away, tighter to me. The cars honked as they slowly and cautiously drove around us. They didn't know that nothing could happen to us, and that we would never be so happy again.

A large, ungainly blue bird was running toward us. I looked closely. It was my mother. She was shouting something, her mouth was opening and closing, the veins on her neck were swelling up. But I couldn't hear what she was shouting, somehow I could only hear the loud beating of her heart.

Translated by Andrew Bromfield

LYDIA   GINZBURG

CONSCIENCE DELUDED

THIS IS THE STORY of one man's guilt. The guilt of a man called N.

*   *   *

Every time he thought about it—it was in a long disconnected stream. He never understood whether they were thoughts that had just occurred to him or whether they had drummed incessantly in his head in those first days after his father's death. For some reason, every time the drumming began it was with a rush of the pale yellow walls of the neighboring house; and then all the rest followed. A whole succession of thoughts, the very essence of which was torture. Two forces directed this stream of thoughts—remorse (which tormented him with ever-increasing agony) and a dull, if logical feeling of self-justification.

Yes, of course, there were objective reasons for his thoughtlessness; he was sick of the poverty, the misfortunes, the wretched family circumstances, and all this had coincided so inopportunely with that new love, which was to be an attempt at a real life. Besides, his love had already entered the stage of catastrophe, when he was destroying one thing after another, and at the same time grasping at straws, only for them to drift out of his reach, and everything that distracted him from that new love was a source of unbearable irritation to him.

So it is!—says remorse. You were irritated. You acted like someone who has these abstract fantasies, who in his heart of hearts has no feelings for the reality of other people's lives. You assumed responsibilities without understanding what they meant in human terms. You uprooted the old man from his familiar surroundings and from his work in order to soothe your delicate nerves—you found the separation at long distance too irksome. And later, when you had set up this rather uncomfortable existence for him—so that you could continue your own way of life—you became indifferent, you started to be forgetful and irritable. Alas, such is the delusion of egoists: I am so near, that at any moment I could stop the hurt that I am causing. What a criminal illusion to think that you can so easily make amends.

But—comes back the monotonous voice of self-justification—perhaps after all, a man should be able to make some sort of life for himself; lonely man that he was, he should be able to build some semblance of a life for two. He took so little for himself, didn't he, in the narrow sense of the word? There were days when he did not have enough to eat (once, he had arrived at his father's place hungry, to find the old man with his sister, sitting over coffee and some appetizing vegetable stew, and this contrast had eased his conscience considerably).

But it is not so easy to stop the voice of remorse—it becomes more and more insistent: "What sort of ignorant talk is this about yourself, in the narrow sense of the word?" it says. "Aren't you trying to take me in with your magnanimity, going hungry in the 'narrow sense of the word' and at the same time buying yourself chocolate in the broader sense of the word?"

This was simply one of those eternal clashes; on the one hand is a relative who is no longer wanted; on the other, your beloved, for whom, whatever you do, you do for yourself. It is the age-old struggle between duty and emotion when the latter, in order to gain the upper hand, uses irritation to obscure the sense of duty. But the retribution is always the same. Judging by all accounts, it seems that the fate of the loved ones, once they are no longer loved, is no longer of interest to the one who had loved them. From now on there begins the wearisome concern for the existence of this unwanted relative, because it was he himself who arranged that existence, and in no way can he now disassociate himself from it.

Remorse is inseparable from the feeling of unrealized power over reality. It is the guilt and the tragedy of conscience. It was Schopenhauer who said that remorse is the punishment of a conscience that has done what it did not wish to do. Deep down, conscience, having merged with other emotions, fails to recognize itself. It has been clouded by the shallow dictates of spite, selfishness, vanity, indifference, sloth. A remorseful Onegin said, "I gave no heed to the voice of love." Why did he give no heed? Why didn't he pay a little more attention to his desires? There is nothing in remorse more heart-rending than the words *a little more.*

There is no better food for remorse than the life and death of someone close to us, and this is because every time we spoke to him thoughtlessly, irritably, negligently, it could not have been that our conscience willed it so, but rather that our conscience was deluded.

And also it is because we have such manifest power over the life of the person who loves us. If we only had the will, we could have changed his whole way of life. It was as though we had had in our hand something precious and through ignorance threw it away. We bear the guilt for everything we might have remedied and did not, as does an artist for the work he has not created.

* * *

For many months N was tormented by painful and insistent memories. It all tallied—his responsibility for that life, which he could have changed and refashioned by an effort of will, but did not, and the reality of that pitiful life.

There are people who have a particularly forceful nature. Just as a healthy physical organism rejects any harmful matter, this sort of person's psychological makeup selects and throws out everything that might destroy it. These are not always inflexible, strong-willed people. On the lowest level they are simply go-getters (there are many women among these), they want to get the best out of life at any cost. They keep cheating, scheming, and lying, covering up their hurt, and are incurably boastful. Do not despise boastfulness—it is the expression of a firmly based optimistic view of life; at its worst it is the manifestation of the will to resist.

N's aunt, the old man's sister, is an outstanding example of this kind of person. When she has been visiting, she will tell you how warmly she has been greeted by the maid, her host's child, the cat, the wife of the superintendent of the apartment building. Returning from the club, to which she goes with her son's membership card, she will recount how the porter bowed low to her and gave her a broad smile. That is doubtful, since she

only gives him 15 kopecks, but that's how she sees things. When she goes
to the bathhouse, after an absence of three days, she actually sees the
nurse on duty and the two attendants nod to her, and hears their "Why
haven't we seen you for so long?" With overwhelming self-assurance she
sees everything through rose-colored glasses, everyone is smiling, encouraging, welcoming. But if she is offended in any way, or meets with
some unpleasantness—whether it is a communal kitchen squabble or a
clear case of her son's inconsiderate behavior—she will keep silent. This
normally talkative old woman, who is always annoying her friends and
relatives with her constant chatter, now has nothing to say; carefully and
persistently she conceals her injured pride.

This was why the aunt was annoyed and irritated by everything that
her brother said or did. He would have seen immediately that the porter
despised him and bore him a grudge, because he only gave him 15
kopecks, because he could not afford to give him any more. This is typical of weak people. They are slow and indecisive, because only strong
impulses can arouse them to make swift and accurate decisions when a
number of choices confront them; they are unsociable, because they do
not have that desire for action and self-assertion that attracts men toward
each other. They are mean, because they are afraid of the future and have
no confidence that they will be able to face it. They are mostly bache-
lors—because family responsibility is the strongest incentive to decision-
making.

At one time the old man had had a wife, but he soon divorced her; their
only son, N, had lived with his mother after that (she had died when he
was still a young man), but he used to visit his father. He was fond of his
father and liked the strange bachelor existence and the atmosphere of ca-
maraderie and masculine trust that developed between them. His father's
lifestyle had turned out to be particularly suited to him, since it was neither completely lonely nor overburdened with responsibility. In his later
years the old man became a bit eccentric. He was peevish and suspicious
and morose, with an ever more marked tendency to stinginess; rather
self-centered and preoccupied with the trivial details of his daily life. He
would moralize a lot, because in people of this type moralizing flourishes
in the vacuum taking the place of sensuality and will.

The substance of his moralizing came from generally accepted convic-
tions of the intelligentsia and memories of his youth—the materialistic,
democratic, atheistic youth of the 1880s. These memories embellished
that comfortable existence with a vague kind of populism, and the natural unsociability of a weak-willed person seemed to him simply a form of

isolation in a vulgar, bourgeois society. He lived well (he had even been wondering whether he should buy a car), but his inclinations were not strong enough to impel him to acquire material possessions. From his moralizing he derived a pleasant feeling of superiority over his acquaintances, who were engineers and doctors, and by means of his moralizing, he maintained around himself the special atmosphere of the old-style democratism of the intelligentsia. And so it continued. Then came the Revolution, which destroyed his socialist sympathies together with his savings in the bank. But he was so lacking in resolve and so strong were his leanings toward populism with its feeling of guilt, that he never allowed himself any inner feelings of resistance. He might consider the revolution cruel, but he could not consider it just. He worked in his former capacity and things turned out quite well for him. Everything collapsed immediately, however, when he gave up work (his son thought it was getting beyond him), as soon as the support of external commitments, to which he had become accustomed, was withdrawn.

It seemed that he had no powers of resistance. Such people of low willpower take the irrevocable step of admitting that they are objects of pity. They are not afraid of humiliation, they offer no opposition to it; on the contrary, they insist on being humiliated. And everything around the old man assisted in this process.

In our harsh and merciless existence, everything stressed and reminded him in many different ways that he had ceased to have any social significance. For example, they gave him a pension of 60 rubles and then suddenly took it away, but then restored it after three months of fuss and bother.

In the early 1930s the cooperative housing societies were typical of the rigid, harsh conditions of that time. It was in the nature of this system to eternally remind a man that he should not live as he wanted to, and that he was always getting more than he deserved. It was a system that denied the rights of man to living space, to air, to a bathroom; this denial of rights was real only in principle, merely a theoretical concept, since in practice the management was compelled to tolerate the tenant. But according to the cooperative housing society, it was quite unacceptable for an elderly pensioner, living alone, to occupy a nice, sunny room. They threatened to evict him, to move another tenant in with him, or to transfer him to another apartment, they extorted money from him and sent officials along with briefcases. All this activity was illegal, absurd, and led nowhere. But this loutish behavior on the part of officialdom somehow accentuated the old man's feeling of pathetic unworthiness. In spite of his obvious social and legal rights, it seemed to him quite right that they should move another tenant in with him or transfer him to another apartment. Depressed by the old man's feeling of unworthiness, N kept complaining to the office of the public prosecutor.

This feeling of pathetic unworthiness was fostered by the lifestyle that N had arranged for the old man. It was a lonely, old-maidish kind of existence (the aunt only visited him occasionally), with a primus stove and trips to the market, where he had to count every kopeck. In theory, it's true, what was so terrible about an old man, who had nothing else to do, having to cook his own favorite vegetable stew? There was nothing terrible in that. But all this had its own inner significance; and like a poisonous discharge, it would slowly seep outward and express itself in the old man's behavior. The fact that he was chopping up a pink turnip would in itself indicate that he was no longer a member of society—a real man. Oh, the utter stupidity of all those excuses N had made to justify himself! After all, the old man had what he needed in the way of creature comforts, more in fact than N had himself. How could he have misjudged the situation, how could he have failed to understand the basic principle of human life, its motivation: the belief in one's own personal worth. And while the old man stirred his carrots and turnips in the saucepan with an unsteady hand, this belief in himself gradually diminished.

About his own creature comforts, and the fact that he himself was less well provided for than his father, N pondered gloomily as he lay on the bed. He would show up there and lie sprawled on the bed in what he considered to be an exhausted state and allow himself to be waited on. There was that incident about the bath he had wanted, a nice, warm bath. Of course, normally there is nothing difficult in starting a fire with the help of a few sticks and logs, but that time the old man could not get the fire going—it kept smoking and dying out. This incident infuriated N—this atmosphere, where everything was difficult, stifled him. He only wanted one thing—a separate existence, difficult if you like, but uncomplicated—so that he would not even notice it. But here, in this house, everything was a problem to the point of desperation. Every piece of wood, every turnip, every bill meant more difficulties and humiliation. And the old man not only did not resist them but in every instance he looked for all the difficulties, all the humiliation that the situation could possibly provide.

N suddenly exploded because he could not have his bath. After all, he'd been tired and had been so looking forward to lying in a warm bath—he should have known that here they could do nothing right (he was thinking of his aunt too). And so, he went out for a walk through the streets covered with grimy snow. He knew that the old man was still sitting by the stove, terribly upset (he had so wanted to greet his hardworking son with a nice, hot bath). N wandered about until dusk, thinking what a martyr he was—but also that he was a rotten kind of son. At home, the old man still sat by the stove in his old summer coat, his felt boots, and his motley colored skullcap; in his hands, waxen pale with hard, swollen veins, he held a log. He was pleased that he had managed to get the stove going. N had had his bath half cold, as he was forced to leave the door open for a long time, so as to let out the smoke.

He felt terribly guilty, each time he remembered that incident. But all this had happened because N did not understand, had not understood that the main thing, the one that underlay everything, was the old man's refusal to recognize that never again would he be able to work.

At home there was a kind of understanding that he was only temporarily not working; regular employment, of course, was too much for him, but he would still write some articles on his subject; he would get in touch with a few publishers. Sometimes he would give N a list of books and journals to look for. N hated looking for anything at all. One day he took his father to the public library—it was most embarrassing. The old man was confused—he did not understand what the librarian said and could not comprehend the simple card index. N remembered that incident with rancor every time the old man gave him a list of specialist literature. He would say "Yes, yes," and stuff the list in his pocket or the desk drawer, instantly forgetting all about it.

Sometimes the old man would tentatively reproach N for his thoughtlessness. One day, they had a rather unpleasant conversation for an entirely different reason. N had now forgotten what it was about. But at the time he suddenly exploded and said something to the effect that he had enough troubles of his own and reminded the old man of the public library incident, "Everything is too much for you." That really was a mean remark—hitting below the belt. It was painfully obvious that the old man was deeply offended.

Usually, N was careful about what he said, but sooner or later this was bound to happen, because so much resentment was bottled up in him, convincing him that an idle, emotionally dependent old age was infinitely burdensome.

N did not come easily to this conclusion. It was an admission of one of his many unfortunate blunders. In his student years, lonely (in spite of his academic prowess), cold, and half-starved years, he dreamed about having a house. Even then, he imagined it as a bachelor's establishment. As a matter of fact, he did not want a house that took all his time and strength; he wanted a separate home, which would not be part of his everyday life, not changing as life did, but a stable home; his father would live there and his aunt would keep house; he himself would show up when he was tired. Ideally, the house was to be out of town. He would arrive there on an evening of soft, sparkling snowfall. There would be a white cloth on the table, a lamp, a teapot, and he would be sitting there, tired from overwork, but with his spirits rising because of the teapot and white tablecloth.

It is a strange thing about longstanding dreams that have matured over the years and that have grown in proportion to a man's longings—they nearly always come true. And this is very sad. The dream of a house out of town, outlined in all its details, coincided amazingly accurately with the reality, even to his arrival on a sparkling, snowy evening. Only one thing was glaringly missing—love. Love had been a natural prerequisite for N's youthful plans. There was the assumption that this love would continue, acting as a link between the aging father, with his eccentric moralizing, and the boy—wild since childhood and searching for his identity. It was a friendship with walks, boating, a bit of sparring, noisy arguments about everything under the sun, in the heat of which the boy would become irritated by his father's intellectual nonsense, his pacifism, or his wrong understanding of Blok. But when years later they met again, everything was different. Here was no longer an elderly eccentric, fond of his simple comforts, his arguments, and his boasting, but a pathetic old man, whose world contracted ever more tightly around him, ever more rapidly turning into indifference, so that in his microscopic world there was simply no room for the interests of the son.

In addition to the old man's absentmindedness and failing intellect N had his own special problems. He was now a grown man, tired, with nerves on edge, disoriented, and in general completely indifferent to everything and everybody, but at the same time, trying in a muddled and resigned way to establish for himself some kind of happiness. These two men met again, expecting, as before, warmth and kindness from each other, but instead were shocked by each other's selfishness. The younger man, who now, of course, was the stronger, realized how difficult it was to be kind. And the older man started to be afraid of him. "You are shouting at me," he said one day, sounding very hurt. By this he meant: In the past, when I was the stronger one, you used to talk to me quite differently. This had happened when they had been arguing about the old man having to get the stove in his room repaired. The old man was saying that it could not be done, because it was too expensive. N said that it was necessary, that he would find the money. And it was just because in his opinion he'd been very magnanimous during this argument ("I don't begrudge the money," he'd said) that he was unable to control his irritation and his bad temper. Or maybe it had happened on another occasion, during a theoretical argument, when he had lost his temper over the old man's "intellectual nonsense." "You are shouting at me." How could he, how could he have allowed himself to act so meanly?

But the most painful scene had been the one with the liver sausage. The old man had come to visit him and together they had had a good breakfast. Then N had gone out of the room; when he came back, he saw that the old man was picking at the remains of the liver sausage with his knife. With a start the old man had quickly left the plate of sausage. He had been ashamed to show that he would have liked some more. N's conscience smote him. The shock was so sharp that for a moment it had almost dispelled his indifference and unkindness. But it seemed to him that the ache he felt threatened to become an overwhelming pain. So, quickly stifling the pangs of remorse, he gave way to feelings of disgust—the meanest possible reaction to the scene of the liver sausage.

Everything about the old man annoyed N, most of all the privations that the old man patiently endured. His Dutch stove was out of order and the room was always cold. N said spitefully that he really couldn't visit him, that it froze his very innards; and in fact, in the winter he did not go there for two months. But the old man lived there. He warmed his room with paraffin stoves that poisoned the air, warmed his hands at them, so that the skin became painfully stretched. The old man assured N that he had gotten used to it and did not feel the cold; it's true he had gotten used to it, yet at home he was always dressed in his skullcap, felt boots, and thick overcoat. The paraffin was a problem, it had to be brought from the town, but quite understandably it was forbidden to carry it on the train due to fire hazard (100 rubles fine). The old man would wrap the bottles in a newspaper and pack them in a basket.

Because of the difficulties about the paraffin, the old man caught a chill and spent about ten days with N. It was just about then that Lisa would arrive almost every day with the express aim of having it out with him and picking a quarrel. The old man's presence in the next room inhibited their quarreling and, more important, prevented their making it up. In the end, N could hardly conceal his impatience; frowning, he would take the old man's temperature—37.3—obviously he could not go home with a fever; and the old man suddenly said in a resentful tone, "Am I in your way?" N felt terribly ashamed and started some kind of explanation in an attempt to gloss over his tactlessness.

At last the old man went home. He left for the streetcar stop—as always with the little bag in which he carried his shopping. N accompanied him to the stop, heavyhearted, vaguely ashamed, and half wanting to take him back and start all over again. But if for some reason they had had to turn back—if there had been a sudden snowstorm or if the streetcars had stopped running—then that wish would have immediately changed to anger, because everything was preventing him from getting on with his life. At the streetcar stop he kissed the old man—spoke to him gently, helped him in, and handed him his bag—then he walked away, feeling desperately upset.

With an effort, one could always see a different aspect of the situation. The old man had a nice room and nice neighbors. The air in the suburb was good, and there was a quiet park where the old man liked to sit and read his paper. He used to say that since he moved there his digestion had improved. One day N had had some visitors and one of the women said that the old man was looking very well and younger and, of course, this pleased the old man.

Obviously, such memories do not come easily to mind—they are dim and have to be forced. The mechanics of remorse forcefully sweep aside everything that does not fit into its structure. On the other hand, it was very characteristic of remorse that N should remember how one day the old man had said, not directly to N but to his aunt—obviously so that she would pass it on, "It would be better if he gave me a fixed sum every month and not whenever he feels like it." It would be better—in other words, it would be more like a pension or a salary, in any event not so humiliating. How could he have humiliated the old man so much?

Last summer N had gone to the country with Lisa; there he devoted his time to his studies. The aunt too had gone to visit relatives. So, the old man had been alone for two months. Suddenly, he did something that he had never done before. In spite of his tendency to consider himself a pathetic figure, he had never complained to N about anything; he had either wanted to spare N's feelings, or he had been ashamed to do so. Thus he had left N with an excuse for doing nothing about the situation. But now he suddenly wrote a letter, in which he said without mincing words that he did not have enough money and that he was very lonely. N knew all this very well, but he somehow hoped that the old man didn't know it—did not realize, for example, that he was lonely. This complaint, which the old man expressed in words, in writing, shocked N to the core. He began to fret, especially because he was so far away, and he desperately wanted to change everything, that very minute. He immediately wrote a letter, "an affectionate reply," for which his father later thanked him. Specifically he pointed out that he too was short of money and was living very frugally. He wrote this not in order to wriggle out of his responsibility; on the contrary, he immediately scraped together all the money he had and sent it off.

For about two days he felt guilty and worried, and then, as he always did, he pushed it to the back of his mind. This was all the simpler because he had chosen not to understand what the old man was writing about, not to comprehend his loneliness. The endless days of reading his paper on the park bench, going to the market, and then at home with his primus stove and the persistent melancholy that had settled in his stagnating brain. They were very quiet days, because there was no one to talk to and the nights were mostly sleepless—like most old people, he slept very little, thinking thoughts that could only be about his loneliness, his uselessness, about death, and about how eggs were more expensive in the market today, and how his leg seemed to be starting to hurt again.

For the old man, those interminable nights were filled with thoughts that in every detail were concerned with his uselessness, his leg, and with death. And in no way could N break the chain of remorse so as to obliterate from his mind the memory of those days, those nights, those thoughts.

It is impossible to solve the tragedy of longing, when there is the clash between longing and fulfillment, but in old age, a yearning for peace can sometimes be fulfilled. People age in different ways.

Ideally, old age as a natural decline of strength occurs very rarely. More often old age is sad, unwilling to come to terms with itself; it is difficult to help, almost as difficult as it is to help the young. But an old age that has lost its purpose, with an intellect that is steadily declining—in this case it is possible to be helpful in simple material ways.

It is possible for old people to remain happy if, though their activities are curtailed, they do not cease to have some influence on the life around them and on the young as possessors and donors of worldly goods. Or when their children, well-off and confident in their achievements, are happy to fulfill their filial duties and grant to old age the comfort and respect due to it. Among the poor, old people were always unwanted and pathetic figures. Now the irritation of young, harassed people with one of their family, who has outlived his time, finally penetrated the world of the intellectuals, breaking through the resistance of those highly sensitive individuals and becoming a problem of psychological parasitism. In the absence of an inborn and lifelong place in the hierarchy, in conditions of cramped and disordered existence, stripped bare of traditional aims and concepts (such as clubs, charities, sinecures, rituals of veneration—everything that the old world in the upper strata of society offered to ensure a secure old age), the claims of old people seem to be quite unreasonable.

One of the saddest laws of life is the so-called ingratitude of children. The value that parents and children represent to each other is not the same. For parents, children are fulfillment and creation, a protection against loneliness and a promise of immortality. For children, parents are objects of duty or pity, or at best of a filial attachment, which is continued in a disinterested and, therefore, somewhat casual way. Passively and indifferently, N proffered what he had. But when it turned out that this was not enough and that besides giving material support he had to give up his time and energy—this he could not endure.

N had never had any faith in money. He did not believe that money could be an effective influence on life and death. Absentminded, indifferent to material possessions, absorbed in his own thoughts—he was poor, without realizing it—he wore his poverty lightly, and it never entered his head to apply the term to himself. And this kind of blatant, unashamed poverty made N feel guilty—it was unbearable to him. Physical suffering is not the most characteristic feature of poverty in the bleak, narrow sense of the word. It is a combination of oppression, dependence, a deep-rooted lack of self-respect and fear. It is, for example, the conviction that it is necessary and natural to wait four hours in the outpatient hospital to get free treatment, so as not to go to a private doctor and pay a ruble. It is a kind of social dogma: "I am not such a lady that I won't go to second-class baths." It is above all a person's feeling that there is difficulty and veiled hostility in everything. It is the same for a poor man as for an artist—nothing in life goes unnoticed. When he is walking, he is conscious that he is wearing out the soles of his boots. When he gets on a streetcar, he remembers that he has to pay so many kopecks. He takes note what stamp he puts on a letter before sending it. He makes not a single spontaneous gesture.

There comes a stage in the eternal struggle between the weak and the strong, when the strong gives up first, because of his remorse. The irresistible weapon of the weak is the shamelessness with which he parades everything that makes him appear pathetic. He torments the stronger one

by his eternal self-depreciation. And the stronger one, in order to continue normal existence, becomes embittered and resentful, refusing to see
what everyone else has seen long ago. And when at last he does see, it is
too late—he feels guilty and condemned and in his heart there is an open
wound. But nothing—neither overwork, nor passions, nor weariness,
can justify him.

A man behaves especially badly to those dear to him, not only because
he is not afraid of them but also because in his relationship with them he
feels a groundless conviction that it is never too late to correct any wrong
he has done. "I am like a balsam, with which I can at any moment ease
the pain that I myself have caused." The very proximity of his relative
can be misleading. When he is sitting there, I can feel quite easy—he is
here and I am here, consequently I can easily put right any wrong I have
done him. But he has only to leave the house for half an hour to do his
shopping and the delicate balance is disturbed. What if something
should happen to him? Maybe it has already happened? And then, that
unkind act, that gesture of indifference, would be the last thing I ever
did.

Those most prone to panic over imagined family disasters are the people who are overbearing and thoughtless in their home life.

*   *   *

The old man was ailing. One day, N was informed that his father was
getting worse and so he suddenly rushed off, having decided that it was
absolutely necessary to get him more nourishing food. He spent all his
money buying a chicken, oranges, and cream. But even as he was buying
them, he was trembling with impatience; he must get back quickly, as
quickly as possible, so as to substitute his chicken and oranges for the
years of hunger. Walking across the yard in the dark with the packages
that hurt his fingers, he stumbled because he was looking up at the windows. He thought that if there was a light in the windows as usual, then
nothing could have happened. If only he could arrive in time to make up
for the past with his love and with the chicken. Before he had crossed the
threshold, his face twisted with anxiety, he was asking, "How are you?"
Nothing had changed. Then the old man said that cream didn't agree with
him and anyway they had already brought milk; chicken broth was no
good for him either as the doctor had advised him to eat only vegetarian

food. So all the shopping had been wasted and the worry that he had experienced while shopping had also been for nothing. N sat with hunched shoulders, downcast, limply answering his father's questions. He longed to sink into solitude, as into deep water.

It was only now that he understood what he had previously failed to grasp. He should have been able to stop the terrible march of events. Now he saw clearly what he ought to have done. It was as though he was sitting beside the old man; touching his hand as it rested on his knee, he stroked the hand, caressing with his fingers the swollen veins (he used to do this as a boy and then in the thoughtless bustle of life he had forgotten the gesture). Within him a strange illusion was growing—it was as if it was no longer possible to be separated from this man who sat by his side. He felt as if he was holding a precious thing, grasping it more tightly lest it should be taken from him. He thought, Now I am acting like a person with hindsight; why didn't I do that before? Why didn't I understand? Why didn't I stop being so absorbed with my feelings of the moment— but then, this situation hadn't arisen before. My conscience did not express itself in that much-needed gesture. Consciousness reverts to a chaos of disconnected moments that incoherently crowd together and cancel each other out. By then it is too late to make amends.

Death tears out a part of our being from the darkness. To avoid being hurt, we do not allow ourselves to understand the life of the loved one. But the pain that is caused by his death is so great that there can be none greater—it brings down the final curtain. We try to make our grief the more intense because the death of our loved one is identified with our own guilt and it demands that we should be punished.

*   *   *

How did it happen—all this that later ended in his father's death? It all began with N's telephone being out of order. Strictly speaking, it all started with N's aunt arranging a party at her apartment in town. The old man had been invited too, but he didn't come. The women were eating fruit pies. N dropped in and had some pastries too. He could not stop worrying that the old man hadn't come. As always, everything got on his nerves—even more than usual because in a few days' time he had to make a report and he needed his mind to be especially free from worries. That utter silence—the telephone hanging uselessly there—all this had become bound up with his father's death. The old man had fallen ill, that is, first, his leg had given him trouble on the very day of the party. He had asked a neighbor (she worked in the town) to telephone his son and ask him to come. But N's telephone was out of order. Maybe if the telephone had not been out of order, nothing would have happened.

The next day the neighbor dropped in after work (maybe if she had called the day before, nothing would have happened). N at once started doing what he always did—shouting at his aunt. He went up to her and accused her of a disgraceful lack of consideration for the old man; he himself had far too much to do; he had to write his report. But it seemed that he had no choice but to give up everything and go there himself. Actually he did not go there himself but made his aunt go. The report was a great success, such as he had not had since his student days. That night there was a celebration at his apartment. In the last few years N had become reconciled to the role of failure; not an embittered failure—he would have considered that unseemly. Success revived in him youthful, long-suppressed ambitions. Now he felt at once stimulated and exhausted. He did not want to work any more; he wanted to talk a lot, to rest, to feel that life was good.

In the morning, Lisa dropped in before work. In spite of her inclination to do the contrary, this time she joined in the spirit of success and agreed to share in it. This unexpected attitude heightened N's rejoicing. They talked together and N was surprised at how easily and fluently he could talk. At about two o'clock in the afternoon someone called from the telephone exchange (his telephone was now working), to say that the old man had been really ill for some days. They hadn't wished to tell N in case it should worry him before his report. He said he would come immediately. His heart stood still. He feared for the old man and he feared his own remorse. He was shattered by it. Instead of celebrating his success he must immediately buy some food and go to his father. But, more annoying, he had to leave Lisa.

That is how it started, his telephone out of order, his aunt's party, and his report, and it was to continue for two weeks—until the end. He traveled there and back by suburban train every other day. N was extremely busy (people had suggested to him after his report that he should follow it up with an article). These trips interfered with his work. Although it was February, an early thaw had set in. In the suburban train it was always half dark. It was impossible to make out anything outside the steamed-up windows. At times, when the car was almost empty, it was terribly cold; at other times the train was so full that he had to stand all the way, pressing his face with disgust into the damp collar of a fellow traveler. From the station he walked through the slush carrying parcels that made his arm ache and deliberately thinking, about his martyrdom, "It is always going to be like this."

He had traveled there full of good intentions and the desire to make amends; regretting that he could feel no love; indeed this regret was so strong that it bordered on love itself. On the way there he was thinking that he would talk to his father about his successes or plans, or about something amusing, but once there, he felt frigid and too weary to say anything and it seemed to him that his father would not be at all interested anyway. He sat there, cold, bored, downcast, figuring out when he could decently leave and wondering if he would miss his date with Lisa. Once, huddled by the half-cold stove, he started looking at the furniture in the room—odd bits of good quality, but lacking in taste, typical old middle-class furniture. He looked at the table and chairs and at the old man who, quietly moving his lips, was lying on the modernist couch with the mirror clumsily set into its high back. He was thinking that it was very possible that the old man would die and that he would have to clear out the apartment and remove everything; what a wretched upheaval it would be, coping with the local housing department and the transport. I shall have to get rid of most of it but perhaps I might take that black thing for myself. What shall I feel after he dies? Maybe nothing—I ought to try and imagine ... maybe—nothing. I certainly don't feel anything at this moment.

What a fool!

But worse than these cynical thoughts was his craven desire for haste. He was cold and bored, and an evening with Lisa should have calmed him and been a compensation (in actual fact it turned out quite otherwise); and he would suddenly begin to show a quite unseemly desire to go. He knew that the sick man was surrounded by disorder, that the room was badly heated and that he ought to get a cleaning woman. He would get angry and demand that matters be taken in hand, he would soothe his conscience by leaving every penny he had. But he did not do the one thing that he should have done—he did not stay with his father and take the responsibility into his own hands. He knew that he ought to speak to the doctor but he couldn't wait as the doctor wouldn't arrive until nine or ten o'clock and by then his evening would be ruined.

The last time, before the beginning of the end, as he was leaving, N took some money out of his wallet and said, "I'll be back in a day or two."

"Your visits are a great comfort to me," said the old man.

The old man was always shy and reserved with N. And this pitiful word *comfort* suddenly made everything all too clear. It was just as unpleasant and intolerable as the old man's groaning when his leg was aching, and N wanted to cut him short. Hurriedly shutting out the annoyance that the word *comfort* had caused him, N, with a harshness that surprised even himself, said, "Frankly, it doesn't suit me just now to come very often; I'm terribly busy."

Having uttered these words, his heart sank. He put more money on the table than he had intended at first, almost everything he had.

"I must go. Now please get better soon."

The old man looked up at him from the couch with its mirror.

"I will try," he said, without a smile.

That was their last conversation.

On the eve of the fatal day N telephoned his father's neighbor at work to find out how things were. The neighbor answered rather sharply, "In my opinion, not good. You ought to speak to the doctor yourself." N did not like this interference. That day he stayed at home. The next day, before leaving, he met Lisa and together they went to buy some oranges for the sick man. Lisa said, "What! Have you spent those 300 rubles already?"

"Yes, of course!" he said, and at once started to feel like a martyr. This was how he managed things—spending money on the old man salved his conscience.

On the way to his father's N did not think about anything. It must have been because so many times he had been tormented by his thoughts on the way and had looked up fearfully at the lighted windows as he approached. If only, if only nothing had happened. ... Many times the door had been opened with much trouble over bolts and locks. Indeed nothing special had happened and his retreating fears gave place to irritation and boredom. By now this sequence of emotional reactions had become a habit. After he fumbled with the bolts as usual, his aunt opened the door. And as always, responding to the opening door with apprehension, he asked quickly, "How is he?"

"Very weak," said his aunt, going back into the kitchen. "His temperature has gone up this evening." She said no more but this time the feeling that once again nothing had happened was lacking. N entered the room. From the couch the old man looked up at him with vacant, staring eyes. N felt disconcerted by this. He greeted his father but the old man did not answer. Even now, N did not want to understand the significance of what was happening. He was opening the packet by the table. Having cut the rind from an orange he offered it to the old man on the palm of his hand. Timidly, he asked the silent man, "Would you like an orange now?"

The old man looked him in the face as if he did not understand. Without changing the direction of his gaze he stretched out a trembling hand toward the orange. N held out his hand toward him. Gropingly, like a blind man, and continuing to look at his son, the old man found the orange, pressed it with his fingers, peeled off a segment, raised it to his mouth, and started chewing it slowly; he stretched out his hand for a second piece. His movements became slower and slower. N stood there, completely numb. Then he put the orange on a chair and, without looking back, went out of the room. In the kitchen his aunt was boiling some milk.

"Why doesn't he speak?" Talking to his aunt, N was unable to shake off his feeling of numbness. "Is he like this all the time?"

"I don't know. Half an hour ago he was talking. I was saying, why don't you come? He said, 'It takes him ages.'"

N interrupted her. "Come and look at him."

They went in together. Lying on his back, the old man was gazing fixedly at the arm of the couch. Aunt said something to him but he did not answer. It was no longer possible not to realize the truth.

"What is this?" said N. He did not dare speak loudly. The horror of seeing his father like that aroused him from his numbness. And at once he began to do what was necessary with a kind of automatic precision.

The doctor who was attending to the old man was now at the hospital. N burst into the apartment below where there was a telephone of archaic design with a crank. To start with, he was connected with the wrong department of the hospital; he turned the crank again and this time they connected him with the right department but the doctor had gone out. The occupants of the downstairs apartment gathered around the telephone. It didn't even enter their heads to conceal their curiosity. The duty doctor informed him that the old man's doctor himself would be unable to call until the evening but that he would send an assistant to give an injection.

Upstairs, the old man lay quietly as before. In a whisper, Aunt was saying that during the night the old man had wanted to go to the bathroom and she had had to help him and the sheet had been slightly soiled. The old man had said that he felt as weak as a fly. "The doctor was here yesterday evening," she said, "and he said that it wasn't necessary to give him any injections," but he had left a prescription for camphor to be taken by mouth.

"And has he taken the camphor?"

"We haven't found time to get any yet."

So they had not had time to get it. Of course it was difficult for her and he had not been there. And then he suddenly realized that if he had not spent so much time talking to Lisa on the way to the station he might have arrived an hour earlier. The old man would still have been conscious; he would have been pleased with the oranges and they would have been able, for one last time, to talk to each other.

N went to buy the camphor. The brightness of the pharmacist's windows, the many colors of the neatly packed medicines aroused fear and revulsion in him. Back home he found the medical assistant, a tall, flabby looking woman, with a syringe. Behind her were two women from the downstairs apartment. Their telephone had been used on the sick man's behalf—now they had every right to come into his house. N realized that the smell of death breaks down people's restraint; doors open and walls crumble before them.

The assistant seemed rather annoyed. Apparently, the doctor had instructed her not to treat him in any way but only to give him an injection. But after all, she was a doctor and not a nurse. So before giving the injection, she made the sick man sit up, supporting him with one arm, and raised his shirt in order to listen to his heart, so that his aging, yellow stomach with its gray hairs was laid bare. The neighbors looked on with interest.

"Would you please leave," said N. "He might not like ..."

As they were leaving the two women looked back in surprise. It was clear that the sick man was unconscious so how could he possibly mind?

N followed the assistant into the front room.

"Well, how is he?"

"I can't really say."

There was resentment in her voice. "I haven't been attending him personally."

"Do please examine him," suggested Aunt, who was always ready to play up to outsiders.

"No," said N. "We mustn't disturb him. All the same, I would like to know what you think. How is he?"

"I can't really say. His condition is serious." Instead of the tone of injured professionalism she now spoke with genuine embarrassment. "Yes, his condition is serious."

For the first time the truth of what was really happening in that room was openly admitted.

In the evening the doctor came and it so happened that a friend of Aunt's who was herself a doctor also called. The two of them seemed to be trying not to lose face in front of each other. The old man was lying with his eyes closed; they felt his pulse, speaking quite loudly as they did so. They were saying that things were bad, that his right side was obviously paralyzed and then, turning back the blanket, they raised and then let fall his right leg, which dropped lifelessly like a stone. While this was going on the old man was breathing heavily but the expression on his face was calm. N was wondering if perhaps his father could hear and understand what the doctors were saying—he had been told that this might be the case—and that he ought to keep them from talking loudly in front of him. But in front of two such self-confident people he was too timid to say anything.

The doctor was by the table, opening a little ampoule of transparent, yellow liquid, and they injected the old man with the camphor, saying as they did so that it was completely useless. N's life, his writing, his failures, his relationship with Lisa, seemed somehow remote and strange in comparison with the new drama, unlike any he had known, that was now revolving around the body on the couch. And the body itself was somehow impossible to describe; it was not that of a living man because everything had gone out of it that constitutes the essence of a man and what remained was clearly and with incredible speed hastening toward its final extinction. But the body was not a corpse because, so long as it breathed, it was impossible to believe in the inevitability of what was to come; it demanded care and aroused an insane desire to keep the old man at all costs on this side of extinction.

N busied himself with all the household chores, taking upon himself any job that came up; he wanted to have as much to do as possible because by now neither work nor exhaustion held any fears for him. On the contrary, he sought them as means to combat the one thing he now dreaded above all else, remorse.

The woman doctor, bending over the couch and looking straight at the sick man, persistently repeated, "Don't you recognize me? Don't you? Please answer." Suddenly there was a slight tremor in the old man's face and in a strangely plaintive voice he murmured the doctor's name. This signified a momentary return to consciousness and N thought—why hadn't he gone over to his father like that, bent over him, looked into his eyes and started talking to him? Why hadn't he spoken loving words of comfort? Why hadn't he sat down beside his father and held his hand? Instead, he stood numbly by the couch. He felt awkward—he didn't know why—and his awkwardness continued to increase. Was it because of his awareness of what was happening in that room or was it because of his worry about the humiliation and helplessness of the dying man, subject as he was to the ministrations of strangers; or perhaps he felt that it would be tactless to show his feelings to the old man and make him respond, because, after all, his father too must be unwilling to show his feelings and embarrassed by the fact that he was dying.

N felt, in short, a veritable tangle of emotions, and there were so many trifling details implicit in the basic confusion. Suddenly N had the idea that the old man had wanted oranges and now it seemed that he had brought them for nothing. He had been pleased when the doctor said that after all the old man needed nourishment and he had ordered sweetened orange juice. They had fed the old man with a spoon—he had swallowed without opening his eyes and everyone had been pleased that he had drunk quite a lot of the juice. Suddenly it struck N that his father had not realized that the oranges he had wanted so much earlier were there now. But it was all of no avail. The old man had vomited and the pink liquid ran down his chin, all over his shirt, and onto the blanket.

Night was approaching. It turned out that that night it was impossible to get a nurse and there was no one to give him the injection. The doctor, Aunt's friend, did not stay. On leaving, she gave an injection, assuring them that the pulse was steadier and that during the night all that was necessary was to check the pulse. She would be returning in the morning but before that, the nurse would come to give another injection.

The three of them were left alone; N, his aunt, and the body on the couch. His aunt, without undressing, lay huddled on the bed, watching fearfully from there. N too did not undress but lay down on a settee. It seemed to him that he kept falling asleep only to wake up again every few minutes. Listening intently, he could hear the old man's heavy, measured breathing. Again he slept and again he awoke, alerted by his fear. He kept jumping up to feel the old man's pulse. The left arm, which was not paralyzed, kept slipping off the narrow couch; pale and flabby, it dangled as though weighted down. For some reason N remembered this especially even many months later; if his own arm slipped and hung down as he slept he would draw it back in alarm. N kept catching hold of his father's hanging arm and would clumsily feel for the pulse. Every time he did so it seemed to him that it had stopped and he felt as if his own heart stopped beating. Then a moment later his thumb, awkwardly feeling for the pulse on the cold, clammy skin of the sick man's wrist, would feel a beat. In heavy, irregular jerks, the vital, hidden artery was beating beneath the touch of his thumb, and N, keeping his thumb pressed on the pulse so as not to lose it, feverishly counted the beats. He didn't understand what was happening; he only knew that there was life in the blood that was pumping and laboring in that motionless body. Toward morning he suddenly fell asleep for an hour or two. When he woke up the room was getting light. The old man was still lying in the same position with his cap on; the arm, which N had so many times lifted and laid back on the blanket, was once again hanging down. N's back was hurting. His early morning sleep had calmed him a little and the feeling of dread had left him. Before making the effort to get up he was thinking that he must go to the market, stop at the pharmacy on the way, and then there were many things to see to. The hopeless, vicious circle of this illness was beginning; all the same the doctor had said that the pulse was stronger.

The doctor herself came soon after.

"No, the pulse is again considerably weaker." She shook her head. "Why didn't the nurse give him an injection when she came by in the morning? It was none of her business to make decisions; she only had to carry out orders." The doctor looked a bit awkward as she gave the injection. She felt guilty for not staying the night as they had begged her to do.

The woman doctor left and then the sick man's own doctor arrived. He stood for a moment, then drew up a chair, looked at the patient, felt his pulse, and said quietly that yes, he was much worse, his right side was paralyzed, a stroke, it was a question of a few hours. All the same it was strange that this should be so since there had been nothing alarming during the course of the illness.

N walked over to the window, turned away, and burst into tears. Behind him, his aunt too was sobbing.

The illusion of uncertainty was shattered and from now on everything that they did could be done only in anticipation of death, in preparation for death, in efforts to ease its coming. Everything that was being done, everything that was happening, was simply—death. And, already in connection with this death there were urgent questions to be considered about the apartment, the cooperative housing association, and some of Aunt's belongings. N had to go into town to get the necessary documents but he did not object to this because he thought it would be better to spend a few hours traveling than to stand by that couch. But standing on the platform under the huge station clock, he had an increasing feeling of anxiety. The journey to town by suburban train and streetcar, the successive delays—though each one was quite short—all this meant that the time seemed to drag interminably.

Barriers of space and time lay between him and the body on the couch. What did he fear? What more was there to be afraid of? That his father would die without him, that he would not be there to see him die?

In town he did what was necessary: obtained the documents, telephoned about getting a night nurse. He acted mechanically, as though numb, but with the single, persistent desire to get back as quickly as possible in case some better news awaited him there.

The neighbors asked him to dinner (they were having pancakes). He realized that he had eaten practically nothing all day, but the moment he sat down he immediately felt that he couldn't stay. If there had been meat he could have eaten it, but the thought of eating pancakes with caviar was quite revolting.

N traveled back, trying to make the time pass quickly so as to shorten the distance that lay between him and his dying father. But no—death had not yet come. Now he could be sure that it would not come while he was not there.

During his absence, life had assumed a new kind of routine in preparation for his father's death. The nurse had sent a woman to help; she was slovenly looking, but silently she cleaned up and put the place in order. The nearer the dying, unconscious man came to the moment when he would no longer wish for anything, the more the things that he had desired, but had never been able to have in his lifetime, appeared around him.

The stove was stoked up, and for the first time in winter, as far as N could remember, the room got warm. It made him realize that that was how the room should have been heated during the winter. They washed the body on the couch and changed his clothes. "Why is he so muffled up?" said the home help. "He must be very uncomfortable."

Everyone became very concerned that he should not be uncomfortable, although they knew perfectly well that he could not feel anything. Several times during the day the doctor sent a nurse from the hospital to give the old man injections (although, in the morning, he had admitted that injections were useless) and to relieve him from accumulated urine.

Aunt cheered up considerably. She was proud of herself for having managed to organize the death process so well. N thought, Why are they doing him so much good now when he is unconscious and it makes no difference to him what they do? How peaceful he looks! Why didn't I get here half an hour earlier that day? Why did I waste time looking for those oranges?

That night the nurse stayed, although by now no one had any doubt that there was no need for her. She was a cheerful soul, with a hearty appetite; she went out into the corridor when she wanted a smoke; she was well disposed toward the dying man and indeed toward everyone. N did not mind her being there. He smoked with her in the corridor and sometimes talked to her. There was nothing crude or fearful in her attitude toward death, and the professionalism of her attitude was tempered by that age-old peasant dignity in the face of the inevitable.

There was really nothing for her to do; she had her meals, smoked, slept on a small cot, which she moved up to the couch. That night the sick man's breathing sounded different; he inhaled now with a slow, steady, rhythmical noise. This breathing did not indicate that he was suffering, but for N each long, almost gurgling, inhalation was torture. After every one he strained to listen for the approach of the next one. At night N made a bed on top of a large trunk in the corridor. He kept going to sleep, waking up, looking into the room, going to the kitchen for a drink. The night nurse occasionally joined him in the corridor for a cigarette.

In the morning the old man was still lying motionless on his back with eyes half closed (it seemed as if his eyelids had ceased to function). There was still the same hoarse, even breathing but his face had changed. It had sagged; his cheeks had fallen in above the toothless jaws. It was the face of a stranger, either angry or bewildered. Only the forehead had not changed; it was still the same characteristic forehead with the two bony protuberances above the eyebrows, between which there was a small, soft wart. As he stood by the couch, N saw only the forehead with its two protuberances—as a child he used to call them bumps and liked to trace around them with his fingers. Now the old man's brow looked very peaceful. The night nurse said that he would die in about two hours.

And now this was the end. There were no interfering neighbors, no jobs that had to be done, no doubts—only death. Nothing but the echoing emptiness of waiting for death. Just as it is in prison, time had no meaning. The body lay on the couch in its last agony. To ease the existence of that body they had taken off his warm clothing, unbuttoned his shirt, revealing the yellow chest with its gray hairs as it rose and fell with the hoarse breathing. N led his aunt out of the room. He shut the door and remained in the room with the night nurse. He somehow had to endure his torment to the very end. At the end, it seemed to him that he had become completely numb and could no longer feel anything. In actual fact he was experiencing such spiritual torment that for years afterward he saw this death in his dreams, appearing in many different guises.

Everything took its course—the dying gasps, the temperature—with pointless medical precision it was taken every fifteen minutes—continued to fall from 39 degrees until it had reached a level that indicated unmistakably that death was imminent.

"What a strong heart he has! How he's fighting!" said the night nurse.

His whole body was fighting; his chest, from which the hoarse breath was coming in increasingly short, quick gasps; the arteries, so visible in his neck that one could measure his pulse simply by looking at them. But the face remained impassive and indifferent to everything that was happening in the body.

"Watch," said the nurse, "when the tears of sorrow begin to flow that will be the end."

N was sitting now right up close to the couch so as not to miss a single breath. What the nurse had said about tears of sorrow had affected him deeply, and he sat there repeating her words to himself and waiting for the tears to appear. But later, he was never able to remember whether he had in fact seen tears on the face of the dying man. The face had become even more taut and now it suddenly seemed to shrink. It stretched and shrunk rhythmically, taking part in the body's struggle against the coming of death. In his death agony there was no sign of conscious suffering, but torments of an inexpressible nature racked his observer. And in a final egoistic outburst N kept repeating to himself, "How should I be feeling if he were conscious?" Death came without fuss or commotion. Life ended with a sigh and a sob. With relief in her voice, the nurse said, "He is dead."

N stood up and bent over the couch, trying to understand what he felt. He did not know if he would be afraid to touch the lifeless body. He was not. He smoothed his father's peaceful brow with the bumps that had changed not at all and kissed it.

*   *   *

Everything that followed, that was concerned with the burial of that body, had for N some falseness about it. He discussed with the undertakers what material should be used for the coffin, he inspected the cemetery to see that the grave would not be flooded in spring, and he listened to his aunt worrying as to whether his father should be buried in his suit or his jacket. He did everything that had to be done; he also had to go to the Registry Office, where they crossed out the first page of his father's passport; he had to talk to the housing manager and borrow some money. He tried to appear relatively composed but in fact he felt anything but composed. For him, the question of death and extinction had little to do with graves and coffins or even with that lifeless body. Perhaps there was a shade of hypocrisy in that moment when he closed his father's eyes and kissed him once more on the forehead. Several times during the course of the day N lifted the sheet from the couch. Under the sheet, the old man lay, dressed only in his underwear, very small and shriveled, in no way frightening, with a gray stubble sprouting from his yellow cheekbones. But all this somehow bore no relation to what was already, in embryo, lurking in his heart and was destined to become something that would fill his whole existence. Perhaps, during the actual course of the funeral, occupied as he was with the final arrangements for the burial, N was calmer and more detached than he would be for many months to come.

It was a quiet funeral, with no guests. When the coffin was being lowered into the grave, Aunt suddenly burst into tears, very mournful tears; pressing her handkerchief to her lips, she kept repeating, "Why do they dig it so deep? Why so deep?"

N realized that she was thinking about her own inevitable death. N sent his aunt back home with the driver; he paid the cemetery workers for carrying the coffin and for lining the grave with fir branches and then he went back alone across the snow-covered field. He knew that now at last he would be able to think, but it was easier to think, walking alone in the icy wind and sun.

And thus began what was to last thereafter for a very long time—the grinding rotation, the flow of fragmented thoughts, already made meaningless by continual repetition, but all of them, in their very essence, supplying never-ending material for his feelings of remorse. The old man had been waiting for him to bring the oranges but he had come half an hour too late. He'd been talking to Lisa ... and on top of that, the previous day there had been no one to go to the pharmacist for the prescription ... perhaps if they had got the camphor earlier. Of course all these conjectures were nonsense—but if only he hadn't lost his self-control, if only he had thought of getting the nurse out from town to give the injections, if only they could have persuaded the lady doctor to stay the night. But he hadn't been insistent enough, he'd been far too timid, he felt that he had betrayed his father. And then he started thinking that they'd paid the night nurse too little, and he felt very ashamed about that. Then immediately he started thinking about how badly he had arranged the life that so trustingly had been put into his hands and how all this would always keep coming back to him.

Père Goriot is not true to life. Are there really, could there really be, could there ever have been children who did not want to go to the bedside of their dying father on account of an invitation to dinner? In fact, the truth is even worse, even simpler—children always go and visit their dying father; they rush to see him after they have made his life miserable while he was alive.

Lisa will understand; she's like that herself. Lisa once said to him, "Have you noticed, people who really love their parents accept their death relatively calmly? It is the selfish ones who get all worked up—instead of thinking about the man who has died, they think about their own guilt."

*   *   *

A delusion that it's never too late to put things right ...

A mind without clear, common aims, naively sees an action as isolated from any connection between sin and retribution. For it, existence is either an empirical jumble of passing moments, all equally senseless, or a meaningless succession of moments that cancel each other out. And the last moment of all is death, which cancels out everything.

Such is the logic of individualism at its life's limit. But stronger than any logic is the practice of life itself. It demands from the transient man that he should live as though his every action were predestined for some unending, historical sequence. It insists upon an irreversible moral code of life—love and creation, compassion and guilt.

Translated by Ludmilla Groves and Mary Plume

GALINA   SCHERBAKOVA

THE THREE "LOVES"
OF MASHA PEREDREEVA

WHEN MASHA PEREDREEVA found out how much IT cost in Moscow, she couldn't sleep all night. She lay there thinking, It's just as well I read it with my own eyes. Seriously if anyone had tried to tell her that people paid 100 rubles* for it, she would have laughed in their face. A hundred rubles! After she finished at the teacher training college she'd be paid less than that for a whole month's work—a whole month! And people were being paid that much money for just a few minutes. It wasn't as if they were being made to hump steel girders or look after pigs. Take her mother, for example. She was a cultural official with the local council and earned 150 rubles a month, including traveling expenses. All that traveling gave her chronic cystitis. The conditions she had to put up with when she made the rounds of the villages! Her doctor had said to her, "Olga Sergeyevna, it's no laughing matter for someone in your condition to be taking your knickers off in freezing cold outhouses or cabins. You must make up your mind. What's more important—your health or your status?" She settled for status. She was known throughout the region— without her there would be no movies, no culture—nothing! "I don't work for money. If we followed the capitalist path, who knows where it would lead."

---

* 1985 prices.

"As if we know where *this* path is leading us," Masha would say.

It was clear to her that her mother's opinions were often motivated by grievance and poverty. She had reached the ceiling of her life's potential, and no amount of battering would break through that ceiling. She could go no further with her secondary education (she was trained as a projectionist). True enough, she had been a party member for twenty-five of her forty-three years, but she wasn't sharp enough to use this to her advantage. She was like a fire extinguisher—producing huge amounts of foam and noise, but never achieving anything. Masha would look at her mother and think, God save me from a life like that. No husband. No money. Ill health. What she did have was an apartment. Yes, a good apartment—two bedrooms, all the modern conveniences, on the second floor, even with a telephone. Her mother worshiped the apartment. She used to take Masha to see the wooden tenement where she had grown up. The people in the tenement still remembered her. Unlike Masha they thought she'd really made something of herself. "I haven't gotten anywhere!" she would say, waving a hand self-deprecatingly. But her eyes sparkled. She desperately needed to be reassured, to have her successes enumerated in detail. And the simple people from the tenement would bend over backward to please her. "Just think about it, Olga," they would say. "For a start you've got your own apartment. Two whole rooms for the two of you, and that's not counting the kitchen—you could easily just live in the kitchen if you had to. It's big enough. Look at us.—Never mind the bathroom! You could live in there too—you've got running water in the kitchen as well, haven't you?" Her mother would laugh, delighted by the conversation. Then the good-natured people from the tenement would heap more praise on her because she had a white-collar job, and didn't have to go out to work with rakes and pitchforks.

"I don't despise any kind of work," Masha's mother would say to them. Ultimately they mentioned the district council. They did not disguise their attitude toward the council—no description was too bad for it, but they tactfully avoided mentioning Masha's mother in connection with it. "You're such a saint, Olga. You don't realize what kind of bribery and corruption goes on in there." Olga would rebuke them. "You ought to be ashamed of yourselves, saying things like that!" But Masha agreed with them entirely. She secretly believed that her mother must share their opinion, she wasn't a complete fool after all! But her mother didn't go to the tenement in search of such primitive harmonizing. She went there when she felt as if she was festering inside, when her boss had given her a tongue-lashing, or when her quarrels with Masha almost reached the point of violence. These were the moments when her mother would put on her best dress, sling a bag over her shoulder, and return to her roots. She would always be warmly welcomed. "You're our girl, Olga! And you're such a pet—you never forget us, even though you've risen so high." And her mother would swallow spoonfuls of praise, soothing away the insults in her life. She heard the same things repeated a million times, the remarks about her apartment and her clothes ("Is that an imported dress you're wearing, Olga? You'd never be able to make that yourself. The cloth is garbage, true, you'd find better cloth here, but the design ... and what pretty straps. Look how they fit together!"). And about the power of the council. "We know you don't take bribes, Olga. But the way the rest of them carry on, it would put the fear of God in you! They're not afraid of anyone."

Masha pitied her mother and despised her. Sometimes the former dominated her feelings, but more often the latter. When she felt pity she dreamed about taking her mother to a Central Asian spa she had heard about so they could cure her mother's cystitis. She would spare no expense to send her mother to a dry climate and put an end to all her business trips. When she was overcome by feelings of scorn, she thought, You're so keen on going back to your tenement, you stupid cow. Why don't you go back there for good? They've got fancy rooms there too. The ones at the end of the corridors have two windows, and even a little entrance hall. Why don't you go and live there! When I get married and have children, what man will tolerate living under the same roof with you? You're nothing but an old windbag—always saying that all men ought to be shot. What are you going to do once you've shot them all? I suppose you like living alone with your cystitis? Or do you?

Her mother was slightly paranoid on the subject of voting. She was in favor of open voting, as a matter of principle, considering it more honest. A long time ago she had been up for election to some kind of committee. They had all heaped praise on her, and then almost everyone crossed her name off the list on the ballot paper. Masha couldn't remember exactly what they were voting for, but her mother was utterly shattered by the experience. Masha couldn't understand either. Why had they praised her so highly if they were then going to cross her name off the list? She tried to imagine herself in a similar situation, but found herself giggling helplessly. Nobody had ever nominated her for anything. Whenever she was at any kind of meeting, ever since she was a small child, she had been prone to collapsing in fits of laughter.

"Comrades! I declare this meeting open."

That was enough to set her off. They would have to take her out of the room. Her mother dragged her to a doctor, who diagnosed nervousness and instructed her to chew gum during the meetings. We have Soviet-made gum now, but at that time it took some looking to find it. Masha's mother used to go to the district center to get it. By now Masha had grown out of her giggling fits, but the memory of them lived on, with the result that she was left alone at meetings. She would sit at the very back, sucking a lollipop or chewing gum, and copy song lyrics. She had a more extensive song book than anyone else at college. It included Pugacheva, Kuzmin, Minayev, Aguzarova—everyone!

Masha thought Soviet culture was a lot more interesting now than it had been in her mother's time, when they used to line up on stage like a load of imbeciles and stand stock-still with their hands on their hips. They didn't move an inch, never mind tap dancing. Nowadays things had changed—it took your breath away, the way some of them could sing and dance. You couldn't deny that the arts were improving in spite of people like her mother trying to stand in the way of change. What bugged her more than anything was that her mother couldn't stand the folk choirs either, but she still organized them, cultivated them, encouraged them. But as soon as a choir showed up on the TV she'd switch to another program, quick as a flash. She tried to justify herself on the basis of Pavlov's dogs, saying people needed variety.

"Those dogs would have croaked if they'd been forced to listen to your choirs," said Masha.

Her mother would scream at her until she was blue in the face. It was just as well they had two rooms. You could always shut the door and turn up the radio. There was no way her mother could outscream Soviet radio.

What brains she had! They'd chew up anything. She jumped out of bed. She'd started out shocked by that article in the paper and ended up thinking about her mother and the tenement. Masha had once said to her mother, "You take up too much space in my life."

"What's that supposed to mean?" her mother bawled. It didn't take much to get her going.

Masha, barefoot and naked, went to the kitchen for a drink of water. As she passed her mother's room she could hear her moaning in her sleep. The nighttime moaning had frightened Masha as a small child. She used to fling herself on the bed, crying, "Mommy, Mommy!" And then she'd get a smack for waking her up. Her mother always said that she hadn't been dreaming about anything that could possibly make her groan. In that case why did she sob, grind her teeth, and toss from side to side in her sleep? She herself admitted that her husband, Masha's father, even used to hit her because of her sleeping habits. Masha could understand the way he felt. When they had lived in the club she hated her mother at night, too. All that u-u-u-u-h, a-a-a-h, o-o-o-h made it impossible to sleep. Masha kicked an armchair in the darkness. The chair creaked. Her mother gave a sob, fell silent for a moment, then began moaning again.

An old mirror hung in the kitchen. They had bought a new pier glass, then didn't know where to put the old one. They tried it all over the place and ended up hanging it above the kitchen table. It looked quite good there. Masha stood by the stove. From there she could see herself clearly in the mirror. Her figure was not ideal by today's standards. She had a big bust and bottom and a fine waist. Her legs were on the heavy side, but straight—you wouldn't have been able to slide a knife between her knees. Her skin was good—not silk, but white velvet with a pinkish tinge. And when tanned, it became a delicate golden color. She had a lovely stomach—oval shaped and with a deep belly button. She'd never had a single blemish or pimple in her life. Her face wasn't as good as her body. A big mouth with fleshy lips, which some people found attractive. For color, she only had to bite her lips from time to time, and she never bothered with lipstick. Admittedly her eyes were rather small. But with a bit of blue on the eyelids and a pencil line to lengthen the corners, they weren't such a bad shape, she looked almost Egyptian—quite stylish. Masha often wondered, Where would we be without makeup? How did they manage in the old days? Her mother said that they had managed well enough with lipstick and powder. But that probably meant that some people managed all right and some people didn't. She didn't believe everything her mother told her. Now of course there was much more to choose from: shadow and shiny stuff to put on your eyes and imported colors of lipstick. If you took a bit of trouble with yourself you couldn't go wrong. Her best feature was her hair. Thick and unstyled, like a fur hat. She didn't have to do anything special with her hair, just leave it alone. Even its chestnut color was natural—they called it "helidraun."

Masha turned her back to the mirror. She had a nice way of turning—quite sexy. There was no question but that she was worth that much money, so she'd better go out and earn it. She'd be a real fool if she didn't make use of her knowledge, now that she knew 100 rubles a time was just waiting to be collected.

Her mother came into the kitchen half asleep. She'd been unable to find the switch in the bathroom.

"What are you doing standing there with no clothes on?"

"None of your business!" snapped Masha.

"Go to hell!" Her mother slammed the door and rattled the toilet seat. Masha dreamed of the time when she would have saved up enough money so that she would never have to live with her mother again. What else would she do? She'd take herself off to the Baltics. Of course Russians weren't very popular up there, but she was better looking than their women, there was no doubt about that. She'd buy herself an apartment by the seaside, and then she'd see. Maybe she'd get married, or maybe she wouldn't. When she was rich. ...

Her mother finished in the bathroom and came into the kitchen. She looked at Masha. "Haven't you stood there long enough? You haven't even shut the curtains."

"They're welcome to have a look—if they're not asleep," said Masha. "Anyone who's not asleep deserves a bit of pleasure."

"I had a better figure than you when I was your age," said her mother.

"You couldn't have!" Masha was indignant.

Her mother took the bait. She took off her nightdress and stood naked beside Masha. Masha moved away fastidiously. She couldn't bear to be close to another person's naked body.

"I'm slimmer than you, for a start," said her mother, examining herself in the mirror. "Anyone would think you were the one that had a child, not me."

"You're flabby," countered Masha.

"Flabby!" her mother cried. She stuck out her elbow and started jabbing at Masha. Then suddenly her expression turned sour and her face drooped. "I don't know how you have the heart to say things like that to your own mother. You're my own flesh. You've taken all my strength, my vitality. You wait till you have a baby. You'll be flabby yourself, and then your daughter will say mean things to you."

"For a start I'm not going to have a baby," said Masha. "Only a fool would give birth to a child that was going to grow up poor. And if I do have a baby, I'll make sure I look after myself. I won't let myself go."

"To hell with you." Her mother sounded indifferent as she walked away, dragging her nightdress along the floor, and Masha—who was fair-minded—noticed that her mother had a beautiful cleft running down the center of her back, and a small, neat bottom. Her legs were slimmer than Masha's, too. From behind she looked like a young girl, if you ignored the chemical bush on her head. Her hair was a real mess. Dyed, poisoned, sparse, and tortured into shape. Masha even began to feel sorry for her.

"You'll do! Still fit for service." Masha tried to sound encouraging.

Her mother froze in her steps, then turned around. "You fucking bitch!" she hissed, clearly but under her breath.

Occasionally her mother's humble origins would come out in the form of foul language. Masha was shocked when she did this. She herself might call someone a fool, or a pain, or if she was really driven to it, a cow. But that was as far as she would go. It wasn't that she deliberately stopped herself from saying anything stronger. The words just didn't find their way into her mouth. In this respect Masha considered herself superior to her mother. In fact she considered herself a cultured person in general. She ate with a knife and fork. She always greeted old ladies before they greeted her, but never greeted men first. Her speech was regularly punctuated with "please" and "thank you." She did not point, nor did she swear. The other girls in her group used to say, "If you're really trying to give someone a piece of your mind, it doesn't mean much if you don't swear."

"You're only lowering yourself," replied Masha.

Her mother was foul-mouthed. A tenement is a tenement—it will always leave its mark. Masha couldn't even walk past it without feeling disgust. Even when the lilac was in bloom—and the tenement was completely surrounded by lilac bushes—a stale smell seemed to hang in the air: a mixture of cabbage, soap, old mattresses, boiled laundry, cats, mice, stale alcohol, gas stoves repeatedly doused with water, and stronger than anything else, a smell that hung stubbornly in spite of the fiercest frost or burning summer heat—the smell of the Tenement Itself. Everyone has their own smell—miners, black people, nurses. So did the tenement. It was a smell that concentrated many things, and it was a fertile environment for bad language, as natural as a fish in water, dust in the air, or a worm in a pile of dung. But the fact that her mother still occasionally came out with tenement-style language, despite the fact that she had long ago stopped living there, simply proved what an uncultured person she was. Masha invariably pointed this out to her.

"You may be a cultural official, Mom, but you're not exactly cultured yourself. You ought to watch your language."

"And you're too cultured for your own good," her mother would snap.

Masha's plan of action was as follows: On the weekend she would go to the district center. There were hotels and even a particular hotel for foreigners there. She would try her luck. In any case, she would have to be a total, complete, utter fool not to seize this opportunity.

Toward morning Masha fell asleep. She did not hear her mother leave for work. Nor did she know that as her mother stood in front of the mirror in the kitchen, gulping down hot tea, she had tried to understand why her daughter had been roaming around the apartment naked in the middle of the night. She felt slightly disturbed. As a woman, and a local council official, she was upset by modern youth. They drank and smoked and took drugs. They believed in neither God nor the devil. They had babies and then abandoned them. Sex did not frighten them in the least. She had recently been shown some classified statistics on this subject at the council. Dreadful. Of course she had total confidence in her Masha. She was a proud girl with a mind of her own. But still, she ought to keep an eye on her. After all, she was fully grown now, and there were certain urges. Masha's mother choked on her tea. She was filled with a malicious fury, rising up from her stomach like bile.

"I'll show her urges! I'll show her what happens if she feels like doing something!" she said to her reflection. "I'll sew up her privates with a needle and thread, if that's what it takes."

After those words she calmed down. For God's sake, whom could she possibly be getting it on with and where? She studied at the teacher training institution—and there wasn't a single boy in the place. There was only one male teacher—the man who took them for PE. And he was due to retire soon, and he had a harelip. He was the kind of man you'd only go for if you'd spent a hundred years on a desert island. Victor Korshunov, one of Masha's schoolmates, used to date her. He was a nice enough boy, polite and well-mannered. But he'd gone off to do his army service two months ago. They'd sent him straight to Afghanistan. God forbid anything should happen to him. His mother Nyusya worked in the shoe shop. She walked around looking completely gray with grief and fear. You could understand it. He and Masha didn't write to each other—she would have known if they did. She was sure nothing had happened between them. They just hung around together, sometimes went to the movies.

Masha's mother felt calmer as she set off for work. The sight of potato peelings on the stairs did not improve her mood. Their neighbor always spilled something out of the bucket when she was taking her garbage down. She'd already had words with her.

"You ought to know better than to throw your garbage everywhere, Mrs. Chebrikova. It's not your own house. It belongs to the state, and you live here rent-free. So please be so good as to keep the place clean and decent." Please be so good—she remembered saying that.

"I'm so sorry," replied the neighbor, slamming her door loudly. What could you do with people like that? She'd apologized, but the potato peelings were still lying there.

*   *   *

Masha arrived in the town at noon. She'd have to while away the time until evening. When the other girls went to look around the shops, Masha realized she had to get her thoughts sorted out, no matter what bargains she might be missing in the shops. She had an aunt living in the town, her father's sister. They hardly kept in touch, but Masha decided to go and see her. She knew her mother wouldn't thank her for it, but nobody was asking her opinion today. Masha bought some asters—a bunch of five, freshly cut and bound together—and headed out. Her aunt lived on the seventh floor of a nice apartment building, with an elevator and a garbage chute. Admittedly running water only reached as far as the fourth floor, but there were plans to install a pump to raise the water higher. So far nothing had been done. At night her aunt collected as much water as she could in bathtubs, buckets, and 50-liter tanks. Wherever you looked there was some kind of container of water. Even mayonnaise jars were filled with water. Of course this made the apartment damp. Wallpaper had started peeling off after a month, and the edges hung down. But apart from that it was a nice apartment. Folding glass doors, a covered balcony, all three rooms separate. Her aunt was a doctor.

"Hello, Auntie Shura!" said Masha, trying to sound as friendly as possible. Auntie Shura stood looking at Masha, apparently failing to recognize her. Then Masha thrust forward her bouquet of asters.

"Good heavens!" said her aunt. "I didn't recognize you. Where did you come from? Come in. I'm just getting ready to go on duty."

Very good, thought Masha. I'll manage without you.

"Where's Uncle Kolya?" she asked sweetly, taking off her shoes and putting on a pair of men's slippers.

"Uncle Kolya's out fishing. He's been gone since last night."

"What a pity," said Masha, secretly trembling with delight. "And what about the boys?"

"They're fishing too. I let them take the day off from school. Get a bit of fresh air in their lungs while the weather's still nice. And if there are children around, the men will have to watch how they behave. It might make them drink a bottle or two less."

"We're supposed to be on a college trip," said Masha. "And I decided I'd already seen everything they were going to show us. If I've visited those battlegrounds once, I've visited them a hundred times ... so I thought I'd come and visit you."

"It was a very good idea." Her aunt sounded uncertain. "Only I have to go to work. You should have written or phoned to let us know. It's better to warn people nowadays."

"I'll wait for you," Masha suggested.

"I'll be gone for twenty-four hours," said her aunt. Then suddenly an idea occurred to her. "Could you mind the water tonight? You could fill the canister. Only you'd have to do it after midnight."

Masha had no idea where she would be after midnight. But she said firmly, "No problem."

"Then you're welcome to stay." Her aunt went into the kitchen, and began taking the lids off cooking pots and frying pans.

"I'm afraid there's only leftovers," she sighed. "I don't really cook when the boys aren't around. You'd go mad, cooking for the three of them every day. But you can help yourself to what there is."

"Don't worry," said Masha. "A cup of tea will do for me."

As she handed the keys to Masha, her aunt asked, "Does your father ever write?"

Masha shook her head.

"I don't hear from him either. I suppose he's stopped paying the alimony too?"

"Last month."

"Oh yes, I forgot you're eighteen already. How's your mother?"

"She's all right."

"Why didn't they stay together?" Her aunt sighed, looked at Masha, and decided that this was the right moment to kiss her—for everything. For the asters, for turning eighteen, for remembering her aunt, for having a scoundrel for a father who had run off God knows where.

*   *   *

Masha began to get ready.

She mustn't waste the water. So she poured a little water into a basin and sprinkled in a few drops from each of her aunt's flasks and bottles. She washed herself slowly and meticulously. As she washed she planned what she was going to do with her first 100 rubles. She decided to put it in a savings bank. The best thing would be to save up carefully and then buy something expensive, like a real fur coat or some gold jewelry. Of course her mother would be amazed. "Where did you get the money?"

But once she had the money, that kind of conversation with her mother would be easy. She'd be operating from a position of strength.

"Your party loyalty really got you a long way, didn't it?" Masha would ask her sarcastically.

Her mother's face would flush, and she would yell—a sure sign that she had nothing to say. Good! It would be crucial to mention the party at the right moment. Masha hated the party even more than she hated the Komsomol. They were nothing but a bunch of windbags who didn't even believe what they themselves said. They just kept playing the same tunes to get ahead in the world. As Masha saw it, the Communist Party was like a highrise building. Her mother was doomed to stay on the ground floor until the day she died, whereas other people could get themselves up to the top. Masha laughed, dabbing at her toes with cottonballs. You could be sure that the people up there got regular water supplies. Her mother would rant and rave. ... She was already over forty, and the ceiling over her head was reinforced with steel beams. There was no chance of her moving any higher. First, if you were honest, you were a fool; second, she didn't have enough qualifications, even officially; third, if she'd had any sense she'd have gotten a job in retail, where it's impossible not to do well. But she chose culture. Broken musical instruments and costumes made of old sacking. When Masha became rich her mother could scream to her heart's content. Scream away! You can have a fit if you like. Masha would tell them all to go you-know-where.

And as for Victor Korshunov—she'd send him to hell in a basket. When he came back from Afghanistan she'd walk right past him and ignore him. ... No, she wouldn't ignore him ... she'd stop and talk to him, but in such a way as to put him in his place once and for all.

Of course he'd earned a few words of thanks. "Thank you, Victor, for your service to the Soviet Union!" Now Masha wasn't afraid of anything. In fact, to be honest, she'd never been afraid of this. She remembered how, just before he left, when he already had his army haircut, Victor had flung himself at her feet. She never would have expected him to behave like this. Quiet, gentle Victor had never said "boo" to a goose, and then suddenly there he was, grabbing her legs and wheezing passionately.

"Be my guest!" said Masha. "Do you think I'd grudge you a little thing like that!"

She had felt a combination of shame, disgust, and pain, but all these feelings were somehow vague and shallow. The strongest sensation was that of Victor's shaved, prickly head rubbing against her cheeks.

Victor had talked about marriage before that. "We could get married tomorrow if you felt like it. Would you like to?" Afterward he stopped mentioning it. At least he stopped suggesting they might get married the next day. He put marriage on a more distant timescale. Masha noticed the change immediately, and thought, "You swine!" But she didn't say anything, because she never imagined she might become his wife, not even in her wildest nightmares. It was the kind of idea that went with war and the end of the world. But she still noticed that Victor had recanted his former position. After he left, he faded away rapidly. He said he would write. "Just you wait and see! And make sure you answer." "Uh-huh," she replied. "Why don't you come to the station tomorrow?" he suggested. "Okay," she agreed. As it happened, she did go. Her girlfriends had said, "Let's go down to the station. There's a brass band."

They arrived. The station was swarming with people. Victor was surrounded by a lot of shop assistants and his mother, who worked in the shoe shop, kept walking around him. The way Victor called Masha over to stand beside him was typical of his character. Masha almost burst out laughing. His mother stopped her frenzied dance and looked at Masha. She took a long time appraising her, but when she had absorbed the information that her son had a young lady standing beside him, she called out in a thin, nasty voice, "Well, here comes the bride! The turtle dove has flown in to honor us with her presence!"

The final curtain fell on the performance of "The Send-off." They all went their separate ways, and that was the end of it. Victor never wrote, and when they were selling imported boots in the shoe shop, and Masha tried to make signs at Victor's mother from the end of the line, she pretended she hadn't seen her.

She bought the boots anyway. One of the other girls got a pair that didn't fit, so she sold them to Masha. She only paid an extra ten rubles.

*   *   *

The local Intourist hotel was located in Pioneer Park. The name of the park was given credence by the plaster figures of girls and boys and classic Marxist-Leninist slogans plastered all over the place. You couldn't move without bumping into one of them. Either a boy reading a book, or a little girl frozen in an eternal salute, or a huge human head. Whoever designed the park obviously thought that Young Pioneers only needed to see the heads of great men—they weren't of an age to benefit from the rest of the body.

Rumor had it that at night in this park, decked out as it was in exemplary fashion with such plaster ideology, things far removed from the ideas represented by those plaster heads were going on. But that's what parks are for—even Young Pioneer parks. Masha sat down on a bench near a fountain. The water came jetting out of the mouths of fishes and poured straight over a pioneer, who stood in the center playing a bugle. Masha deliberately posed in a way that would make it obvious she was alone, but that would also allow her, in the event of an unforeseen occurrence, to run around the fountain and rush down one of the paths, where every third person was a public-order volunteer wearing a red armband. Not that you could rely on them. The worst kind of racketeers wore armbands. Their armbands were nothing but red herrings.

It was already getting dark, but the park was not yet lit up. The local authorities had launched a campaign to save electricity. A special duty officer was responsible for giving the order to switch on the street lights. The duty officer stood at his window and watched the streets getting darker, and the Pioneer Park turning from bottle green to dark blue, then grayish, and finally plunging into total blackness.

The first man broke away from the crowd and walked across to Masha firmly and confidently. He was quite a handsome fellow, but definitely a Russian, not even a Georgian.

"Feeling a little bored, are we?" he asked, plunking himself down on the bench beside Masha.

"I'm just sitting here." Masha was nothing if not truthful.

"How about if I suggested something a little more interesting?" asked the Russian.

At this point there was a gap in Masha's well-planned scheme. She didn't know whether it was expected for her to name her price up front, or wait to mention money after everything was over.

Masha was afraid of making a tactical error. She had been concentrating so hard on doing and saying the right thing, that for a moment she forgot where she was, why she had come, and who was waiting for her answer.

She sat as if turned to stone, like the plaster girl who sat nearby reading a copy of *The Young Guard*. She didn't even notice when the man—he was surely a Russian, not even a Georgian—suddenly jumped up shouting, "Nellia! Nellia!" and disappeared.

That's great! thought Masha. As soon as anything happens I lose my head.

Then she sighed with relief. After all, she needed a little while to get used to sitting on the bench.

Luck was with her. Another man came up to her. He was a Soviet too, but this time not a Russian, he was very dark. He could have been a Moldavian, or perhaps an Armenian. Who else could be that dark? Anyway, he certainly wasn't from the Baltics.

"How about it?"

Scum, thought Masha. He's some kind of country bumpkin. What a fool. "Get the hell away from me!" she said quietly.

"Watch it!" said the dark man, but he kept his distance as he sat down on the bench. Two people could have sat between them.

"Where do you come from?" asked the dark man.

How can he tell I'm not local? Masha was alarmed and began eyeing the passers-by nervously. The girls looked classy, dressed to the nines. Masha made a quick assessment, comparing herself to them. She couldn't see that she was any worse-looking than them, nor was she any more attractive. Why had he asked where she came from? "From here, of course! I come from the seventh floor, where there's no running water," she countered wittily, just to show him what kind of person he was dealing with.

"You can't fool me," said the dark man. "You can't have left the village more than two hours ago. You still smell of cowsheds."

"Are you mad?" cried Masha. "I've never been near a cowshed in my life!"

She leaped from her seat just at the moment when the duty officer, with a heavy sigh, decided that it was not within his power to save the council any more on its electricity bill.

Masha, furious at the dark man's unkind words, was bathed in yellow light, which made her look rather attractive. Anyway, one of a group of boys who were amusing themselves by throwing their cigarette butts into the mouths of the spitting fishes came over to her. He was a strong, well-built boy, Russian of course, but he looked quite like an American. That was how Masha described him to herself—an American type. If you can't get the genuine, pedigreed article, you might as well get something along the right lines.

He took Masha's hand firmly but not roughly and turned her around to face him.

"Hey, where are you going in such a hurry?" he asked.

"Some guy is bothering me," Masha replied.

"Not your type, eh?" asked the "American."

"A piece of scum," said Masha.

The young man looked Masha up and down, he even walked around her, in order to examine her from all angles. He made approving clicking sounds with his tongue.

"Will I do?" he asked politely.

"We'll have to discuss it first," Masha spoke precisely. The conversation was moving along in a satisfactory, businesslike way. It was a relief to discover that some people could get on the right track immediately.

"What would you like to know?"

"A hundred rubles," said Masha. She mentally congratulated herself and gave herself credit for the calm way she had said it. Everything was going very nicely indeed!

The young man rounded his lips and let out a bird-like, whistling sound, but he didn't let go of Masha's hand. He whistled a strange tune, using his lips skillfully like a musical instrument, then asked, "Is that a contract for the whole family?"

"What do you mean?" Masha didn't understand.

"Boyfriend? Husband? Father? Mother? Who's on the payroll?"

"What are you talking about?" Masha exclaimed. She realized now he was joking, but he'd thrown her off balance for a moment.

"Okay," said the young man. "I agree."

As Masha had expected, there were no lights in the seventh-floor window. But she looked up just in case. She didn't want to take any chances.

As they went into the apartment the young man immediately turned on the light, which meant, thank God, that they avoided tripping over any buckets of water.

He made himself at home. Masha didn't know whether to be pleased about this or not. He was strolling around as if he owned the place. Well ... it was someone else's house, after all. He quickly figured out everything about the family. There were two teenagers living in the apartment—both of them boys. And their father was a fisherman.

"None of your things are here," he said. "How are you related to them?"

"She's my aunt," Masha replied.

"Ah!" he said. "So you're on tour ..."

"What?" She didn't understand. She didn't know what he meant by the word *tour*. She knew the word of course, but she couldn't figure out what he meant by it.

Later, while it was going on, Masha wondered where he was going to get the money. He was lightly dressed, and there was no sign of a bulging wallet anywhere on him. It couldn't be in that little pocket closed with a zipper. If it was, then it had to be just one, high-denomination banknote, because the pocket wasn't bulging. Masha began to feel a little anxious about the question of money, even though everything was going according to plan. When she had undressed and lain down on her aunt's double bed, he had looked at her cheerfully, and said, "Not such a bad hundred-rubles'-worth, for a country girl! What a lovely, strong little calf you are!"

She didn't like that. It reminded her too much of the cowsheds. Making sure not to mention her first name or surname, she pointed out that she came from an educated family, and he had no call to talk like that. They'd never kept cows or even goats. And they didn't know anything about such things.

Once again he rounded his lips and whistled his birdsong in her ear. It tickled, but she managed to say that she wasn't some kind of cowherd.

He jumped lightly from the bed, lightly slipped on his trousers and rattled the bracelet of his watch. Masha watched with satisfaction. There was definitely something American about him.

"Hey!" said Masha, as he headed toward the door.

"Oh, I'm sorry!" The "American" tapped his forehead, and, as Masha had guessed, he fumbled in the zippered pocket.

He stood over her, strong and handsome, and tossed a ruble coin in the air.

"Here!" he laughed. "Catch it!"

Well, Masha wasn't the kind of girl who would put up with that kind of treatment.

She grabbed hold of him. For a moment he was taken aback, confused, which gave her the advantage long enough to rip his shirt.

"Pay up, you snake!"

His shirt parted down the middle from the collar to the belly button.

He came to his senses and sent Masha sprawling across the bed. Lying down is not a strong position from which to fight, and unfortunately the principle that you should never hit someone when they're down has been consigned to history. The young man had no qualms about hitting Masha. He hit her proudly and confidently, from a position of strength and justice. Masha did not want to cry out and breathed hoarsely. The bastard realized that there was no danger of her making a noise, and he hit her for a last time, particularly painfully. She couldn't help screaming but he was clever enough to cover her face with a pillow.

Masha heard him close the bedroom door. For a while she howled into the pillow, but, typically for her, it was more from humiliation than from pain. She could stand pain, but what she couldn't bear was any kind of insult or humiliation. Everything had gone wrong! He had twisted her around his little finger as if she were a small child. She'd fallen for it like a complete fool. She should have questioned how a young guy like that would have a spare hundred rubles. That had been her mistake. Of course the article she had read didn't mention age. Mainly it talked about foreigners. But where was she supposed to find a foreigner? Never mind, thought Masha, let this be a lesson to me. In a minute she would get up and start over. As her mother would say, you get two new plates every time you smash one. That's the law of life. Masha switched on the light and looked at herself in the mirror. Her face was all red, but apart from that she looked all right. It could be worse. Now she would use some more of her aunt's water—a bit more than she should. She'd have to bathe her eyes, and anyway … almost swaying, Masha went into the bathroom, and what she saw nearly made her cry out loud.

All the water had been poured out. The buckets and jars had been neatly turned upside down, and on top of one of the jars lay the bouquet of asters she had given to her aunt. Even the teapot lay on its side. So that's how he'd tried to get even. Even the mayonnaise jars had been emptied right down to the last drop. Masha rushed to the tap, which was making a rustling sound, then a promising gurgling noise, then a furious howling of pipes, followed by a silence broken only by the sound of Masha's beating heart. The only water left was in the toilet. Masha drank a little, washed herself and bathed her eyes. Then spitefully, she flushed away the remaining water and walked out of the apartment.

She dropped the jingling keys into the mailbox. In another burst of spite, Masha thumped the box with her fist and headed for the station. She'd gotten nowhere this time. Never mind! She was glad she wasn't the only one who'd had a bad day—her aunt hadn't been too lucky either. If everything had gone well for Masha, she would certainly have taken care of the water and filled the canisters. But as it was, all she'd gotten was a slap in the face, and if they still expected her to do the decent thing, well they'd picked the wrong girl. She didn't care what her aunt said or thought. The next time Masha wouldn't use her apartment. She'd learned her lesson. It was amazing how that guy had figured it all out: "There are none of your things here," he'd said. Meaning, I can cheat you, you fool. You haven't even got the right to live here. Next time she'd plan everything out, right down to the last detail. She'd know better next time.

For now she had to go home. She could catch the night train her mother always rode when she'd been to town. Masha bought a ticket and sat down to wait. The places where he had hit her began to ache, and she could feel her eye swelling up as people looked at her. Masha covered her eye with a handkerchief. "Those hooligans in town," she would say to her mother, who would start shouting. "Young people nowadays have no discipline! They deserve what's coming to them! We go on fussing over them, dancing to their tune. They ought to be shot as an example to the others, the bastards."

Masha's mother was strongly in favor of execution by firing squad, on principle. She believed this to be the only way of restoring order to the country. She had even worked out a precise, arithmetical system for the process. "If you shot one in ten, the other nine would behave themselves properly. Now you can't say that people in general wouldn't benefit. One sacrificed for the good of nine!"

Masha was convinced by the one-in-ten formula. Admittedly, when she proposed the system in class one of the girls had said, "And what if you turn out to be the one?"

"What for?" Masha was indignant. "What have I ever done? I'm not a thief or bandit, am I?"

But, to be honest, she did start to feel a bit uncomfortable about it. There were thirty of them in her class. Which three should be shot? Masha was no better or worse than twenty-five others in the class. There were five who always got top marks for everything, and it was sickening to see them working desperately to get their excellent exam results so they could get into college. To be fair, they should be the ones to be shot. But you could look at it in a different way. For this reason, Masha became rather more wary about repeating her mother's words in public.

Her eye had swollen completely shut by the time she got home. As soon as her mother saw her standing in the doorway, she said, "You can tell people you've been stung by a bee. There are some really poisonous ones around these days. It's something to do with the chemicals they spray on the fields."

Her mother did not believe the story about hooligans, but for some strange reason she did not shout or throw herself at Masha. She just became quiet, then she thought up the idea of the bees, and finally she blurted out, "You know Masha, if you're thinking of getting married, you needn't think I'm going to let you live in this apartment. There's no room for two families in here. So just bear that in mind. You haven't got anything."

"No," Masha agreed. "I haven't got anything."

Then, somewhat illogically, her mother began to enumerate indignantly all the things that Masha did have—two pairs of high boots, a coat with a mink collar, and another light one made in the GDR, a Polish raincoat, and a fox fur hat, and a pair of jeans, and about five jumpers, an anodized watch, and the gold pendant she'd been given for her eighteenth birthday, and the turquoise earrings. Is that nothing? Is it? What have you ever done in your life? You've never earned a single kopeck. How dare you say you haven't got anything. What you haven't got, my dear girl, is the apartment—and you can put that in your pipe and smoke it. Masha calmly told her mother where she could stick her rotten apartment.

So that would have been that. Except that bees can't make you pregnant. Not even with the chemicals they spray on the fields nowadays. And that's what happened to Masha, even though she refused to believe the doctor at first.

"What do you mean?" she said.

The way that old cow looked at her made Masha itch all over. She could hardly keep from scratching herself.

"You're already heavily pregnant," the doctor said nastily. "Four months gone, young lady."

The whole thing didn't add up. That meant she'd gotten pregnant a month too late for the father to be Victor, and a month too early for it to be the "American." So Masha could meet the doctor's contempt with her own scorn. So much for science!

But there was no denying it was a major nuisance. Of course, if Masha had been prepared to behave differently, burst into tears or act frightened, she could have gotten herself out of the situation one way or another. But Masha was proud. She decided, for the time being, to treat the diagnosis with skepticism, since there was confusion about how long she'd been pregnant. It couldn't have happened to her. She wasn't such a fool. She always kept track of her safe days. True, it had been a spontaneous thing with Victor, but it couldn't possibly be him.

Masha's mother was preparing to go off to a big regional conference of cultural officials. Masha had long believed that her mother had some kind of personal interest in these meetings. She gave herself such a thorough cleaning in preparation, you'd think she was being paid for it. She wasn't being paid. She was the one who was paying. She always came back from the meetings having run up debts of about 200 rubles. And she never had anything to show for it. Which must mean she was paying her own way, the old fool. But Masha was indulgent toward her mother. Let her carry on like that, if that's what she wanted! How much longer did she have to go? Obviously, when she was near home she had to keep herself on a short rein. But everyone has to let their hair down sometime.

Her mother came back from the hairdresser with so much hairspray on that when they sat down for a cup of tea and the draft from the window blew toward Masha past her mother's head, Masha felt so nauseous she only just made it to the toilet in time.

Her mother launched into a diatribe against modern food. God knows what they put in it nowadays! Nitrates, chlorates, radiation. To say nothing of the water ...

But Masha knew that the only reason she felt sick was because of the smell of her mother's hair.

"Are you going to go and see Auntie Shura?" asked Masha, apparently out of the blue, as she lay on the sofa with a damp towel on her forehead.

"What have I got to talk to her about?"

That was exactly what Masha needed to know.

Then Masha threw up again, and again, and she said to her mother, "Just stay away from me, okay! It's your hairspray that's making me puke."

Her mother moved farther away and said, "If it was anyone else but you, I would say they had a bun in the oven ... it was just the same with me when I was expecting you."

Masha said nothing. Her mother also fell silent. She walked to the door, and stood looking at Masha from a distance.

"You go off to your conference!" Masha waved a hand. Her mother left without another word, and Masha started thinking. She thought hard. Abortions, she believed, were bad for one's health. Once you've had one you're a sick person for the rest of your life. On the other hand, having a baby is a nasty business too. Not always, but in her situation. You'd be stuck with the label forever. Masha had an irreproachable reputation. No one could find a bad word to say about her—but if she had a baby, she could forget her good reputation. She was in a real mess.

Toward evening, the day after her mother had left, Masha knew for certain what she needed to do. She dressed herself smartly in a light coat and a crepe de chine dress with shoulder pads, a bright scarf tied to one side around her neck. She even wore a pair of sheer stockings and she sprayed on some on her mother's "Sardonix No. 3" perfume.

Masha walked along the street, delighted with herself. What a gorgeous young girl, she thought. It's a lucky boy who gets her as a wife. She's sure to have beautiful children too.

The Korshunovs lived in the part of town where the private houses were. They had a brick house with a verandah, a big garden, a garage, a shower in the yard, and a huge water tank painted orange.

Masha took it all in at a glance. It would be a good place to bring up a child. Better than living in a concrete box. Victor's mother was standing on a stool under an apple tree, pulling branches toward her with a stick and picking the autumn apples. Masha noticed how carefully the shop assistant worked. She had only to shake the tree a little, and all the apples would have fallen off. But she took great care. She laid the apples in her apron, which she held up with one hand.

"Good evening, Auntie Nyusya!" said Masha, opening the gate.

Nyusya stood on the stool and looked at Masha, her face completely expressionless.

"I've come to see you, Auntie Nyusya," Masha continued, even though she knew it sounded stupid. Who else could she have possibly come to see?

"What do you want?" asked Nyusya. She didn't sound hostile, just completely uninterested. Masha sighed secretly, regretting that she could not find exactly the right words, tried and tested, to say to Nyusya.

"Please come down from your stool!" Masha suggested in positively angelic tones. "Come down!"

"Victor, my darling son, what's happened to him?" cried Nyusya in anguish. She flew, rather than climbed down from the stool, scattering her harvest of apples as she went.

"Nothing's happened to Victor! Calm down!" said Masha. "What a state you're in ... now be careful."

Nyusya, terrified and panicked, was fidgeting, her mouth half open, her apron aslant, and the stick in her hand dragging on the ground. She looked completely idiotic.

"I've come to tell you some good news," said Masha. "Some very good news."

"Well then?" At last Nyusya began to breathe freely. "First she terrifies me, then she says she's got good news. What are you trying to tell me?"

"I didn't mean to frighten you." Masha spoke clearly.

"Just tell me why you've come!" shouted Nyusya. "You've made me drop my apples all over the place. What kind of news can you possibly have for me?"

Masha gave a merry laugh. She thought to herself, I'm doing well here. Any other girl would have come in tears, but I come bringing joy. "I have joyful news for you." Those were Masha's exact words. "I'm expecting Victor's baby. Congratulations on becoming a grandmother, Auntie Nyusya!"

Nyusya collapsed onto her stool and sat frozen to the spot, her eyes gaping. Masha picked up an apple from the ground, went over to the tap that stood nearby, washed the apple carefully, and took a big bite.

At this Nyusya came to her senses. "Oh yes, my Victor! Oh yes, as if he wouldn't have told his own mother! Oh yes, if every tart from off the street came in here! Oh yes, pointing the finger at my son, who's never done a thing wrong!" She ranted on in this fashion, placing enormous emphasis on the words *Oh yes,* in a way that began to annoy Masha.

"Stop saying 'Oh yes' like that! You sound as if you're on parade! Victor promised to marry me. You can ask him yourself if you want, but I'm not insisting on getting married. I just came to do the honorable thing and tell you. Your blood is already flowing in my body."

Masha had struck upon this phrase the day before, after her mother had left. It seemed to her the most crucial of all the things she could have said. She mustn't play for pity or sympathy, but on the idea that the blood was already living, pulsing within her, just waiting for the right moment to come into the world, that there was no looking back.

She threw the apple core over the fence into the neighbors' garden and walked out of the yard, as proud and beautiful as could be, and Nyusya ran after her, shouting, "Prove it! How can you prove it? Anyone could say that. You could pin anything on any honest boy! Prove it! Just you prove it!"

"Just wait till you see the baby!" said Masha. "Then you'll see for yourself!"

As usual, Masha's mother returned from her business trip with new debts. She seemed somehow old and exhausted, but the first thing she said, even before she said hello, was, "Have you been feeling sick again?"

"Only if I smell gasoline or hairspray," replied Masha.

"So who's the father?" Her mother's voice sounded dull and weary. Masha had been expecting a fight, and this took her by surprise.

"It's Victor Korshunov," she answered.

"Try telling that to other people, not me." Her mother made a strange laughing sound, as if she was being strangled and tickled simultaneously.

Masha was silent. She'd said all she had to say.

"Victor's got nothing to do with it," her mother sighed. "It was that time you came home with the bee sting."

Masha turned on her. "Why do you keep talking about bees?"

"It was those bees," her mother repeated. "Have you been to see the doctor?"

"Yes," said Masha. "And I've been to see the Korshunovs. I've told them."

Her mother looked at Masha like a mother looking at a newborn baby, amazed and fascinated by the creature that has issued from her body. "And what did the Korshunovs say?"

"Nyusya started screaming at me. She didn't believe it."

"She's no fool. But we'll bring her around. They've got their own house, haven't they? Quite a big one. I wonder how she's going to get out of it?"

"She can't get out of it," Masha said calmly.

Again her mother looked at her as though seeing her for the first time. "You should go to your grandma's in the country to have the baby, and then we'll bring it back here and show it to them."

Masha was impressed. It was a clever plan for confusing the dates. Her mother had reached check and checkmate in one move.

Then her mother made another important move. She went to see the Korshunovs herself. The whole family ganged up to drive her away. Nyusya had enlisted her husband, Victor's stepfather—a great bull-like man who worked as a driver, the bull's daughter—a sharp-tongued little twelve-year-old, and Victor's Grandma Sanya, who had spent her entire life selling sunflower seeds outside the movie theater. At first she had sold them for 10 kopecks a glass, then they went up to 15, and now the resourceful old woman had increased the price to 20 kopecks, at the same time reducing the size of the glass by almost half.

They called Masha's mother every name they could draw from their knowledge of plain Russian speech, attracting quite a crowd in the process. But she might as well have been covered in armor plating. She spoke to them clearly and precisely. "Stop your shouting. You can't change the facts. If you're determined to take such an inhumane attitude to a future Soviet citizen, you will find yourself in big trouble. It's possible that the police will decide to investigate your whole family. As for you, Nyusya—a shop assistant! Your husband's a driver and your grandma's a profiteer. I could have all of you brought up on more than one count. And we wouldn't hear another peep out of you."

They all continued yelling, but Masha's mother walked away proudly.

"They've got a nice place there," she said to Masha later. "Did you notice? They're building an extra floor onto the house."

"Really?" Masha was surprised. "I never noticed. Who'd have thought it!"

In short, the visit to the Korshunovs cleared the whole thing up. Masha registered at the prenatal clinic, making sure all the evidence pointed to Victor, and went around in a state of great tranquillity, which was most important in her condition. She had the following conversation with her mother.

"So who's the real father?"

"Victor," said Masha. "What are you talking about?"

"Oh, tell me." Her mother waved a hand. "I only want to make sure he wasn't a drunk or something. It can affect the baby you know!"

"He wasn't a drunk," Masha replied.

"And he wasn't sick?" Her mother wouldn't give up.

Masha remembered the well-fleshed body of the "American"—smooth, gleaming, strong. A hot, dizzy sensation boiled somewhere down in her stomach and rose up to her head, fogging her brain, and her heart cried out, her lips were moist, and her teeth chattered.

Masha shook her head drunkenly. "As healthy as they come," she said hoarsely.

But her mother couldn't leave her alone. "And what was he like to look at?"

Masha tried to remember what he looked like, but she couldn't. She could see the torn shirt, the hairy chest, the chain around his neck, the white strip from the watchband on his suntanned wrist. But that was all. She couldn't remember anything else. He was handsome, not like Victor.

"Victor isn't so bad looking either," her mother said. "If the army doesn't ruin him. You could do worse. And he always did well at school, didn't he?"

"He wasn't bad," answered Masha.

"Maybe this will give me a chance to get my own life sorted out at last," her mother sighed. "Once you've gone I'll have a bit of space of my own. There is someone, but he's got nowhere to live. He's stuck sharing an apartment with his ex-wife. And there's no way he'd come here. He doesn't want to cope with you. Where he is now may be a dump, he says, but at least he's with his own ex-wife and his own daughter. You can understand him. As soon as you started acting up, what could he do? Go back to his ex-wife? She would have already notified the authorities that he'd officially moved out."

"You ought to go ahead and get your life sorted out," Masha agreed. "If you wait much longer it'll be too late. I'm not planning to sit around here much longer. I don't want to rot in this hole till the end of my days."

"What's wrong with it, if you've got a nice place to live? I don't understand you."

"Nobody has a nice place to live here." Masha spoke emphatically. "It would be a lie to say they did. What about Auntie Shura—she's got an apartment on the seventh floor. There's an elevator, but no running water. Is that what you call a nice place?"

"What do you want?" her mother was amazed. "There's a shortage of water everywhere. They even turn the water off in Moscow sometimes."

"Moscow isn't the only other place in the world," Masha said mysteriously. "Take the Baltics for example. That's where you find real culture."

"What have the Baltics got to do with anything?"

"Oh they've got something to do with it," said Masha, even more mysteriously.

"What are you scheming?"

"Oh nothing," said Masha. "I'm just thinking out loud."

After some time Nyusya came to call. She came in but wouldn't sit down. She stood by the coat hooks and said, "Victor doesn't agree with your story. I'm telling you once and for all. You'd better find yourself another fool."

All of which was very amusing, particularly because Masha had received a letter from Victor that very morning.

"Dear Masha!" he wrote. "My parents have just told me the news. As an honorable man, of course I am not going to deny what happened between us. I admit what happened. But I still have my doubts. I hope you're not trying to take me for a ride, Masha! First you say no, then you say yes. It doesn't quite add up. If it's my child, then all well and good. If it's someone else's—thanks but no thanks! I'm telling you straight. I could get killed out here any day. War is a matter of life and death, so I don't want to risk my life for no reason. You must write to me and explain everything. And I don't want you trying to make a fool of me. Although, I repeat, I admit what happened, another man could have denied everything in my place. But you know me, Masha, I'm not like that. I believe in certain standards, but you must believe in them too. So write and tell me the truth.

"All the best—Victor."

"So he doesn't agree with my story?" Masha laughed, producing the letter. "That's very strange. In his letter to me he admits everything." And she read out the phrase "I admit what happened."

Nyusya stretched out her hand toward the letter, but Masha's mother shielded it.

"This is an important document," she said. "If you don't want to settle everything pleasantly ..."

At this Nyusya burst into tears and said to Masha's mother, "You're just taking advantage of the fact that you work for the council. You think that just because you've got some power, poor people like us have no rights."

"Poor! Don't make me laugh!" Masha exclaimed.

"Why can't we sort this out pleasantly, Nyusya?" Her mother's tone was irreproachable. But Nyusya gave a sob, called them a few unprintable names, and left, slamming the door.

"There's nothing they can do now," said Masha's mother. "Give me the letter, and I'll get a copy of it made tomorrow. And you'd better get yourself off to the village. To hell with the lot of them. You're better off as far away from the scene of the crime as possible."

*   *   *

Life in the village was intolerable. Two tiny, low-ceilinged cells steamed up in winter. Masha's room was separated from her grandparents' by a spotted calico curtain. The old woman came in carrying a bucket. "You can use this for your business."

At first Masha was revolted by the idea, but after she'd tried running outside through the muck once or twice and squatting over a stinking hole, she accepted the bucket. She even got used to the idea of them carrying it out for her after she'd used it.

"Don't you worry," her grandmother would say. "I'll take it, it doesn't weigh anything."

One thing tormented her. The old couple woke up very early and began talking in loud voices, noisily eating last night's borscht, carrying on loud discussions about what they should feed "her with the big belly." These long, noisy mornings filled Masha with such revulsion that she found herself thinking quite seriously, What possible reason can there be for people like this to live? Why? What earthly purpose do they serve? From the cow to the vegetable garden, from the vegetable garden back to the cow. Is that really a life? No interests, no pleasure.

"Have you washed out the jars for the tomatoes?"

"Of course I have!"

"Last year you didn't do it properly and they went bad."

"Stop fussing."

"You listen to me. You only made that borscht yesterday, and it's already going off. Why's that, then? It's the tomatoes, isn't it!"

"You're going off yourself. There's nothing wrong with the borscht. It's supposed to taste sour. It's not just any old soup."

"Shall we kill a chicken?"

"Well, I'm not sure. We can't feed her nothing but chicken."

"Well, what the hell are we supposed to feed her? She won't eat the same as us."

"So sorry, madam! We haven't got any fancy-schmancy sausages."

Masha pulled the quilt over her head. Here, under the blanket, her feelings of hatred melted away. She remembered how her mother had brought her here as a child, and how deeply and peacefully she had slept under this same quilt, after having had to sleep on boxes with brass instruments stored in them. She remembered when her mother had left her father. "There were lots of reasons, but the main reason was his jealousy. I wasn't even allowed to smile at another man, or shake his hand. He was suspicious of everyone." Perhaps he had reason to be suspicious, mused Masha, when she was a little older. But her mother's behavior never gave any real cause for suspicion. Anyway, she always felt her mother had the right to relax a bit. But she never got involved in anything. There was some man on the scene now, but in the past ...

After she'd left Masha's father she'd gone to the council looking for work as a projectionist. They said to her, "We don't want to hide you away in a box! A lovely lady like you ought to be put on display."

So they appointed her director of a club and gave her a room in the tenement. Once she had had a good snoop around, she found the room in the club building where all the musical instruments were stored, lined up in rows. Adjacent to the room was an indoor toilet (which had never worked) with some mops in it, and there was even a little storeroom with a window and a couple of electric sockets, which could be used as a kitchen. Masha's mother had dragged in a couple of display boards showing milk yields and livestock weight increases and fenced off a little passage of private territory in the public foyer. Here they moved in, having secured a water supply to the bathroom. Her mother calculated correctly that they stood a better chance of being allotted a decent apartment if they were living in the clubhouse than if they were living in the tenement. After the stifling, stinking tenement, the club seemed like paradise. They could watch the movies for free, it was quiet during the day. The only inconvenience was having to sleep on boxes— and even that only seemed uncomfortable after Masha came back from the village, where her grandmother had put her to sleep in a soft feather bed, covered with a quilt. She used to sleep until noon, unable to wake up until her grandmother came in and started dragging the quilt off of her.

"You'll get a headache," she would say. "The sun's already high in the sky. It's time you woke up. You'll sleep through the day of judgment."

Sleepy and sluggish she would go out into the sunshine, onto the warm, wooden porch, sit down, screw up her eyes in the bright light, stroke the cat. There was a smell of earth, grass, apples, and milk. Her whole body felt relaxed, heavy and light at the same time. It was a feeling she would remember all her life.

Her mother used to say, "I hate that village."

And Masha would reply, just to spite her, "Well, I like it."

Now she realized that she hated it too. She hated everything: the people, the houses, the animals, the plants. What was it all for? What was the use of it?

But when she was under the blanket something incomprehensible happened. The hatred disappeared, dissolving in the stuffy warmth and giving way to a kind of sweet, pervasive weakness, even tenderness toward those two old fools who had never seen or experienced anything good in their entire lives. And it was in this state that Masha found them a little niche in the wealthy, independent, radiant future she had created for herself on the shores of the Gulf of Riga. Why shouldn't they come too! They could live with her, water the flowers, and feed her chickens. Of course, she would divide the house up so they had a separate entrance, but there was no reason why they shouldn't come and live there. Only she'd have to get them to dress like human beings, decent clothes and shoes. Masha poked her head out from under the blanket to get some air, and caught sight of her grandma's calloused heels, and her shuffling toes, which seemed to have become welded into a solid mass, the nails so thick that no scissors could have cut them. All her life the old woman had walked barefoot, all year round, except when it was cold enough for felt boots. Her grandfather, on the other hand, wore rubber boots winter and summer alike—squelch, squelch, squelch.

"Have you got your eyes open then?" asked the old woman. "Will you have a drop of borshch?"

Dear God, why are they alive?

"Is there any tea?" asked Masha.

"Well, the water's boiling. ..."

"I'm talking about tea, not water!" Masha retorted.

"I know I made some yesterday. Now where's it gone? We never really drink it ourselves."

"You have to make fresh tea," Masha explained patiently for the umpteenth time.

"Whoever told you that?" Her grandmother sounded angry. "That's nothing but a pointless waste of money."

"Have you always been poor?" asked Masha. She made some strong, fresh tea just to spite them and drank it with cherry jam and biscuits.

"What do you mean, poor?" The old woman didn't understand. "We're no worse off than anyone else. You've never seen real poverty. We've never gone hungry since 1933. We've always had bread and potatoes."

She became pensive. "Things were bad after the war. There's going to be famine again, I thought to myself. But your granddad knew what to do. He went off to work in one of the little mines they were digging out around here. He earned good money—well, even though the money wasn't worth anything, we weren't going to die of hunger. We kept rabbits. And when he had an accident, when the mine caved in, it was already Khrushchev's times."

"No it wasn't," said Masha's grandfather, squelching around in his rubber boots. "The mine collapsed in '52, at Whitsun. ..."

"You don't know what you're talking about," the old woman interrupted. "Whitsun was the time you cut your arm because you were drunk. The pit caved in two years after that. Your arm was all crooked. And I said you ought to stop going down the pit ... but you always were a stubborn, Ukrainian so-and-so. And then they started closing down the smaller pits and driving prospecting shafts. It was dreadful work. But you couldn't say anyone was poor. No, we've always lived very well."

Masha was beginning to perk up. "What do you mean by 'very well'?"

"I mean we've always lived very well," the old woman said proudly. "We've always had our own house and our own vegetable patch. We've never had to go running to the neighbors. I couldn't abide that. We've always managed to feed ourselves and keep ourselves in clothes and shoes."

"You're nothing but paupers!" Masha screamed at the top of her voice. "Just take a look around you!" She jabbed her finger at the iron bedstead, the chest of drawers with no handles, which the old woman had inherited from her own grandmother. How old was it, for God's sake? She pointed at the smoke-blackened iron stove, the green cooking pots, the tapestry with swans worn away in the years since the war. How many times had the edges been turned under to hide the holes worn by the nails on which it hung from the wall? It was nothing but a bunch of old junk! Nothing that a normal person wouldn't have felt ashamed of.

"Listen to her!" shouted the old woman. "We're not good enough for her! Well you were glad enough to come here to have your baby. Why hasn't anyone invited you to stay in their luxury apartment?"

"The only possible reason for coming to a place like this is to give birth or die," Masha laughed.

"How can you say those two words in the same breath?" Her grandmother was outraged.

"That just about sums it up!" Masha shouted cheerfully. "You're born and then you die. And if you want to live, you'd better avoid this place like the plague."

As winter approached and the old woman had already taken to wearing her felt boots, a letter arrived from Masha's mother. "Nyusya refuses to say hello if she sees me in the streets, and she's doing her best to blacken your name right, left, and center," she wrote. "I'm afraid you're not going to get anywhere with her." Enclosed was a letter from Victor.

"I'm not admitting that it's my baby yet." The word *yet* was underlined. "A blood test will prove it one way or the other, and that way no one's going to be taken for a ride."

Masha wasn't even slightly upset. There's nothing Victor can do to get out of it, she thought. She tore out a yellowing page from the notebook where her grandmother wrote down the dates of religious festivals according to the new calendar, and wrote Victor a brief, unambiguous note.

"You're a fool, Vic! It makes me wish you weren't the father of my child. No one could say fate dealt him a good hand as far as his dad's concerned. We can do as many blood tests as you like. Send them through the post."

After she had written the letter she walked around in the first fall of winter snow, unable to stop laughing.

One day her mother showed up, she'd caught a lift in a van. She could hardly bring herself to look at Masha, and when she did, her eyes were dull, as though covered by a film. Masha was surprised. What's gotten into her, looking at me like that? To be honest, she could have arranged an abortion if it came down to it. Of course, Masha didn't want to, but her mother hadn't suggested it. If her mother did raise the subject of an abortion, she was going to say: "Childbirth is a healthy process. It's good for the system, whereas an abortion is like an explosion. It can cause so much damage that you can spend the rest of your life putting yourself to rights. And I've only got one life."

The last words were not her own. She'd met a beautiful young woman on a train once who had said this to her. She made sure she had a good look at the woman, checked out her tights, her outfit, her earrings. Watched how she combed her hair and rubbed cream into her skin with her fingertips before she went to sleep. And it was this woman, a single mother, incidentally, who said these wonderful words to Masha: "I've only got one life."

Her words cut Masha to the quick. Masha couldn't resist asking a question about the child, and the woman answered, "Every woman ought to give birth, for the good of her own health, otherwise you don't get rid of bad blood. No one knows what happens to it. It might turn into cancer. That's why you've got to live as nature intended. I've got a gorgeous little boy. I love him so much—he's a real joy. And I'm in perfect health. You can see for yourself!"

With that, she pulled down her pants to reveal her suntan. For the first time in her life, Masha experienced a sense of rapture at the sight of someone else's well-groomed body. Her stomach was so beautiful. And the band where her suntan stopped was well below her belly button, just above where the pubic hair started. You had to hand it to her! She must have been over thirty, and she was so perfectly formed and groomed—you almost wanted to sink your teeth into her! That was the right way to live!

Her mother said, "You're going into the Dawn of Communism maternity home. I've talked to them already, and they've got an experienced midwife. And I've persuaded the foreman to take you there in his car. He'll drop you off."

"God help you!" said the old woman. "He can promise anything you like, but he won't take his car out in winter. He saves it up. I'll talk to the gypsy for you. He's got a good horse. If you leave the money to pay him."

"How much?" Masha's mother asked.

"Maybe 10 rubles." The old woman seemed unsure.

"A taxi would cost less than that!" Masha's mother squealed. "You think we've got enough money to start paying out 10 rubles for some dirty old horse!"

Her mother left 5 rubles.

Masha went to see the foreman herself. He made a lot of clucking noises with his tongue and looked Masha up and down at length, "Well you have grown up into a fine girl!"

Masha accepted the praise and allowed him to touch her here and there—it was for a good cause. She found it quite interesting to see how a man reacted to a situation like this, and to discover how easy it was to manipulate him.

"Of course I'll take you to the hospital!" he promised. He spoke ardently, squeezing Masha's breasts at the same time. "It wouldn't be right not to help out, would it?"

Masha went and had a look at the gypsy's horse, just in case. It wasn't such a bad little horse—smooth and well-built, which was more than could be said of the gypsy. "How much would you charge to take me to the 'Dawn of Communism'?" asked Masha bluntly.

"As much as I feel like!" answered the gypsy. "We're not a taxi, you know. We're living creatures. We'd have to see."

But in the end it didn't happen like that at all. One morning before she had given birth, having just sat down on the bucket, she overheard her grandparents talking. They were under the impression they were talking quietly, but in fact—bu-bu-bu, bu-bu-bu—she could hear every word.

"It would have been a disgrace in the old days, for a girl to get herself pregnant without a husband—the kind of disgrace you'd never live down," said the old woman, as she ate her morning borshch. "But nowadays they spit in your eye, and you don't give a damn."

"What do you mean, she hasn't got a husband?" Masha's grandfather didn't understand. "He's off at the front, fighting the Afghans."

"You don't believe that story do you?" The old woman laughed. "Are you really daft, or are you just pretending? They just picked him out of a hat ... they don't know who the real father is ... there's no doubt about that."

"That can't be right." The old man was outraged. "Her mother would never allow that kind of thing. She's a party member."

"For heaven's sake!" The old woman went on gulping down her soup. "The party members are the first ones to get up to those kind of tricks. Who's always out on the tiles around here then? That Komsomol secretary! That's the way they all carry on. And Maria's no different. She knows how to handle men. But you're such an old dolt, you don't even see what's in front of your eyes. If you ask me, the best thing would be if that baby was to die."

Masha's grandfather spat three times, indignantly, to keep the devil away.

"There's no two ways about it. That's the best thing that could happen!"

Masha was amazed at her grandmother's grasp of the situation. Who would have thought she was so sharp? She may have been stuck in a village all her life, but that didn't stop her sniffing out what was going on. Obviously Masha took after her. Her mother didn't, she wasn't particularly bright. Otherwise she would have made sure she had a better life. True, the kind of life her grandmother put up with didn't exactly suggest a great intellect either. But Masha explained this to herself on the grounds that in her grandmother's day no one had any idea about decent living conditions. They just thanked God if they didn't starve to death. You had to take things like that into account. But if the old woman was young again today! She'd make something of herself, Masha was sure of that.

And the very next day it happened. It was all over in a flash. The old woman only just managed to grab the baby as it came out. For a moment Masha thought she was going to drop it. And there was a moment when Masha's grandmother looked at the baby as she was cutting the umbilical cord, and thought, a lovely, healthy little great-granddaughter—what a waste. But all these were only passing thoughts. They were too busy to think—cleaning the baby with a cloth, wrapping her up, helping Masha expel the placenta, giving her something to drink, changing the sheets on her bed—tiny, insignificant acts to do with preserving life.

"Just look at her!" the old woman said happily. "She's a little darling!"

On a page from her grandmother's notebook Masha drew a chart, showing when the baby had supposedly been born. It was for the benefit of those misbegotten Korshunovs. Just as well she was a big baby. There would be no problem moving her birthday forward a bit.

Masha's mother asked, "What date shall we put down?"

"Here," said Masha, holding out the sheet of paper.

Her mother looked at the baby for a long time. Masha watched her and saw in her eyes none of the murky confusion that clouded them when she turned her face toward her own daughter. The old fool! thought Masha. Well, there's no point getting angry with her.

Giving birth had done Masha's looks no harm at all—quite the reverse. She had become ripe and voluptuous. She tried out her new appearance on the foreman. When he saw her he swayed slightly and stretched out a hand toward her. But her situation had changed now.

Masha said to him sternly, "You watch where you're putting your hands!"

And she went proudly on her way.

The gypsy too, made approving clicking noises when he saw her. "D'you need the horse then, gorgeous?"

"Leave me alone!"

Everything was going very well. She was too attractive for her own good. Masha gazed at herself in the mirror, and thought, Yes, I'm too attractive for my own good. If only it would last.

When spring came she went back to live with her mother.

"Let's make this clear from the start—this is only a temporary arrangement," her mother said. "You get yourself fixed up at the Korshunovs. They've already got the attic ready." And then she screeched, "I've done my bit! You got yourself into this mess, you can sort it out yourself. I'm in no state to carry your burdens for you."

In the same breath, she began cooing sweetly at her little granddaughter, "You're my little doll, aren't you! My little chicken! Who's Grandma's precious flower?"

Masha didn't resent her mother's attitude. She knew herself that they couldn't go on living in the same apartment. They would end up poisoning one another. So Masha dressed the doll up in her best finery, put her in the carriage and set off for the Korshunovs' house. Since her last letter, in which she had wittily suggested that Victor send a blood sample through the post, Masha had heard nothing. Masha considered the problem at length and finally decided to send him another letter.

"Hi, Vic! How are you enjoying army life, soldier boy? Made any good friends? You're making a big mistake not writing to me. It doesn't look good. You'll have to come back here sooner or later, and the whole town knows you're the father of my child. Everyone's congratulating us on our gorgeous daughter—she's a real stunner and well-behaved too. It's no trouble putting her to sleep. You should also bear in mind that I've registered you as the father on her birth certificate. Things will only be worse if you make a fuss. When it comes down to it, you and I are both Komsomol members, and the Komsomol never turns its back on one of its own. Just try getting around it when you apply for a job or a place in college. They gave me a layette at college. We couldn't use it because our baby's a big, healthy girl, and the diapers and jackets they supplied were made for some poor, skinny little thing. A big thank you to your parents, who haven't given me anything for the baby. All I want to know is, what are you planning to do? There's no point burying your head in the sand—you're a father now, with family responsibilities, and that's the long and short of it. See if you can't find me a sheepskin coat—I hear there are tons of them in Afghanistan. I'm a size 48, medium height, or a size 50 would do if it's not too wide across the shoulders. Make sure you get something for yourself too. You'll have to have shoes and clothes to wear when you get back, and the shops here are totally empty. You certainly won't find any real good stuff. Your parents have built an attic onto their house. They've done quite well for themselves. Could share a bit. If you think about it, I'm sure you will agree that you'd prefer your child to grow up in a brick house, not a concrete box, breathing air scented with trees rather than gasoline fumes. Don't disgrace yourself by turning your back on a helpless woman and your own child, Vic.

"Your own Masha."

Masha was pleased with this letter. She had always been good at writing essays, avoiding clichés, and managing to find the right, human touch. If it weren't for the commas, she would have been a top student in literature, but she was never too hot on grammar. Commas, and especially dashes were the death of her, and for that reason she never liked literature. The better you manage to express something in words, the greater the danger of missing out on some punctuation marks. But she had a good style. That's what her teacher used to say to her. "You've got a good style, Masha."

Masha pushed the carriage, aware of the admiring glances of passersby. People kept coming up to her, wide-eyed, saying, "You look great, Masha—like a film star!" She knew they were telling the truth. She was imbued with a film star's beauty. And her little doll was all pink and lacy. The two of them together were a real picture.

The Korshunovs wouldn't even let them into the yard. Masha tugged and rattled at the locked gate. On the other side of the gate a huge dog leapt at the end of a chain, barking so diligently that eventually he barked himself hoarse. The house stood as if abandoned—not even a curtain twitched. It was a Sunday, and Masha couldn't believe there was no one home.

Masha crossed to the other side of the road, only for the sake of the baby who was upset by the dog's barking and was beginning to thrash about in her lacy nest. Masha sat down on a bench to wait. Sooner or later someone had to come out of the house to go to the bathroom.

But the Korshunovs proved to have great stamina. Nobody emerged. Masha had time to give the baby a bottle, change her diaper, and still the house was silent. There was a net curtain hanging at one of the attic windows, but not at the other. Masha imagined Nyusya, her nose pressed to the curtain, waiting for Masha to go away. But Masha sat and sat, and if Nyusya was frozen forever in that absurd position by the window, then it would serve her right for treating other people, that is to say, Masha and her doll, so badly. They ought to take her into their house—it was the least they could do, if only to do the right thing by their soldier son, Victor.

That day Masha waited in vain, although she certainly was winning the public over to her side. Apparently everyone turned on Nyusya afterward, saying they didn't know how she could be so hard-hearted. What do you expect, Nyusya? They all do things the wrong way around nowadays—first they have the baby, then they get married. What are you being so stubborn about, Nyusya? What do we live for at all, if not for our children and our grandchildren? And you've been presented with a granddaughter ready-made.

In short, everyone started crying shame on the Korshunovs. And when Nyusya tried to say that no one could prove it was Victor's baby, they answered reasonably that, indeed, no one could prove that sort of thing. Maybe in the old days it was one boy and one girl, but now they all had two or three boyfriends, if not seven or eight. Everything was going to the dogs, but you could be sure of a girl like Masha. She'd grown up into a fine girl. And everyone knew her mother—that dragon down at the city council. She never would have stood any nonsense from Masha, she'd given her a strict, old-fashioned upbringing. So it's more than likely that baby is your granddaughter, Nyusya. And she's such a little doll—just like a baby out of a fairy tale. The spitting image of Victor. Same eyes, same nose, same eyebrows. Anyone can see she's a Korshunov. You don't need blood tests.

"She'll come around," said Masha to herself, thinking about Nyusya.

She was still waiting for a letter from Victor. She was sure it would bring good news. After all, he wasn't such a bad guy. Not too much of a wild fly-by-night. He will do for the time being. Masha had him pretty well pegged. And he was bound to love the baby. Masha even considered the possibility that when she was very rich she might keep him at home. He could busy himself around the house. She would have a large house by then, and there would always be plenty that needed doing. Masha tossed her head, and from her throat issued a strange sound—neither singing, nor the shriek of a bird—it was impossible to describe, and quite involuntary. It was the kind of sound a bud might make, if a bud could speak as it burst into leaf; or like the jubilant shout of a flower, if a flower could shout, as its petals opened in the morning.

"What's the matter?" Her mother was frightened.

"Nothing." Masha covered her mouth with her hand.

"You were making a funny noise. Maybe you've got polyps?"

"What are you going to think of next?" Masha shuddered fastidiously. Polyps? The very idea!

Since the baby was born, Masha had been in a state of exuberant good health. She experienced a sense of delight, for example, at the wonderful ability of her own legs to walk, to climb, to run. How well her fingers moved! She couldn't get over her legs! Every cell in her body seemed to be bubbling and singing, and Masha thought, I've come through childbirth so well. It must mean everything else will go well too. I'm going to get my house on the Gulf of Riga! I'm really going to start living!

The Korshunovs were not prepared to give in. On one occasion Masha pushed the carriage to the shoe shop and stood outside the glass window just opposite where Nyusya was working. As soon as she caught sight of Masha, the old fool stormed off to the other end of the counter, forcing the entire line of customers to turn around and face the other direction. Masha was left looking at a sea of backs.

Masha also liked sitting by the fountain on the square outside the council building. Here, more than anywhere else, she found herself filled with confidence in a wonderful future. The dark blue fir trees, yellow sand, the fountain lined with colored tiles. The council building was cleaned up to a spotless shine out of fear and fawning respect. Masha thought and thought and at last remembered the word she was looking for—*oasis*. It was an oasis. It was true that few people gathered or spent time sitting there. Mostly they hurried across the square. What could an oasis like this offer to an ordinary person? People just came and went, with only one purpose driving them: food and clothes. Masha had different goals, for the moment she was a nursing mother. Her only aim was to breathe the air, and of course to attract the attention of passers-by. But this was so simple, so superficial it could hardly be called a goal. A goal was something different, something you struggled to achieve. Masha was content simply to sit on the bench—with obvious consequences: Who is that charming young mother? Which family is she from? And so on and so forth.

Before they heard the news that Victor had been killed, something happened.

It was a fine day, and Masha had taken her doll for a long walk. When she came home she found her mother reading the same old newspaper with the article giving details of the rates they paid in Moscow for IT. In all her life Masha had never seen such an idiotic expression on her mother's face. She was sitting there like a half-witted servant girl with her mouth hanging open, flabbergasted. She might have turned to stone.

"Have you read this?" she asked Masha.

"Ummmh," Masha replied.

"Who would've believed it!" Her mother's voice was almost inaudible. "So much money just for one time. And here we are, running ourselves ragged."

Masha grinned to herself. She couldn't believe the stupid old fool was considering a change of career. She really had lost her marbles this time!

Masha's mother went into the bathroom and started crashing around with basins and splashing water. Masha knew what was going on. Her mother sometimes did this to hide the fact that she was crying. If she'd had a quarrel with her boss, she would come home and make a huge racket in the bathroom. Eventually she would emerge, flushed and red-eyed. It was as well to be careful with her on these occasions. Masha prepared herself mentally for any attack that might be coming her way. She was expecting a tirade to the effect that her mother was sick of having Masha around the place, that her life was her own, and there was no reason for the two of them to be constantly in each other's hair. They must each take responsibility for themselves. So take your precious baby and get yourselves off to where you belong. They've already put net curtains up in the attic. Expensive, German net curtains, what's more. Those shop assistants are nothing but a pack of thieves. They always seem to have the best of everything—and you can try every trick in the book, but you'll never find anything decent to buy.

At first it looked very much as if things would go as Masha expected. Her mother came out of the bathroom, red and puffy, but the speech she made followed very different lines.

"Is that what we're building communism for? So they can live in the lap of luxury, in private apartments? What kind of system is this? The whole nation sweats blood, and what do they spend their time doing? How much does a miner earn compared to what those hookers are getting? This kind of thing didn't go on when Stalin was in charge. He would have packed all of them off to the camps, and they would have had to tie up their privates for good. What we need is another Stalin! I can't believe we've sunk so low. Those brave young women who fought with the partisans in the war—you wouldn't have caught them carrying on like this! And now they're all at it! They deserve to be shot or hanged. Immediately—without trial. Where did you get this paper?"

Masha was shocked. It was all so primitive. She had never thought of her mother as an intelligent woman, but she hadn't believed she was quite such an imbecile.

"All work is worthy in this country," she said. "You know that."

"You call that work?" cried her mother.

"What do you call it? Relaxation?!" cried Masha.

They stood facing one another, breathing heavily. Masha's mother was considering the possibility of grabbing her daughter's luxuriant hair, while Masha prepared to seize hold of her mother's arm and shake her until her stuffing came out.

At that moment the doorbell rang, and they both twitched violently, forcing their faces back into normal expressions. And there's nothing so surprising about a bit of breathlessness these days: They could have been washing clothes, cleaning the floor, ironing ... there are thousands of things a woman might have been doing to make her breathless.

A young girl was standing at the door.

They didn't recognize her at first, but she didn't keep them in suspense for long. "Our Victor's been killed in Afghanistan. Mom's yelling for you to come over."

Masha's heart pounded as it had never pounded before. Everything's working out perfectly! she thought. This is absolutely perfect!

"Dear Lord!" her mother sobbed. "Our darling boy!"

Masha was horrified. What was she carrying on about? Then she realized. Her mother wasn't so stupid after all! Why hadn't she realized herself that she should start weeping?

Masha turned away. She didn't want them to see her bewilderment. She decided that she should neither howl nor weep. She would opt for a state of stony-faced shock.

And that was how they arrived at the Korshunovs' house. Masha's mother, sobbing with all her might, so you never would have guessed she was both a party member and a council employee. Masha, frowning and silent, her lips compressed. And the baby playing with the lace on her clothes and blowing bubbles with great delight, entirely oblivious to the historic moment she was living through.

After that everything went so smoothly that Masha found herself repeating, "May he rest in peace!" It could scarcely be better than what was happening here on earth!

Nyusya swept up the baby out of the carriage and hugged her close, calling her "my own flesh and blood." And that was only the start ...

It turned out that the news of Victor's death had arrived at the same time as a letter. Victor had written,

"My dear family, Mom, Uncle Volodya, Grandma, and Vera! I am writing to tell you that I am still here in one of the most dangerous places in the world. Somebody has to do the shooting. The men here are all determined to do their best to make sure the forces of progressive Afghanistan are victorious. To put it bluntly, I'm fighting. And so I spend even more time thinking about the peaceful life at home. Especially about the baby—which might be mine. Of course we can only get definite proof when I come home and they do blood tests. But as it is, I can't deny she might be my daughter, and I want to do what I can to help her. I see a lot of children here, and I feel so sorry for them. How can I let a little child grow up an orphan, even if I'm not a hundred percent sure she's my daughter? Please, Mom, don't say anything horrible to Masha—you'll feel so ashamed if we eventually get married. I'm coming around more and more to the idea of marrying Masha. She's a serious girl, and I know she wouldn't be a millstone around my neck. So you do your bit, and I'll write and reassure the young mother. She's asked me to get her a sheepskin coat, but I haven't seen any here. Maybe you could ask at the shop and see if you can buy one, Mom? You'll have to give her some kind of present anyway. I want to see you all. I'd love to taste some home cooking. It's not that the food is no good here, but I'd just like to taste some of my favorite food. Pickled eggplants maybe, and roast pork with potatoes. It's strange, the things I miss most out here. My love to you all.

"Your son, brother, and grandson."

*   *   *

They had prepared huge amounts of food—eggplants, and roast pork and potatoes, and wine and vodka to drink, because they had decided to celebrate everything all at once: Victor's funeral, a housewarming for the attic, and a christening for the baby. They were amazed to discover that Nyusya had personally, of her own free will, written out a will, turning over the attic to the baby, and she'd deposited some money in a savings bank for her. And she said to Masha, "You finish your schooling. We'll take care of the baby. After all, she's our own flesh and blood."

She also presented Masha with a sheepskin coat—only a Mongolian one, but none the worse for that. It was a bit on the stiff side, but what could you expect from the Mongolians?

"Not bad, as leather goes," said Masha's mother, but Masha could see she was envious. She'd never had a leather coat, nor was she ever likely to on the money she earned.

The Korshunovs said to Masha's mother, "Well, we're practically related now. Don't you worry, we'll leave you to live your own life, but you won't be too proud to help us put in an order for some corrugated iron to build our garage. It's nothing to you after all."

You mustn't think that Nyusya was a hard-hearted woman, more preoccupied with the thought of getting ahold of some corrugated iron than with her grief. But her sorrow was eating her away. In the past month she had lost almost thirty pounds and had taken to wearing her daughter's clothes, which looked rather strange on her—all bows and frills and baubles. But Nyusya was the kind of woman who took everything to extremes. If she decided to hate someone, she did the job properly; if she lost weight, she practically starved herself to death; and if she loved someone ...

When she came home from work she would kneel down beside the baby's crib, and stay there for hours and hours. She would kneel there, talking to the baby. "You've got our Vic's nose ... I can tell already. When you're older it will get a bit broader, then everyone will see. And your little eyebrows ... thick until the middle, then nothing at all. Never mind, my darling ... we'll buy you a French eyebrow pencil, and you'll pencil them in, won't you?" And without pausing, she would start speaking to Masha. "And don't you even think about buying makeup off those gypsies. You'll poison yourself. They ought to be shot, those gypsies—nothing better to do with themselves than wiggling their bottoms at men and spreading their lice around."

Masha went back to college. Her life was calm and orderly. But Masha had not forgotten her dream. She would have to make another trip into town. The only thing that held her back was the thought of facing her aunt. She didn't think she should poke her nose in there again. Or perhaps she should ... her aunt had bumped into her mother in town some time that spring—her mother was on one of her conferences for promoting culture and was running along the street. Masha's aunt stopped her and started crying.

"Why did Masha have to take it out on me, playing that dirty trick with the water? It wasn't my fault you split up with my stupid brother. What have I got to do with it? I've always got on well with you and treated Masha as if she was one of my own, and then she goes and does that to me."

"Why did you pour all her water out?" Masha's mother was mystified. "What's she ever done to you? She always tried to smooth things over between your father and me. She's a good woman."

Masha almost burst out laughing, but she managed to contain herself. She contained herself to such an extent that she said nothing at all.

Nyusya was summoned to the local army recruiting office and told that she was to go to Moscow to receive some kind of posthumous medal for Victor and meet some of the men from his regiment. They were meeting to unveil a memorial, or something of the sort.

"I haven't got the time to be going up to Moscow," said Nyusya, waving a hand. "You ought to go, Masha, you're his wife. And I haven't got anything to wear. Everything's too big for me. Look!" Nyusya put on her new leather coat and practically disappeared inside it. She looked terrible.

The coat fit Masha perfectly. The expensive garment looked dazzling on her.

The recruiting office didn't care one way or the other. They wrote down Masha's name on the invitation and issued her a third-class train ticket.

Masha was stunned, not to say deafened, by Moscow. She took to cleaning her ears out in the evening, wondering whether perhaps they had been blocked up by the dust. Or maybe they were producing more wax than usual because of the change in the climate? There were soldiers, songs, demonstrations. They drove around Moscow in a stuffy minibus—the kind of dirty, dusty vehicle you traveled in when you were hired to help with the harvest. The hotel was, as Masha discovered, uncomfortable and far from the center of town.

From the window Masha could see a gray, depressing station platform. Looking at the scene, you'd never think that Moscow was a capital city, and not some little provincial town. Even the people waiting on the platform were the same—loaded down with shopping bags. Masha had not expected any of this. She watched the people crowded into the foyer of the hotel, all of them in Moscow on business; and they were just the same—weary and exhausted. Masha began to entertain doubts about the veracity of that newspaper article. There wasn't even a whiff of the wonderful life Masha was seeking. Where was she supposed to find people playing for real stakes in this pit of human perspiration where happiness was measured in terms of grabbing a seat in the bus, tracking down a piece of sausage in the shops, and sleeping on a cot in a hotel? It occurred to Masha that there were simply too many people.

They once had a meeting at school to discuss national food supplies. Everyone had to propose a solution to the problem. Some people came up with ideas for vegetable gardens, rabbits, or simply eating less. Then Zina got up. She was the kind of girl who didn't care what she said. And she said, quite bluntly, "Some people shouldn't be allowed to live."

"What do you mean by that?" they asked her. Zina began to count on her fingers. "We don't need cripples. We don't need loonies. The same goes for people with terminal illnesses."

They argued themselves hoarse. It turned out to be the most interesting meeting they'd ever had. Even their teacher joined in the fray, shouting and screaming with the rest of them. She was in favor of getting rid of loonies, but insisted that the cripples should be left alone—someone might love them, after all. Then the principal showed up—he had always been a little weird—and started shouting at their teacher. "Do you realize what you're saying? Have you any idea what this means? It's practically tantamount to fascism." The teacher burst into tears, saying she had joined the party before he was even born. Anyway, they started ranting and raving between themselves and never gave the rest of the group a chance to finish the discussion.

But here, in Moscow, Masha remembered the meeting, and started thinking about Zina's idea. Zina was the kind of girl who took everything to extremes, but this time she had really gotten to the root of the problem. Somehow, the number of people had to be regulated. Take old people for example. There were more old people than ... it would be quite fair to make a decision on how long people should be allowed to live. Say, sixty-five years ... and then that would be it. ... A cutoff point ... make way for someone else. Of course there would be exceptions made for really great people. It could be put to the vote, and if there was a majority saying you were truly great, then you'd be allowed to go on living. Someone like the comedian Arkady Raikin. Obviously everyone would vote to keep him alive. Masha mentally removed all the old people from the Moscow crowd. Immediately the scene improved. Why had the government never hit upon such a simple idea? There was nothing heartless about Masha's scheme. In fact she was being very humane in setting the cutoff point at sixty-five, which was, if anything, too generous. Eventually Masha came to the conclusion that the newspaper article had been nothing but a pack of lies. None of the things it claimed actually went on in Moscow. At least Masha hadn't seen them, and she couldn't imagine where to begin looking.

The days passed quickly and pointlessly. Masha did not join the crowds of mourning women at the meetings and demonstrations. Of course she was sorry about Victor. He hadn't been concentrating, the stupid fool. He'd done a great job, leading a whole group of soldiers out of an ambush, and then once they were well out of it he'd jumped out of the undergrowth and shown his face. Who would have expected Vic to do something so stupid? One of the men spoke very nicely about him and was polite and respectful toward Masha.

"Don't forget, Masha, wherever I am, if you ever need anything for yourself or your little girl, I'm always ready to help. Igor Kostin, at your service!"

Masha looked at this Igor, and didn't know whether to laugh or cry. He was a puny, weedy little fellow with a skinny neck and bluish pimples on his face. He had a patchy beard, which he was stupid enough to allow to grow. He was so small and scraggly. It was embarrassing the way he kept coming up to her. Masha began to avoid him. Fortunately he was so thick-skinned he didn't even notice.

Her mother had given her some money. For some reason she had decided that they would be taken to special shops in Moscow. This was not the case. The people who knew the city went under their own steam, but Masha was in Moscow for the first time. Once she followed the crowd into some department store or other and then allowed herself to be swept out again. That's not to say that she was some kind of wimp with no idea how to get herself a place in line. But Masha had other things in mind. If none of what she had read in the newspaper article was true, she must clear her head of the ideas the article had planted there and find an alternative route to wealth and a life beside the Gulf of Riga. Perhaps she should consider going into trade? Nyusya had already said to her, "Where's your high school education going to get you? Of course you must finish your studies—people respect a few qualifications. But then you ought to come and work at the shop. I can get you a job on the haberdashery counter."

Masha grimaced. You scratch my back, I'll scratch yours. What kind of a life was that? Shop girls never stopped being shop girls. She wanted to do something where she'd be her own boss. That was the main thing—to depend on no one but herself. Taking no favors, and giving none either. She wanted independence.

Shop work would be a last resort. She hadn't come to that yet. There must be other ways to get on in life!

Masha was faced with the problem of finding out exactly what they were.

Masha was sharing a room in the hotel with a woman from the western Ukraine whose son had been killed. Masha, who was nothing if not objective, thought to herself, If I looked like that, all the wealth in the world would come running to me if I so much as whistled. This was despite the fact that the Ukrainian woman was, by Masha's standards, already quite old, namely thirty-seven. But she looked like a queen, even though her clothes were nothing special and her face was expressionless with grief. It wasn't that she didn't see Masha, but somehow she failed to take her in. On the second night, as they were going to bed, she said, "You'll find another one. ..." and she waved her hand. Masha wasn't sure how to take it. She decided the woman was right, and she wasn't about to try and prove her wrong. They're not crazy, those Ukrainian women. She had come across them from time to time and noticed that they had a way of always getting right to the heart of the matter. If the two of them had met in happier circumstances, Masha would have asked

Sophia's advice about many things. She had a good head on her shoulders. But now it was a bit tricky to know how to start. Eventually Masha got her chance.

Sophia came back from church in the evening. There were some Georgian men, or maybe they were Armenians, who had already started pestering her in the hotel. Anyway, they were from the Caucasus and they were rich. Sophia was so pale that Masha gasped. She looked like death but so handsome, Masha couldn't take her eyes off her. And then these Georgians or Armenians came knocking at the door. At first they knocked gently, then harder, and then they started kicking it loutishly.

Sophia cracked her knuckles, whispered something to herself and opened the door. They stood there in the doorway, a crowd of dark-skinned, lustful men with lecherous eyes, big noses and jaws. Sophia covered her face with her hand, and said one word. She said it twice: "Git! Git!"

Masha could not see Sophia's face, but she had a good look at the way the men fell back, their impudent energy drained away. She was impressed! Afterward Sophia went into the bathroom for a long time. When she did emerge she was as silent as ever, her eyes downcast. Evidently she had no desire to discuss what had happened, but Masha wanted to.

"These Moscow girls," she said. "You wouldn't believe how much they charge. That's why the men try it with anyone from out of town. They earn a hundred rubles a time! I read it in the paper."

"They're not human beings, they're animals," replied Sophia and lay down on the bed, turning her face to the wall.

Why aren't they human beings? Masha wondered. Everyone's a human being. What about models who walk about on stage in swimming costumes? Probably Sophia considered them to be depraved creatures too. Masha felt angry with herself. You've picked a great person to pour your heart out to, you fool! What can you expect a woman who's already thirty-seven years old to understand about modern life? It's true that Pushkin died at that age. Masha felt sorry for Pushkin. There was no denying he was an ugly-looking man, and he didn't have much money either, but he had married a beautiful woman. You make your bed, you have to lie in it. Of course poetry's all very well, but to be honest, you can't really call it work. She pitied him—a good man in his own way, but irresponsible. A superfluous man, to put it bluntly. And superfluous men get shot. Masha was rather proud of these ideas—they were entirely original, not taken from anything she had read. But she deliberately said nothing out loud. Nobody ever tells anyone else their innermost thoughts. But that doesn't mean they don't think. Masha looked at Sophia, lying on the bed with her face to the wall, and wondered what the main thought in her head could be as she hurried to church. Perhaps she cursed the Soviet government, which had taken away her son first to battle and then to his grave? Would she ever say such a thing out loud? Not likely! But you can always think. You can turn your face to the wall and think. And that was how Masha was going to follow her thoughts. She had no particular feelings about Soviet power—in fact she was perfectly satisfied with it. If she'd lived in a capitalist system she might have been a servant, but as it was … all roads were open to her. All she had to find out was whether the newspapers told the truth. There was no time to lose.

Masha had noticed the major a long time ago. She had noticed the way he kept looking at her during the first meeting she went to. Amid the crush of bodies, the tears, the embraces, there was this major, who had never fought at the front himself. He was ginger-haired, strong-looking with glinting, steely eyes, small but well-built. Anyway, there was this major, who had never fought at the front, and he looked her up and down from head to toe. Then he looked at her again, this time walking around her. Masha sneered to show her irritation and suspicion. After that, whenever he saw her he would fix his gaze upon her, and stare, like a cat staring at a baby chick. There is no denying that Masha was pleased by the attention. Of course this was a sad occasion, but there was no reason for everything to be gloomy. It was important to her to know she was attractive enough for a man to look at her in that way. She wasn't forcing the major to stare at her after all. On their last day in Moscow they were taken to Red Square. Masha gasped—it was so beautiful. Far better than any of the pictures. She stood there gaping, and the major hunted her down and attached himself to her. He started pointing out different buildings, showing her what was where.

"That's an exhibition hall. Have you heard of the artist Glazunov? The line waiting to see his exhibition went right around the building. That brick building is the Lenin museum. And over there is the university. The main part of the university is out on the Lenin Hills now. But this is the original building. Can you see the Intourist? It's a first class hotel."

"And they stuck us out in the back of beyond!" Masha felt insulted. "We never got a chance to see Moscow at all."

"You can only stay there for foreign currency," replied the major. "Foreign currency is worth more than ordinary money. What the government is trying to do …"

Masha let down her guard at the point where he started talking about foreign currency and the government's plans. Two forces seemed to have collided within her. The powerful force of the beauty surrounding her, which had momentarily knocked her sideways, and the secret force burning within her. The beauty of Red Square had paralyzed her, but her secret, inner force attached itself to the major. This might be it! Why not? And it had all happened so suddenly!

He led Masha around, holding her by the arm. They didn't seem to be going in any particular direction, but all the time they were moving farther and farther away from the group. His hand was burning hot. What did it mean? He looked around and hustled her into the minibus. Inside, it was empty, dusty, and grimy.

As Masha yielded to him, she managed to say that nothing in life was free—she wasn't an idiot, and she'd read ... but either the major didn't understand her, or he didn't hear, or he didn't take any notice. He muttered something to her about the advantage of being dead—because then you don't know anything. Masha wondered what he meant and who he could possibly be talking about. Then she realized he must be referring to Victor. The major was slightly inhibited about the idea of taking a dead soldier's girlfriend—but not so inhibited as to stop himself from doing it!

Afterward he shot out of the minibus like a bullet from a gun, without so much as a backward glance at Masha. And then he disappeared, as if into a crack in the ground!

She was filled with hatred. Is that it? she thought. Is that the way it is? Just because she came from the country, they could treat her like that? She wasn't going to stand for it! She could have that major reduced to a pulp on two counts.

She would go straight to the Central Committee and tell them what had happened. He wouldn't get away with it! But in her heart she knew there was no one she could turn to. She'd been a fool. What she needed was experience, and that was exactly what she didn't have. She'd have to get her brain into gear. She wanted big things, and not just a little sex! Sex as such left her cold.

When Masha climbed down out of the minibus, she realized that the whole thing had only taken a couple of minutes—just enough time for the traffic lights to change once. The sun was setting. Masha wiped her flushed face with the hem of her slip. "Damn the lot of you, I don't care if you look at me. Parasites, bastards, vermin!"

She took a deep breath and walked away, following her nose. Her nose led her toward the Intourist hotel.

They can just wait, she thought. When I'm rich, when I'm very rich, I'll strangle all of them. All of them! One by one ...

Translated by Rachel Osorio

IRINA   POLYANSKAYA

THE GAME

I SAW THE GIRL for the first time near the Pushkin monument. It was the beginning of October and the city was immersed in a thick, gray fog, broken only by intermittent drizzle. Trees with yellow leaves shone weakly. A group of schoolchildren, restless and bored, surrounded their teacher or tour guide, who was pointing toward the monument, but the children were ignoring her lecture and having more fun studying the pigeon perched on the bronze curls of the figure on the pedestal. I was waiting for someone and all my thoughts were focused on him. Only my eyes, alert and perceptive in those moments of bitter indecision and fog, were taking in the people around me. I was glancing at the identical faces of the children, wanting to single out at least one to interrupt my train of thought, when I saw her. Fate presented me with her face. A girl came up to the monument. She was in her teens, I think, and everyone who saw her that day must have remembered her and told their people at home, "We saw a crazy girl walking around town today."

Despite the cold weather she wore a short pleated skirt, a T-shirt, nylons and high-heeled patent leather shoes. She was holding herself upright, as if her back, spine, and entire soul were withstanding a colossal trial that could crush anyone but her. Looking at her I recalled a motto from our youth: "The important thing in life is to hold your head high." Such a stupid motto for stupid girls like us. The most important things were not what we thought they were. Life, with the tenderness and insistence of a mother bathing her child, taught me differently. You could read the girl's face. "I am not aware of anyone around, I came here only to see YOU." This was addressed to Pushkin. The solitary flower she held in her hand was for HIM. A rose, giving off a radiance that his glum face was lacking. There was animation among the schoolchildren who noticed her and began nudging each other.

The teacher stopped her well-memorized recitation momentarily. The people sitting on the benches and the passers-by registered her presence but were better mannered than the students. I felt I knew everything the girl was going to do, as if she was acting on my orders and with my blessings. I felt as though we were there together. I was the only one who could understand her, and so precisely that it was impossible to smile or be surprised or even look at her. We were rehearsing a scene.

She stood there for a while, just looking up at HIM (the capitals are hers, not mine). She then bent her rigid back to place the rose at the foot of the monument and stepped back a pace. Again she stood there motionless, trying, as it were, to come to an agreement with the skies above HIM.

I already knew what she was going to do next. The girl put her hand into her bag, took out a small notebook and pencil and scribbled (I can bet on this) the following: "Today at eleven hours fifteen minutes (he was already fifteen minutes late) I met with HIM for the first time." Dear Lord, this poor little thing imagined that her main asset was independence. This was obvious from the tortured and stony expression on her face, an expression that fielded the jokes from people on the street. "Aren't you feeling hot, young lady?" It was a rather cold autumn and the people whom she arrogantly defined as "normal"—including me—walked by, sat, smoked, talked on the phone, got in line, embraced each other, wore coats, sweaters, and leather jackets, and did not feel hot.

She began walking away, putting a distance between herself and my impression. Her legs were too thin for her miniskirt and patent leather heels; her back reproached all of us. I swallowed her reproach and stood up to meet the bad news approaching me. He was lighting up a cigarette and searching sluggishly for me with his bored eyes.

My meeting with him also left me feeling weighed down with sorrow and I wished to ease the sensation. I came across a movie advertisement that said *Carmen,* a two-part, French opera film, was being shown in one of the halls on Kutuzovsky Prospect. I decided to walk there. Once, when I was as young as that girl, I also carried my head high so that everyone around could see my challenge to the Fates; I wore dangling and sparkling things to match the challenge. I was quite impressed with Carmen in the film, with her dark looks and part-black blood, which made her look exactly like the girl from Mérimée's novella, and quite unlike the Queen of Spades, the big-breasted matron you usually see in opera productions. The fog had now enveloped me and I walked on, taking no notice of anyone or anything till I found myself standing in a little cafeteria, eating a cheese sandwich and having a glass of juice. Tears were streaming from my eyes and the people around looked at me as if I was not all there.

It's not so bad hearing people say, "Young lady, the zipper on your skirt is undone." It is far worse when somebody sees your tears.

A crowd of unknown people, tears close at hand, like handkerchiefs in their pockets, was running toward me. Each of them was carrying something deep in their heart: the death of a father, sheer bad luck, dismissal from a job, a cardiac problem, a picture of a loved one who had run off, unsatisfactory marks at school, suspension of a driver's license, cirrhosis of the liver, autumn asters for a birthday ...

I wish I were someone else, I thought. I can't survive being me. I imagined all of us, enveloped by the fog, taking out our innermost belongings—like opening up cards—and sorting them out and exchanging them. The man with cirrhosis agrees to trade places with me, so I lay out my sorrow in front of him with, let's say, my knowledge of English or my easygoing nature. As I accept his cirrhosis and—more importantly—get rid of my lumpish sorrow, I stand up joyous and unburdened, and those who see me that day cry out, "Why, you must have come into a fortune!" But the former owner of the cirrhosis now walks with my gait, holding on to the walls of buildings with my sorrow, which he had imagined was a light one. My sorrow bears down on him and bends his back. He loses weight, wanders around, not knowing where to go and whom to see in order to lull my (his!) anguish. While he is enjoying himself at a friend's place, laughing his head off—the way I do when I'm not having any real fun—his liver will start feeling at home inside me. It will start talking, moaning, and hurting, flooding my soul and body with pain. He leaves his hospitable friend's home and I fly from mine and we rush to meet each other, propelled by the pain that pushes us like a snowstorm. In the pitch dark we find each other—me, to give him back his liver, and he, to return my sorrow. Perhaps it would have been better to have swapped with the woman who had bad luck exchanging her old apartment for a new one. But as soon as I do it, I can discern her ex-mother-in-law appearing on the horizon, and beginning to gnaw at my life. No, we had better keep what we have. With a wave of my hand I disperse the crowd converging in front of the building and the people rush off in all directions, dragging their sorrows behind them.

There were two tiny auditoriums in the movie theater. The first one was showing an English comedy and everybody there was taking shelter from the fog. In the lobby, in front of the entrance to our auditorium, was a snack bar.

I immediately sensed that the people sitting there were my kin. Unlike those who had come to see the comedy, this crowd had not gathered accidentally. There was a special atmosphere there. We had flocked from all over our great capital to see this particular film. There was a handful of old women in worn-out fur coats, one of them on crutches; a young, nice-looking couple; three college students; a young man with *The Hockey and Soccer Review* in his hand (he was the only one who came here by chance, not realizing it would be an opera film, unaware of the unpleasant surprise awaiting him, his 50 kopecks wasted. I could hear an annoyed knocking at the door under the glowing red "Exit" sign); there was an old man with the impassive face of a cooperative director, and another old man with his elderly wife—a very ancient, very old-fashioned couple who behaved toward each other in a grand manner. "How are you today, my friend?" "Thank you, my dear, quite well. And you, my love?" When I came in, they smiled at me conspiratorially. Enveloped by this gentleness I sat down and, remembering the cheese sandwich left untouched in the cafeteria, asked the barman for another. He gave a nod of understanding and asked if I cared for a cup of coffee.

He also understood us. I thanked him and sat near the old women, joining in their conversation about Maya Plisetskaya. I had always had this roof above my head, this sanctuary: the music. It was thoughtless of me to have tried swapping lives with cirrhosis—I would have inherited his video recorder and his spaniel, which I would not have known what to do with. And what would he have done with this music of mine? If I were asked "Would you like your sorrow to vanish into thin air—but only together with the overture to Carmen?" I would cry out, terrified, "Not a single bar! Not a single note! Let this sorrow be cursed, let it stick like a splinter in my throat!"

So, united by a feeling of kinship, we were sitting and drinking our cups of coffee and reminiscing about Placido Domingo, when suddenly she entered. Just as the musicians were clearing the throats of their instruments. She had obviously walked all the way from Pushkin Square and her hands and legs were covered with goosebumps, but she still carried her head as high and arrogantly as she had before. We were saying just then that only Tchaikovsky and Liszt had really appreciated this opera, while the rest of their contemporaries had hissed at this music. She asked for a cup of coffee, but not for a sandwich, and sat down at our table. There was a pause in the conversation and speaking each word distinctly, she said to me, "Excuse me, is this where they are showing *Carmen*?"

Suppressing a smile, I replied, "Yes, it is."

She nodded, took a sip of coffee and ceremoniously put the cup back on the table. I knew that she was desperate for a sandwich and perhaps had the money for it, but she was unwilling to give up her act. The bell rang and we all drifted in and sat at a distance from each other. Our furs may have been faded and a bit bald, but our feelings and perceptions remained intact and we decided to give the music enough room, to make it flow freely and unhindered around us. Stendhal insisted that one should not listen to music in a big gathering. We sat apart so as not to disturb the aura created around us by the music. Nodding to the old women I took my seat in the second to the last row near the wall and saw the girl take hers in the middle of the first row, flapping her seat noisily. Even here she decided to challenge us all.

I can't say the vigorous overture carried me away into a world of dreams, like that girl had. All my thoughts remained with me. I am not much of an opera-goer, because of the outward discrepancies between the music and the appearance of the cast, to say nothing of their voices. In this case everything was just right. I always go to see such films, there are not many of them, and their audience continues to diminish. This has long since ceased to bother me. But it probably bothers her and led her to take the front seat so as not to see the empty auditorium. The performance was excellent and the tears were real. No one disturbed us. Even the young man with *The Hockey and Soccer Review* had gone away without waiting for Carmen to appear on the screen.

The film ended and we filed out toward the exit, exchanging impressions. On the way out an old woman recalled Tamara Talakhadze singing the part of Micaela. We said good-bye to each other and went our separate ways. She was running in front of me, slicing the human flow in two, shivering as she ran and unwilling to make her peace with either the people around her or the cold. We entered the train station together and changed our silver pieces for 5-kopeck coins. Going through the passageway that led to the Arbat line I slowed down, unwilling to lose sight of her.

She also slowed down and headed in the direction that I was going to take.

The rumbling of the train sounded like falling rain. I entered a car and sat opposite her. Why was she so strangely dressed, so out of season? Could it be only for the complicated game she was playing with life and people, with people and her own life? Could it just be the cracking voice of young extremism ringing in her ears, deafening the other warm and natural voices, which she was unable to hear? Was she resisting them? What was she after? Glory, roses, barricades, or her little name, which must have been Zoya or Tanya, although she would probably introduce herself as Stella. But perhaps everything was much simpler: She was a provincial, she had lost her old-fashioned, tasteless raincoat or it could have been stolen, she had no one to go to in Moscow apart from me. She had an aunt, though. And her mother had begged her to stay with her aunt in the capital. But the girl had visited the aunt, brought her an expensive cake and a bunch of flowers, and displayed her independence by mumbling something about a nonexistent girlfriend who lived in an apartment in Moscow, which had a separate room ready for her. She had just enough money to buy herself a ticket back to Bryansk, on a hard-sleeper, covering herself from head to toe with a second blanket at night. But she had nowhere to spend the night and she was riding the train without any destination. I had a place to take her to, and just then I had no one staying with me. I could offer her a bowl of soup and a collapsible cot. Yes, this was the thing to do. We got off at Kievskaya station and again I followed her.

A young man I know likes to walk the streets of Moscow with a map of the city in his hand. He has tremendous fun pretending to be a lost tourist and accosting all sorts of people to ask them in heavily accented Russian how to find his way to the Central Department Store, near Red Square. He testifies that we are hospitable. We put our bags and purses down on the pavement and start gesticulating and speaking in broken Russian, shouting directions in the tourist's ear, as though he were deaf. This friend of mine bothers peaceful passers-by—sometimes women with babies in their arms—for about ten minutes, trying to find out the way to the "Czar-kennel," and people happily correct him, saying it is the "Czar-cannon" and show him the way. He mingles shamelessly among crowds of people pretending to be a foreign tourist, tossing up the ends of his long knitted scarf. Only he, who is small, wretched, and poor, is inclined to impersonate someone he is not.

We changed from the radial line to the circular line and took the train to the Park of Culture station. I made a mental promise to myself: If she came after me, I would offer her my collapsible cot. I would even lend her

my raincoat, which she would certainly send back to me, when she returned to her little hometown.

She got off the train, following me, and we walked quickly along the
passageway. Suddenly I realized that I was not following her, but she was
steering me, keeping a short pace ahead and sensing my presence with
her back. I slowed down. She looked back. I was frightened. It meant
that she had sensed something in my expression and had become aware of
something within me, as I had of something within her. She recognized
me. She wanted to ask me a question: Will I look like you, when I grow
up? I wondered if my life would suit her. It didn't suit me at all. Like an
actor, who continues playing a part out of habit, whatever the cost and
the effort, I was sticking my stupid neck out, although I had long since
shed all my dreams and aspirations. I was some fifteen years older than
she was. Again we got into the train and sat opposite each other. She
opened a book, *Gravity Without Formulas,* which again proved the darkness her soul was wandering about in. She was still a little girl, a very
foolish one, mistaking the blood throbbing in her ears for noble ideas.
Her dreams were as shapeless as clouds. Her eyes were sightless. Her
tongue lied. I knew her type well: grim and reticent. If you made an attempt to talk with them a little, their childish foolishness would pour out
like peas. I knew what kind of poetry they wrote. What kind of books
they read. And what kind of notes they left in the margins. I knew how
their boyfriends jilted them. How their parents worried about them. I
knew if she happened to find herself on my collapsible bed, the girl
would torture me with her infantile nightmares, with the confessions of a
creature unaware of itself, with that tragic playacting of hers. She would
stick to me like a leech, would start writing letters to me, would send me
(on her miserable salary, for she failed to make it to college and now
works as a junior assistant in some laboratory) expensive art books. She
would put herself out to buy me Goya's *Capriccios* if I made even the
slightest mention of my dream to have this book. She would begin to con-
fide all her secrets in me, which would bring tears to my eyes and put a
lump in my throat.

She was already staring at me, the book folded. There was an arrogant
expectancy in her eyes. She could not afford to speak to me first: "We
seem to be going the same way?" with the nonchalant air of a girl who
had an aunt living somewhere in Moscow. She was waiting for me to say
these words, following which we would start chatting, oblivious to
everything around us, two birds of a feather. She was staring straight
ahead, severely and hungrily, and I averted my eyes and tried to take a

short nap. Her stare was burning through my eyelids. She couldn't believe my treachery. But I already knew that if I fell into this trap, this instant temptation of kindness, if I gave her a bowlful of my soup, I would steal from her a thousand times more. What would I say to her? Why must I lead her on?

I opened my eyes, her scorn had been unbearable and I could stand it no longer. I felt happy that she had gotten off the train back at Kievskaya station and that she was nowhere around. Only some soup, a raincoat, perhaps a sandwich. There was nothing else I could have given her. But she would not have believed me if I'd told her that her game, like a wave rolling over sand and pebbles, would slide smoothly into real life, and become life itself. That she would have her fill of grief yet. ... That everything comes true as soon as you utter a word. That a head held high teases more than bare legs and a miniskirt. ... That the Fates are never dormant ... and that everything would then go up in flames, and there would be no hiding from it, no use covering your face with your hands, like those stowaways on a bus, caught by a shot from a camera. ... You'd remain this way for ages—your mouth contorted by a cry of terror, your fingers cramped, a look of utter misery in your eyes.

I went home and said to my mother, "I saw a crazy girl walking around town today."

Translated by Ayesha Kagal and Natasha Perova

NINA   SADUR

WITCH'S TEARS

SOMETHING LIKE THAT HAPPENED to a girl I knew at college. She had a boyfriend, Alec Gorokhov. He wasn't much to look at. At the cottage, where they first met, she didn't even notice him at first, especially since he'd brought his girlfriend with him. They were all sitting around roasting meat and my friend Olga—a real go-getter who, to be blunt, never wastes any time—was sprawled out, sizing up these kids who'd gathered for the barbecue. Suddenly she felt someone's eyes on her. She looked over. It was Alec staring at her. Olga snorted—he was so skinny, ordinary-looking, his little nose red with cold. She had had a little to drink and went out through the garden gate for a walk to the lake. She soon heard someone trying to catch up with her and somehow she knew right away it was Alec scrambling after her.

"Well, what do you want?" Olga said.

"Nothing, really," answered Alec.

They walked toward the lake together, but Olga hates it when young guys she didn't choose chase after her. Olga is a pretty little thing. She dresses well too (her mother works in a department store), and with her personality, she doesn't suffer from any shortage of boyfriends.

"What do you do?" Olga asked him.

He answered that he had tried getting into an aviation school but he hadn't done well enough in the entrance exams so now he was going to be swept into the service on the next draft.

When they got to the lake it was already late and pretty cold. They wandered up and down the beach for awhile. There was no one around, only some dogs running loose who kept looking at them.

Afterward, they went back. Everyone had drunk too much by then. Alec's girl sat motionless by the fire. She was quite pretty too. All the time Alec and Olga had been walking by the lake, she had sat by the fire, and she didn't even turn her head when she heard the gate shut. As for Alec, he just went dumb: Only now did he remember his girlfriend.

"I must see her home," he said to Olga. "I'll call you tomorrow."

"That's all I need," said my Olga.

"What's your number?" said Alec, and Olga gave it to him, to get rid of him. Then he called his girlfriend over and they left.

Later, he started phoning Olga and, when she didn't have anyone else, she would agree to go out with him. They would go for a walk, or to the movies, sometimes they drank a little, and Olga would die of boredom. Meanwhile, he was trying to talk her into marrying him.

One day, they happened to drop in on some friends, and Olga spotted the perfect man, went after him, got drunk, and told Alec to get lost. Then, in the morning when she got up, she remembered what she'd done and decided to call him, just in case. He was human after all.

She phoned him and he told her that everything was okay, fine, no offense. Another month passed. By that time, naturally, Olga had broken up with her man, but she hated being alone so she was waiting for Alec to phone. He may have been a bore, but she was waiting all the same; she was used to him.

But he didn't phone. Olga got furious, waited some more, then phoned him herself. They met, they went out, just like before. He walked her home. It went all right. Then she called him again. So they got together again. Again, it was the same old story. Again she called, and this time he said to her, "I've got someone new. I'm going to marry her." Olga tracked down the crowd they used to hang around with, on purpose, to have a look at his bride-to-be. You couldn't imagine anyone uglier. About that time Alec got his summons from the draft board. His monster was there to see him off too, and Olga said to him, right there on the platform, "She won't wait for you to come home from the army, but I will." He didn't say a word. That's exactly how it turned out. His bride couldn't wait, married someone else, and he came home to nothing. Olga phoned him again and they started going out again, spending time together. And it turns out that he always agreed to see her, but wouldn't phone her himself; that he was actually forcing himself to go out with her. Olga cried and she raged, but in the end, she somehow managed to stop phoning him, and then came something altogether different. She began to sense him.

For instance, we'd be going somewhere. Olga would be fine, talking away. Suddenly she'd shut up and say: "Girls, right now we're going to run into Alec." We'd say, "Come off it! Wise up!" Then bang! Gorokhov, in the flesh, would be coming toward us. We'd be so scared our knees'd be shaking. They'd square off like a couple of rams. We'd manage to drag them apart somehow, and we'd give Olga hell. Life goes on. Again she'd sense him. Again we'd come across him in places he'd never been before.

She's stopped studying by now. We're taking notes for her in school. She's driven all her boyfriends away. We're telling her to do just the opposite: "You'd better find someone steady; you're starting to look a real mess." And she says, "I think I should too, but I can't. They all pretend I don't exist." And it was the truth. Lately, the other kids had begun shunning Olga. They could take her once in a while, but on a regular basis—no thanks.

Meanwhile, she's in a terrible state. She doesn't just sense him any more, she's started "seeing" him. "There," she says, "someone died today; someone close to him, but he doesn't know it yet. And he's going to trip and sprain his ankle and they'll tell him about it later, in the hospital." Naturally, that's exactly the way it happens.

I went to see her once. Her mother wasn't home. Olga was sitting there by herself. I said to her, "Either you're a complete idiot or you'd better phone him right now and start over again."

But Olga says, "I don't want to. I don't like him."

I had no idea at all what to think. "Then what the hell are you doing having premonitions about him all the time?"

But she just shrugged and didn't say a thing.

Once, later on, we were on our way to the post office together. By then I couldn't stand being around her either. I was scared that she'd start "seeing" him again and, sure enough, she starts shaking, grabs me, and says, "There, around the corner." I poked my head out and there he was, standing, looking so dejected, like some burned-out old tramp, but he was still young, the same age as us. And he looked like he was forced to wait for someone, not of his own free will.

Just then, Olga came up behind me, but I didn't let her get any further. I said, "There's no one there. Let's go back." She listened and we went in another direction. But I felt uncomfortable and not at all myself. I put her on a streetcar and went home.

Half a year later, Olga got married after all. At her wedding she took me aside and said, "I'm sick to death of it all. I'm stopping." I said to her,

"Thank God!" And then she went on. "Alec's going to be a cripple soon anyway." And that's just what happened. He got hit by a car and became a "Category 1" invalid. Meanwhile Olga had a child, a girl, Marina, and then she separated from her husband. But she's doing all right now; she's got her mother to help her, and she's re-registered at school. And it didn't go any further.

Dear Little Redhead

There was another girl we knew, Natasha Solovyova. She wasn't from Moscow. She rented a room from this old woman, more like half a room, since the old woman only had a one-room apartment. She let Natasha have it for 15 rubles. Basically, it was okay—the subway was nearby and the old woman often gave her meals—but the old woman herself was odd. Natasha says there were times when the old woman wouldn't take money from her, not for anything in the world. She'd be handing her the rent, for instance, the 15 rubles, and the old woman would start screaming at her and throwing the money around like an idiot.

Natasha would say, "What's the matter with you, Granny? Don't you remember? I haven't paid you for November yet." Then the old woman would spill flour on the floor, as if by accident, and scream that Natasha had bumped into her on purpose, so now she could sweep it up. Sweeping flour isn't much fun. An awful nuisance, but Natasha would start sweeping. What else could she do?

Another month, she'd take the money, then count it a hundred times over, grumbling that it wasn't enough. The old woman had a cat, naturally. No, it wasn't black; just a common, gray tom. It went slumming for weeks at a time and came back through a little casement window, its mug mauled, all dirty, a fright to look at. In short, an ordinary, good-time cat.

Now, my Natasha happened to notice that, whenever the cat wasn't home, the old woman would take the rent. But when the cat was home, she wouldn't. She also noticed that when the cat was around, the old woman behaved differently. When the cat was there, she was somehow more efficient, meaner, more hardworking. The old woman was shrewd, a wheeler-dealer, and tough too. She used to crash around in the kitchen, cursing and swearing at God knows who. Natasha also remembered how she always used to say "For good or for ill?" addressing something that only she could see. Say something on the shelf went crooked, she'd go right up to the thing and ask it, "For good or for ill?"

One time, a washbasin came crashing down in the bathroom. It made Natasha jump from fright. The old woman ran to the bathroom and saw it lying on the floor. She looked at it and said, "For good or for ill?" Natasha went to see too and she thought it was ridiculous—the basin lying there innocently on the tiles with the old woman standing over it, demanding a reply. Natasha gave a great snort. The old woman jumped, turned to face her, then just stared. Natasha was really frightened then.

That old woman wouldn't let Natasha have any of us come over. Once I had to get some history notes from her in a hurry, so I went there anyway. But I couldn't stay in that place! I just couldn't! Natasha even said to me, "What's up with you? The old woman treated you all right—oddly enough." Actually the old woman hadn't said a thing except "Hello, young lady," and then had gone straight to the kitchen and didn't show up again to meddle in other people's business, the way old women usually do. But I just couldn't stand it! I said, "Give me back my notebook, I'm going." I took the notebook, went outside, and right there, while I was still on the porch, I felt as if I'd been released ... as if none of it had happened, not the fear, not the anguish, not the horror. I could breathe easily again too. I even laughed a little. What had come over me?

I said to Natasha, "How can you stand living with her?" But she wouldn't look me in the eye and said, "It's all right."

Then I said, "And at night?"

Then she said, "Well, I got some sleeping pills. I take three at a time and I nod right off."

"Uh-huh, I see. Now, what's the real story?" I said.

But she wouldn't look me in the eye and she never said a word, as if she wasn't allowed to answer.

Later, though, we found out all about it. Out of the blue, Natasha married Sergei Koloskov, moved in with him, and then told us everything.

That old woman divided off half the room with a curtain, so that Natasha could have part of it for her own use. And every night someone made squeaking noises on the old woman's side. She either spoke with those squeaky voices or cursed and swore at them.

And every night Natasha would die of fright. Then, in the morning, the old woman would study her closely, as if to see whether Natasha had heard anything or not. Of course the old woman knew perfectly well that Natasha could hear every word, but she needed her not to give herself away and Natasha knew it.

Then once, it was a night in October, it was pouring rain, windy, and thundering somewhere. Natasha starts getting ready for bed. She's turned out the light and she's lying there. But she doesn't have the pills yet so she has to get to sleep on her own.

Suddenly she hears someone fussing about—there it is. A solitary voice starts squeaking; it seems to be asking something. The old woman begins to toss in her bed and mutters something back sleepily. The voice stops bothering her. Meanwhile, the rain falls harder and harder, like a thing possessed, crashing down on the window sill. ... It was sheer hell!

Natasha has crawled under the blanket, head and all, and she's just lying there. Suddenly the voice starts squeaking again and, the thing is, though she can't tell just what it's squeaking, it seems to her that they're words of some sort, but she simply can't make them out. And she wants so badly to find out—what are those words it's squeaking? The voice sounds like it's out of a cartoon and all the more frightening for being so obviously alive. And she wants so badly to make out what words it's squeaking. You'd think a tiny voice like that wouldn't know any words at all, but it's saying something anyway—and it's so absurd, so frightfully absurd!

Natasha has thrown back the blanket, just a little, and lifted her head off the pillow, listening. They're really going at it now! The old woman thunders back in her deep voice, while the tiny voice keeps telling her off, just like our principal at school. The old woman tosses and turns on the bedsprings, droning and groaning away, but the tiny voice won't leave her alone and keeps driving its point home. Now Natasha, maybe because she's used to it already, or maybe because she's getting into the spirit of things herself, sits up in bed, shivering, her teeth chattering, dying of curiosity. And she can't stop herself—she's being drawn toward the curtain, so irresistibly that she's almost sick to her stomach.

By this time those voices are raging completely out of control. The rain is trying to smash in the windows. Everything is creaking, rumbling, groaning. ... Natasha's sitting there and suddenly the curtain begins to billow, as if a draft had blown through the room. But there couldn't have been a draft. The old woman was afraid of drafts and all the windows were shut tight. Natasha wants quickly to get back into bed, but suddenly she can't move, she can only sit there as if something has taken hold of her. The curtain goes on billowing and all of a sudden—thump—out jumps Kitty with his soft paws. He sees Natasha, stops, stares at her with his enormous eyes, and she stares back.

Kitty stood there for a bit, glanced back at the curtain, then made his eyes into slits, yawned, and came over to her, jumped onto the bed,

sniffed at her, and started purring. Natasha stroked him and he got all affectionate, poking his head into the palm of her hand. And all the while
the voices were squealing there, behind the curtain. Natasha pulled him
close to her and sat trembling. But Kitty kept an eye on the curtain, his
ears working away, his tail slapping. Natasha pressed him tighter still,
even though he had fleas and was dirty from hanging around the garbage
dumps. She didn't care. Tears were running down her cheeks and Kitty
thought it was funny. He sniffed at them, but soon grew tired of it, broke
free, and left her, jumped down onto the floor, stretched, and went back
to the other side. Natasha literally collapsed back onto the bed. She was
drenched with sweat and she nodded right off.

The following morning the old woman looked at her oddly, question-
ing her with her eyes. And Natasha felt that today she could finally say it.
"I heard all, I saw all." It was as if the old woman was allowing her to, but
Natasha didn't want to and that was that. As soon as she remembered
how she'd sat there with tears pouring down her face, she just couldn't!
The old woman danced around her all morning in vain, right up until
Natasha left for school. Later, Natasha bought herself the sleeping pills
and started taking them and that seemed to be the end of it.

We have this class at school—we make all sorts of scale models, minia-
tures, useless little things. I, for instance, was building a stairway for an
apartment building, wasted away all my time, and got a 'C'. I was supposed to make a teeny, little stairway using matches, cardboard, and
wire, just like a real one, but for little people about the height of an
amoeba. Anyway, I got a 'C'. Natasha, on the other hand, had to make little outfits, for those little amoeblings who were supposedly going to
crawl up and down my stairway. Well, Natasha ended up with a 'D', because one of the shirts made out of a hanky disappeared altogether and
they wouldn't accept a suit without a shirt. She was furious. She searched
far and wide for that tiny shirt and, mainly, she felt bad about wasting a
hanky, ruining it for nothing and getting a failing mark anyway. But later
she did sew another shirt and then they gave her a passing mark. She
came very close to repeating the year.

A month went by like that, all quiet. The old woman ignored her completely and Natasha went on blissfully gulping her sleeping pills and
walking around like a zombie, because the pills never wore off and she
was really out of it, sleeping on her feet and staring off into space.
Natasha used to keep those pills on a chair beside her bed.

One day, she sees the old woman standing there with the pills, sniffing
them, turning them to the light, licking one even.

"What do you think you're doing, Granny?" Natasha asks in a sleepy voice. She always spoke in a sleepy voice by then. At school they even nicknamed her "Sleepy."

"Looking at your pills," answered the old woman.

"Those pills are for ..." says Natasha.

"For what?" says the old woman.

"For colds," lied Natasha.

The old woman gave her an angry look. Then she curled her lip and snarled, "The sleep of the soul! Devil's brew!"—and she threw the pills down and went and spilled the flour again, and then made Sleepy sweep it up. Well, Natasha, of course, took half the day to do it because she had no strength left, she needed to sleep so badly.

That same night Natasha is getting ready for bed again, but she can't find the pills. And she's so afraid. She realized that the old woman had stolen them! And everything started all over again: the voices squeaking, the old woman bickering with them, the curtain dancing. ... Natasha is shaking under her blanket. She's pulled it over her head and she's afraid to breathe. Suddenly she hears someone come running up: pitter-patter, pitter-patter, and he's standing right beside her. She can feel his presence but she can't even cry she's so scared. She just lies there biting her fingers, bug-eyed in the darkness under her blanket. And whoever he is stands there at the foot of her bed. It's grown quiet on the old woman's side, you can even hear her starting to snore, but he keeps on standing there. Natasha begins to pull up her feet carefully to get away from him. She wants to curl up into a ball, but suddenly he pulls the blanket, ever so gently, but Natasha is clutching at it too. He tugs his way and she hers. He jerks at it, but she won't let go and, when she sees that she's stronger, she isn't so afraid any more, she even starts to get angry at his outrageous behavior. But right then, she feels that her arms have fallen asleep, she has no strength left, she feels prickly all over and her fingers have gone numb. At that very moment, he gives a jerk and the blanket slips off her face. Well, she decides to cautiously have a peek at the foot of the bed—who can it be fooling around like that down there? She raises herself up ever so slightly and sees a tiny, little ... it isn't clear what. He has a little face all right, but he's all sort of red-haired, and dirty, wrapped in some sort of rag. The rag looked familiar and, when she got a better look, she saw it was her little shirt, the one that almost got her expelled from school. The shirt was so big on him that he was swimming in it. It was torn at the seam in front (she had stitched it only temporarily), and through it, reddish tufts of fur stuck out, like peasants have, and the little shirt itself looked like nothing on earth, as if he'd slept drunk in the gutter in it. He stood there, jerking at her blanket, frowning, pouting, and didn't even notice that she'd already been watching him for a while. Natasha opened her mouth wide, but she couldn't get a breath. She saw that he looked a little like her and then a warm feeling came over her, but she was still scared to death. At last she had to breathe. She breathed in carefully and he suddenly shuddered. He'd seen her. He dropped his arms to his sides and stared at her bug-eyed. But he wouldn't leave. He just stood there, then he frowned, looking out from beneath knit brows and his little face was just like Natasha's: little nose, tiny brows, just like her own! The little shirt kept slipping off his shoulder and Natasha just lay there, mouth gaping, eyes wide. Several minutes went by that way, then suddenly someone whispered right into Natasha's ear, "Go ahead, ask, or I'll let you have it!" And then, in a voice hoarse and crazy with fear, into that tiny, dirty, yet human little face, she croaked, "For ill or for good?"

And he answered in his tiny voice, without hesitation, instantly, as if by rote, "For good."

And right then someone whacked her over the head. She fell over, screwing her eyes tight, and when she opened them again, there was no one there, only Kitty sleeping at her side.

In the morning, when she gets up, the old woman is walking around angry as a toad and it happens to be rent day. Natasha hands her the money, the old woman takes it, counts it, and says, "You're short."

"There's 15 rubles there," says Natasha.

"What am I supposed to live on?" the old woman screams.

"What have you lived on till now?" screams back Natasha, "I paid 15 rubles from the start and I'll go on paying 15 rubles!"

Then the old woman gets furious. She hurls the frying pan, spills the flour, and starts cursing under her breath. Natasha picks up the broom, but then the old woman goes totally berserk, tears it out of her hands, and throws it out of the window. All day long they tramp through the flour; they leave footprints all over the place; they dirty all the scatter rugs with it; Natasha just doesn't know what to think any more.

And two days later, literally, Sergei Koloskov proposes to her and she moves in with him.

That's all there is to tell.

Rings

There is something to rings of course, just as there is to dreams. If dreams reflect our lives in one way, then rings do in another.

Dreams present us with images and we begin to understand those moments of our lives that held a promise of something or else those events in our lives that went wrong. Rings, though, mutely encircle our entire lives, without emphasizing any particular moments. I could give many examples of dreams and rings, but I'd get confused. That's why I'll just give my love and my friendship as examples.

My very best friend, Lyubka Vakheta, is seventeen, three years younger than I am. We live in the same apartment building, and it was she who first made friends with me in the elevator. I was in grade eight and she was in grade six. She caught up with me in the lobby, started riding up with me, and said, "Hello, are you going out to play today?" I was amazed—a lowly sixth-grader. But later I got used to it and now even our mothers mix us up. We've come to look so alike.

My Lyubka leads me astray. I miss classes in school, but I look at my classmates and they're all so prim and proper, whereas for me every day is a holiday because of Lyubka. She's totally ignorant. She doesn't even know what year the war started. She says, "Twenty million ..." I say, "That's right, killed." Then she says, "Who is the president of America? Kennedy, or something?" I say, "Where have you been? It's Reagan!" And she says, "I wonder what made me think of Kennedy?"

Lyubka's very pretty. She has fine, sharp, little teeth and blue, blue eyes. She dreams of taking drugs, is perpetually overexcited, and refuses to lose weight. She eats so much. I've never seen anyone eat as much as her. She's bursting out of all her clothes. She comes to me for a candy and ends up eating the whole box, but I don't mind because I happen to want to lose weight.

Lyubka ruined her reputation in the Blacklands. She was always ruining her reputation somewhere or other, but in the Blacklands she ruined it for good. It was there that we both fell in love—I with Levan, and she with Sasha. I was mostly afraid for Lyubka because she's totally incorrigible. This Sasha was all right, as Sashas go. He never did anything vile to me. He was polite and proper, but he treated Lyubka like a prostitute. And she's a virgin. Now that is vile. At first, everything went all right for them in the Blacklands ... he really liked Lyubka. But when he found out she was a virgin, he cooled right off and that's when Lyubka went crazy. His group of boys were staying in camp number two and at night Lyubka would ask one of us to go with her all the way across the fields to their camp. She'd pick up drunks from there and they'd stagger after her over the ruts into the darkness. Then, at the loading ramps, she'd leave them, drunk and lonely. Sasha used to say to her, "Right. I've got thirty minutes for you." Afterward, she'd make her own way back. But even that wasn't so bad.

We were there harvesting watermelons and Lyubka found a ring, black and deformed, with a dirty, watery, little stone. We had a giggle about it but she put it in her jacket anyway and then forgot all about it. How could anyone find a ring in a field of watermelons? Only Lyubka could.

Later, we went back to Moscow and Lyubka began getting ready to give herself to Sasha, because she had no other way out—he wouldn't agree to be just friends. Her mother began smoking, her father began taking heart drops, and her grandmother lost the use of her legs. Lyubka doesn't know how to keep a secret. She goes straight up to her mother and says, "Mommy, buy me some white panties." Her mother bursts into tears. "Do you think I don't know what you want white panties for? You little idiot, you cow! Go and find yourself another boy if that's what it's come to! The dirty bastard!" But Lyubka phones him anyway and their conversation goes something like this:

"Hello, Sasha!"

"Well, what do you want?"

"Why don't you phone me any more?"

"I'm busy."

"But in the Blacklands I thought everything was fine between us."

"You promised to deliver, and you're not delivering."

"But I've told you already, I'm still a virgin and you won't have any fun with me. I don't know how to do anything yet."

"You've got to do it first and talk about it later."

"You'll drop me right away. But I can't go on like this either."

"Then stop phoning me."

That's how he always spoke to her, so I phoned him myself and said to him, "First, I'm asking you not to tell Lyubka that I phoned and second, I want to tell you that there's a law in the criminal code against the seduction of a minor. That's just for your information."

The next time Lyubka phones him he says, "Don't call me anymore. As a woman, I find you repulsive."

And, for the time being, the ring lies there in the forgotten jacket.

Now, about Levan. Why does he have a name like that? Well, he was born in Georgia and they all have names like that there, but he's Russian; he's even baptized. He's married. I fell in love with him accidentally, after Lyubka started going out with Sasha. She'd go off to the other camp and I'd be left alone, and Levan would be sitting there by the campfire, and he wasn't like any of the other boys. On top of everything else, he was married and he wore a silver wedding ring on his finger shaped like two snakes, with a little gap between them. A gap in the middle with two identical little snakes, one on either side of it. At first I thought there were two rings, the kind that interlock, but there was only one, it just had that deep gap in the middle.

One day Lyubka said to me, "I don't mind you two kissing but stop petting!" She said that! To me! And it's no use arguing with her either, she starts trembling and calling me names. If she sees a black marketeer, say, and he has something she likes, she'll buy it for sure, even if you get down on your knees and beg her not to. Then, afterward, she'll say, "You know something, you were right, we've been cheated." But it's no use arguing with her; she gets so excited and starts shaking and screaming—it's best to let her have her way. So there she was, beside herself, screaming for me and Levan to stop crawling all over each other. I managed to calm her down a little and we arrived at the club. The farmers have a club. We sit on a bench. There's a dim, hanging bulb. Our friends are all up at the front dancing, and Lyubka and I are sitting at the very last desk ... I mean bench. Then out of nowhere, Lyubka said, "Listen, Larissa, what exactly are we worried about? Just look! We're the prettiest ones here! Obviously! And we're the tallest. We're the very prettiest! We're the very best-dressed!" And she was all over me and kissing me. And how? The idiot! It was absolutely indecent! Everyone was staring at us but Lyubka had glued herself to me like a drunk, and you couldn't have pried her off if you tried. Lyubka was pretty but the boys we knew always treated her oddly, not exactly mocking her but with just a hint of pity. And they began treating me the same way too, but for some reason I didn't care. They somehow didn't interest me anymore, because of Lyubka.

Levan used to go on and on about his daughter. He had a little girl and he didn't love anyone but her. He told me, "Once you and I are married, I'll be making 300 rubles a month and I'm going to teach my daughter foreign languages. I suppose you think that's funny." Somehow, I couldn't quite picture it. How was it going to work? Me—Levan—his daughter and her foreign languages ... What about my daughters? But, for the time being, I didn't explore that particular subject any further. Lyubka and her excursions into the nighttime fields distracted me. The thing was that she kept losing our drunken boys in the fields and would come back alone, absolutely beside herself. And let's not forget the locals—collective farm workers. And the wolves ... And they had all caught the scent of Lyubka and were closing in on her. We went back to Moscow just in time.

It was in Moscow that I had the dream. I walk into a room, and I know I've been there before. It's very crowded. It's full of obese, middle-aged women. I sit down in a chair and know that I've found happiness at last. And all of these women have gathered together because of my happiness. Then in comes Levan. He comes in behind me. I can't see him but I know he's entered because everyone falls silent. My joy comes from him. I turn and suddenly see him standing there. No, he's sitting too. I rise and go to him. "You see, Levan, everything is just the way I wanted it to be." But he doesn't say anything, he slumps in his chair as if he's dead, lets his head fall backward, and his lips part slightly in anguish. But he can't speak, so he closes his eyes. I start yelling at him and shaking him in his chair, trying at least to make him angry, but he submits to my actions. Only his face becomes twisted because he's about to cry. That was my first dream about Levan.

The next day he came to visit me. We had a lovely time. We sat and dreamed about how we were going to live together. We kissed, Levan and I, and he told me he loved me. In the evening Lyubka came rushing over and we went to a bar, but didn't stay long. We went back to my place and talked about our boyfriends. That night I had another dream. Again there are lots of people, all yelling. I have to fight them off, argue with them, and Levan is there again sitting on some sort of bench, half dead. I force my way through the crowd to him and, as I'm passing, one of the women stabs me in the thigh and I begin to bleed. So I yell to Levan for help. "Why don't you do something, Levan? This is my blood! My blood!" But he remains silent and again some power starts throwing him back and forth in his chair, and again he submits to someone else's actions, and only his face is distorted by weeping. Finally, I get close to him and show him the blood running down my leg and as soon as I say "Look," he looks, but if I never said anything he'd just go on sitting that way, swaying slightly, letting his head fall backward and twisting up his face. He stares at my thigh but doesn't do anything. Then I take his hand myself and place it over the wound and say, "Stop the bleeding." And exactly as I placed his hand over the wound that's how it stayed. But black streams of blood came seeping through his limp fingers, running all the way down his arm to his elbow, and that really terrified me.

That evening, I said to Lyubka, "You know, we're both probably going to die." Lyubka was ecstatic. She was all over me in a flash. "Oh, how wonderful! Larissa, darling, let me kiss you. As for Levan, he's a fool! A married one! Ugh! And he's ugly too! A man. We'll look so beautiful lying there in our coffin together, so young and sweet, just like twins." "What about your Sasha?" I asked, and Lyubka said, "I'll call him tomorrow. I'll let him do it, then we'll die together."

And then I dreamed of Levan again. Again, a lot of furious people, and they're all talking about him. "How can he behave this way?" I push my way through the crowd and then I see Levan, standing in profile in some sort of doorway, barely catching the light, the rest of him lost in the depths of the room he came from. It's very dark where he came from and they're holding onto him; they're showing us just a little bit of him and he's swaying on his feeble legs and smiling involuntarily because of our light and our noise. I know that all I have to do is call to him and from out of that dark room they'll order him to respond quietly, lift his head and whisper a word or two. And I love him very, very much; much more than I know how to love in real life, with a love I'll never understand as long as I live and I start thinking of nothing but that—what can I do to remember this love I feel, so I can accomplish something? I start thinking about that so intensely that I look away from Levan swaying there in the doorway, so timid, emerging out of the dark doorway not of his own free will. And I think, Does it really have to be like this? There is another way! Find a nice young man. Have children. What good is all this to you? And when I open my eyes again I see a half-shut door, an empty doorway. Levan isn't there. There's only a thin wisp of smoke drifting just above the floor.

I got up, I went to school, and I couldn't stand the sight of Levan any more. By that time he and I had just about split up too. He had been avoiding me, spending all his time with his wife. He was afraid of me.

One day Lyubka and I went for a walk. It was warm and she put on the jacket she had worn at the Blacklands. We walked down the street and all the men stared at us and Lyubka was intoxicated by their glances. Her walk was full of insolence, hands stuck in her pockets. Suddenly she pulled out the ring and we immediately remembered: "the Blacklands." Lyubka got all excited and said, "Oh, Larissa, the Blacklands. I'm going to die of love." Suddenly, right there in front of us is a pawn shop. Lyubka suddenly makes up her mind. "Let's go in and see, maybe it's worth a few rubles, enough for coffee, then we can sit somewhere awhile." Well, I knew there was no use arguing. We went in. Lyubka gave the ring to the man in the window, who took it and started examining it, and he looked and he looked. ... I got really angry so I said, "I'd rather be in some bar than here all day." But the man poked his head out and said to Lyubka, "Come over here, young lady." Lyubka went over to him and he said something to her. Lyubka shrugged and we left together. He told her to drop in tomorrow. But she never got a chance to, because they came and got her first, with a big black car, and a police escort, and they took her to the pawnshop. They grilled her for a long time. Lyubka didn't know if she was coming or going. She lied nonstop about the ring, just in case, until she didn't know herself what the truth was. And in the end they took the ring away from her and instead of paying her for it—I know this sounds like fiction—they put Lyubka and her entire family on a state subsidy and said that Lyubka's children and even her grandchildren would live off the money that the ring was worth.

Now we have everything we ever wanted. Lyubka's getting fat because she eats more than I've ever seen anyone eat before. She'll eat anything you put in front of her. We don't know what to do with our lives anymore because Lyubka refuses to study "in just any old tech school" as she puts it, and what that means is that all her time is now spent on that Sasha. And Sasha did something really strange too. What he said, when he found out about the ring and the state subsidies, was, "Get out of my sight! You're such a slut!" And ... and who should show up but Levan. I didn't think he would. I wasn't expecting him. He came over, took off his fur coat and walked right into my room; he went over to the table, saw a book, reached to get it, and suddenly, something on his finger gleamed with incredible brilliance! Such brilliance! Such vulgarity! It made my head spin a little. I thought to myself, He can't be wearing a different ring, especially not one of those signet rings! He can't help being Levan but he does have some taste. Then what could it have been? It was one of those strange moments, the kind I have never understood: Something coarse and oppressive had for an instant revealed itself to me. When I looked closer I saw that it was his old silver wedding ring. It had just caught the light in a way that made it seem like some other ring. It was as if the silver had spoken to me and was now cooling off, growing duller on his finger. Two snakes, Levan and his unloved wife and a gap between them—me—unloved by anyone. And at last everything was clear to me. Everything. Since the ring had been created that way, and since Levan kept on wearing it, nothing would come of it. Not a thing. I don't know how to explain it. But nothing would ever come of it. Ever.

Translated by Alexander Maidan

STEPS

H<small>E</small> <small>STEPPED</small> <small>TOWARD</small> <small>US</small> out of the darkness. We only noticed him when he jerked open the door of our car, raised the knife, and demanded the keys. It would have been far worse if he'd started dragging us out of the car one at a time. But that old car—your legs and our home—was so valuable to us.

Just like that—gimme the keys—and the gleaming, narrow blade at your breast, and it was night, and there was almost a mile to run to the nearest house. Besides, who'd have helped a woman and an invalid in a wheelchair? As long as he didn't think of dragging us out of the car.

God, I wasn't even really afraid right then. There was just a dull fury against the lights of the city, over there beyond the ring road. It was the city that had cast us out to this deserted parking lot. What had we done to it? Never mind the fact that we couldn't go anywhere together, or the way people ogled us on the street, or nosy parkers peered into the car, attracted by the sight of a wheelchair on the back seat: Look at that, a cripple with a woman, wonder how they manage it? That wasn't enough. Even here, outside the bypass, behind the scrap-metal dump, in this absolutely deserted place there was no peace for us—this pithecanthropus with a knife comes looming out of the darkness. And the steps were to blame for everything, that accursed town with all its steps.

For some time now the thing that has most interested me about all apartment buildings and public buildings has been whether or not they have steps at the entrance. I'm also concerned about whether there's a staircase by the elevator, whether it has handrails or not, whether there's a shallow ramp provided at the road crossing and whether the curb is high or low.

All these subtle points of urban design are questions of vital importance to me, because I work in an organization that deals with people with disabilities, and my closest friend is confined to a wheelchair. Even a short flight of steps without handrails makes any building—movie theater, concert hall, or plain, ordinary snack bar—as inaccessible to us as the President Hotel, which is completely out of the question: loads of steps and the kind of people who wouldn't think of helping you up them.

I don't rely on my memory, I write it all down, noting the presence of a kind ticket woman in a theater who will open the other entrance, or a kind doorman in a cafe, who is prepared to give the wheelchair a push if we get stuck in the doorway.

What more can we do? Man is a social animal. Urbanized man, born and raised in the city, is a special type of *Homo sapiens,* poorly adapted to a solitary life. We curse the lines in the shops and the jostling on the streets, the crush in the buses and the subway, but we couldn't live long without it all! We'd be bored to death. Just try sitting at home for two weeks without going out, and dirty, crowded Moscow begins to seem like the best city on earth. After a month's life as a hermit the sight of the yard of your own house or your own street is positively overwhelming. And what if you stay at home not just for a month or two, but for a year or more, after leaving behind the blank, white walls of two or three hospitals, which were the only sight you could contemplate between operations on your spine?

"D'you know how much the trees had grown when I came home from the hospital?" Igor asked me, and I understood a truth that is hidden from every person who can walk.

So there it is. The climate and the glances of the curious make it impossible for us to be together in the open air. A person in a wheelchair is a rare sight on the street, and Igor could have earned a living by carrying advertisements if he'd wanted to. Our few friends also live in houses with steps. When someone comes to see Igor, it's like a visit to a sick person. But my friend is not sick. He's simply a person in a wheelchair. His life has its attachments, enthusiasms, and worries—all the things that make up a normal human existence.

But his sphere of habitation is restricted to his own apartment and the box-space of a frail little car. And every way you turn there are steps, steps, in the clinic, and in the building where they decide about pensions, and even in the most important building, the Ministry of Social Security, there is a semicircular flight of steps, the place is an impregnable fortress.

Anyone who has ever seen a person in a wheelchair climbing a staircase by pulling themselves up along the handrail, will never forget it. Once the elevator broke down in Igor's house, and he had to tug himself up five flights, one step at a time, with his arms ...

You can jump off a high curb in a wheelchair by turning your back to it and leaning the chair back on its large wheels. Not a sight for anyone of a nervous disposition. Extra high doorsteps can be overcome with outside help. But how can you finally overcome your own pride and come to terms with the idea that you, a grown man, are condemned to go through life asking for help at every step, always relying on somebody's charity? Better to leave this city, just go. But where to?

Charity isn't all it should be, either. It seems social consciousness also passes through certain stages, ascending from degrading pity to a civilized attitude toward people with disabilities. Everybody has apparently noticed that people with disabilities exist, but they don't acknowledge their right to a sense of their own dignity and their own life, the right to have a job, friends, happiness, and to acquire all of this all you have to overcome ... that's right, is a flight of three steps at the entrance.

You won't hear the word "cripple" behind your back very often any more. But the bureaucrats often use the phrase "what for?" What do people with disabilities want clubs, sports competitions, and exhibitions for? It all requires resources and effort. Why not wait until the country gets a bit richer?

But how long will Igor and I have to wait until we can meet like normal people and simply go somewhere for an ice cream, as we've been dreaming of doing for almost two years? They say the human race has been waiting even longer for happiness. But our happiness—mine and Igor's—can be built with a few bricks and two buckets of cement, and a railway wagon of bricks and a tank of cement would be enough to bring happiness to all the city's people in wheelchairs, at least downtown.

*   *   *

For an entire year we were planning to go and see some cartoons. We found a quiet little movie theater and took some friends along to lift the wheelchair up the steps. But we got nowhere. The manager explained to us logically that the presence of an invalid in a children's theater was undesirable, it would spoil the mood of the audience.

We didn't argue, dissuaded less by the logic of the argument than by Igor's cool, ironic glance. He was sitting in his wheelchair wearing a jacket with the outmoded inscription "USSR," because he's a member of the national team in one of the sports that are open to people with disabilities. He defends the honor of this country in international arenas, at the same time convincing international public opinion that humanism and charity are alive and well here. It's only the steps that are a problem.

*   *   *

Night, and the blade of a knife at the chest of the person you love. Night, and no one there to help ... That incident ended well enough for us, he was just a robber and we bought him off by emptying all the cash we had out of our wallets. Then afterward we drove into town and stopped for a long time at the side of the road, recovering from our fury and despair and wondering whom we would meet next, and where, and whether it would only be a knife next time.

Translated by Andrew Bromfield

A MARRIAGE
OF CONVENIENCE

A GOOD THING YOU CAME," said Sergei, drawing me into the dark depths of a communal apartment cluttered with the junk of ages. "It's time I had a decent meal, too."

Somehow, Sergei always managed to get the wrong end of the stick. The one good thing about communal apartments, everybody knows, is that they are all situated in the center of Moscow. But the view from Sergei's window was onto the heavy traffic of the Outer Ring Motorway, and, moreover, onto that ten-kilometer narrow stretch of it that is notorious for its head-on car crashes and the almost total death-rate of those motorists involved in them. Nor could the window be rightfully called his own. He had gotten this room out of a complex "chain exchange" engineered by some slick operator who kept saying, "It's just a matter of greasing a few palms, and everybody will be happy." When the deal was eventually concluded, everybody was happy—with the exception of Sergei, who found himself sharing this room with an old lady, who, after the proper palm had been greased, was pronounced to be his grandmother. She had been expected to die before the deal went through, but proved to possess an aristocratically tenacious hold on life. To be honest, she also possessed an equally aristocratic probity. She apologized to Sergei in French with a shrug, offered him tea, and promised to burden him with her presence as little as possible. She was as good as her word, too, though nobody knew where she spent all those hours when she was away from home, waiting for death to catch up with her.

What does he mean by a decent meal? I wondered. I had thought we were going to the tennis court, which Sergei's firm rented for an unknown purpose, since Sergei was the only one who ever played tennis there, except for me who tagged along in the hope of learning at least the ABCs of the aristocratic game.

"You could at least have warned me that you expect to be paid for the tennis lessons with food," I grumbled.

"Sorry, no tennis today. I'm thinking of getting married. This evening I'm going to negotiate."

Luckily we had by then reached his room, and I had the old lady's settee to faint on. This bum, this workaholic, for whom any effort outside work was a bother, was thinking of getting married! Unbelievable. Okay, I could imagine him bringing a wife into this den of his, but calling the girl on the telephone, taking her out, making a declaration of love—no, he just wouldn't be able to go to all that bother.

I discovered that there actually was something to eat in the place—my function was simply to cook it. Sergei finds cooking an excruciating drudgery. Even boiling noodles is too much for him, involving as it does the pouring of water into a pan, lighting the gas stove, taking the pan off the heat, and then straining the noodles.

So I decided to cook him lunch just out of curiosity. On a full stomach he was prepared to enlighten me. "There's nothing for it but to get married," he pronounced in the tone of a Podkolesin. "It's marry, or die. Earning money is one thing, but standing in food lines, cooking … I made headcheese once. It's supposed to never go bad, but after two weeks it had the consistency of glue and began to stink, too. And it's not only the question of cooking either. A married person feels less vulnerable. My foster grandmother, roommate that is, is also thinking of getting married. Another resident in this room. Between them they'll get rid of me in no time. I've met the prospective husband—a racketeer if ever I saw one."

"And does your future wife have somewhere to live?"

"Absolutely! This very room. She's my former wife, you see. That same Valentina whom I divorced five years ago."

"But why the hell should you marry your own wife all over again?"

"Oh, there are plenty of good reasons. All you women have kinks, but at least I know hers and she knows mine. It costs a lot these days to get a new passport when you take your husband's name, and she's already got mine. And do you know how much wedding rings are? We've still got the ones we bought last time. And generally this is a bad moment to start on any new ventures, plow up the virgin lands, so to speak. There've been all these beauty contests, and women expect a lot. Why, a bunch of roses would make a horrible dent in my budget. Let alone a honeymoon. ... Where can you afford to take your young bride to give her something to remember? And my ex may still remember all the good things we had during our first honeymoon. The trip down the Yenisei ... almost a cruise."

"I see. What about love?"

He looked at me commiseratingly, as much as to say, What are you talking about? What love? The main thing is to survive.

"You know my pal Yuri?" he asked. "He's making a lot from his business trips abroad, so he thought he could afford a new wife. And do you know what this new wife has gone and done? After love had paled a little, she invited over some of her burglar pals. They picked the apartment clean. Even carried off the computer he borrowed from the firm. So he lost his job too."

So when Sergei left for his "negotiations," I went along, and even made the sign of the cross over him.

And get married they did. When the photographer at the registry office tried to bully them into posing for a "newlyweds" picture, they showed him their old ones, saying they were even better, because they were younger then. Valentina, a thin, nervous woman, looked content.

Translated by Raissa Bobrova

MARINA   PALEI

CABIRIA FROM THE BYPASS

W H E N   T H E R E   W E R E N ' T   A N Y   M E N around, or men's voices, or the scent of a man, she would sit with her legs spread wide apart and listlessly pick at the chipped polish on her fingernails.

Her name was Raymonda Rybnaya, but everyone called her Monka or Monechka. She picked up the surname from her husband; for the first name she was indebted to her mother, my aunt, Gertruda Borisovna Faykina. Nature had endowed my aunt with a strong taste for beautiful things, as a result of which she was invariably carting from apartment to apartment (and there and then would hang up in the new place) a portrait of the writer Hemingway, a calendar for August 1962 with a lemon-faced Japanese girl reclining in her birthday suit, and a 3-ruble Christ dying on a plaster cross. My aunt's other innate weakness was her uncontrollable passion for lying. Our weary relatives said that she couldn't take a breath without lying. As a result of this predilection of hers there arose the touching legend, according to which she had chosen the name for her daughter solely in memory of her brother Roman, who had died at the front. (When she told the story, my aunt, where necessary, would make significant pauses.) A slight flaw spoiled this legend. The fact is that Gertruda Borisovna had a son who also came into the world after the death of this heroic uncle and, by the way, before Monechka's birth— Gertruda Borisovna had tried out names for him ranging from Askold (Asik) to Erazm (Erik), and finally settled on Nelik. Kornely (Nelik) subsequently became a policeman.

149

Here's a photograph. Monka's fourteen and I'm, correspondingly, four.
We're standing next to a snow-covered spruce by my grandfather and
grandmother's house. Monka has a broad forehead, dimpled cheeks, but
her eyes are frankly wily, or rather, they're already quite lascivious. I
only go up to her waist, I peer demandingly—and look a good deal like a
wise, stern, and stubborn old woman.

From the myriad, scattered fragments, the stream of oblivion for some
reason retrieves the one where Gertruda Borisovna is getting Monka
ready for Young Pioneer camp.

My aunt is standing in the kitchen, hurriedly cramming ruby-colored
salad into a fruit jar with a wooden spoon and with a lovely nuance of fa-
talism, shouts very loudly, since the neighbors had gone out, to her
daughter on the other side of the communal apartment.

"And you better remember! I only drank one shot when I was sixteen!
And I got Nelik with that glass!"

But Monka is already rushing down along the bank of Obvodny Canal
with the laminated suitcase.

She's running, smiling, skipping, her skirt, as always, much shorter
than the customary length, Monka doesn't change, she's forever fourteen—the only things that change are the posters and slogans (I can't
make them out too well through the shroud of time, dust, blue-gray ex-
haust, and factory smoke): A man in a heavy space suit is making the
Roman gesture for victory, the gesture is intercepted by a decorated war
veteran with eyebrows as thick as a moustache—she's running, smiling,
skipping, the curves on the diagrams undeviatingly creep upward, road
signs are glimpsed fleetingly, the canal is having a hard time pushing its
turbid waters forward to God knows where—she's running, smiling,
skipping, a model youth displays his white teeth, picture-perfect, and
there's the Olympics bear, suspended over a sea of round loaves of bread
and embroidered peasant women's headdresses, diligently aping the cos-
monaut, the old man, and the youth—she's running, smiling, skipping,
alongside the road monotonously stretches a red fence: XXVI XXVII
XXVIII, without breaking stride she picks up a twig and loudly runs it
along the fence: dr-r-r-r-r-r-r-r-r-r-r-r-r-r! All of a sudden the parapet
comes to an end, and the flat, unusually deserted bank lures her toward
the quiet water. She looks with fascination at her dissolving reflection.
The plash of a solitary oar is particularly distinct in this stifling sound-
lessness. "Fare"—the oarsman demands in sign language. She throws
open the small suitcase. A fountain erupts—green stockings mended
with blue thread, a red skirt with a safety pin instead of a clasp, wedge

shoes, makeup, a bra that's been ruined from too many washings and with a torn shoulder strap, a bright-colored blouse with the triangular vestiges of an iron, a gauze kerchief, worn-down boots, a ginger wool dress all nubby from wear, when she flings over the sleeves she displays the dark semicircles at the armpits. "You don't have to," the oarsman says soundlessly. She pouts like an offended little girl. Her confused expression fluidly spills over into a languid, naughty, coquettish one and finally is frankly inviting. She playfully giggles and smirks suggestively. The oarsman is immobile and old. Beaming, she narrows her eyes—in which legions of blue devils dance frenziedly—and shielding herself with her palm she whispers something to him, but I can't hear what. The oarsman begins to laugh. He laughs for a long time, light-heartedly—for the first time in a century of monotonous, joyless labor. His loud laughter cuts open the red carcass of the sunset, and the sun, scandalously violating the law of the universe, sharply makes a backward movement, illuminating for a moment the rapid-flowing water. "Fine," the oarsman says boldly. He even looks a bit younger.

*   *   *

Monechka's talent, as is the case with infant prodigies, manifested itself early, tempestuously, and noisily.

We would often sleep together when we went to grandmother's dacha. Once, accidentally, I felt a rough triangle of hair on Monka—in a spot where, to my mind, hair couldn't grow. I was even more surprised that she clearly approved and encouraged my discovery. But then my aunt sat me down on the chamber pot.

Monka hadn't used a chamber pot for a long time. More often than not she wasn't home at night. She would run off to late-night dances and in the morning somebody wearing a cap would help her off his bicycle.

"That's Vladik!" she would explain with extreme righteousness, of course judiciously not approaching the porch. "Don't you recognize Vladik? ... It's Vladik!"

It was a tough job keeping Monka home on a summer night. She would already have disappeared by morning. And if they tried to keep her home in the morning, then in the afternoon she would volunteer to go to the market, the center of the dacha settlement, to help grandmother carry the groceries—and she'd be gone for several days in a row.

They would thrash her. Monka's daddy, Arnold Aaronovich, a hero of the Finnish campaign, would unhurriedly wind his army belt onto the hand with the missing fingers. His pants would fall down and he'd step out of them. Wearing just his underpants, this snorting beast would start to approach his teenage daughter, who would have already knocked over chairs and was pounding at the door that had been locked earlier. Fixing on Monka his only eye, the cyclops-tarantula effortlessly accomplished his capture. Monka was rooted to the spot, frozen stiff in the corner. Her parent worked her over silently, with pleasure, from time to time voluptuously crying out and panting hard.

But her wet panties didn't have a chance to dry before Monka would be off once again.

I still have the tenth-grade anthology of Soviet literature that was supposed to be hers. Gertruda Borisovna picked it up secondhand from a warehouse, along with a box of compasses. As befits an old maid, the anthology is decrepit and chaste. Nobody had attempted to cut its signatures, the pages remained virginally clean, the dates of the lives of the classic writers aren't underlined, and there aren't even any doll-like eyes with implausibly long, curly eyelashes in the margins. True, the gray cover is stained reddish-lilac, like port wine, and on the flyleaf some simpering fool has set forth in cloying penmanship:

> Study, my dear,
> After all, time passes,
> And the years go by.
> You won't notice,
> When you've become grown up,
> And it will be late
> To study then.

This book contains a number of valuable bits of information. Gorky, comfortably settled in between Zhdanov and Molotov, confidentially informs them that Man has a proud sound, while the perpetually agitated Stepan Shchipachev holds his slogan up high: KNOW HOW TO VALUE LOVE!!! LOVE IS NOT SIGHS ON A BENCH!!! Monka was delighted with this dictum, which she dragged back from a prenatal clinic during summer vacation after the seventh grade. The dictum was beautifully written on a health poster, which in the style of charades linked together a bottle of 40 proof, a nefarious park bench, and an inexperienced couple as well as the moon and the equivocal shape of an infant. I don't think that

Monka ever learned the name of the author of this text. She didn't endure
the tedium of learning to the end, so the vacation after the seventh grade
became the last one.

"What can they teach me!" she declared contemptuously early in the
summer of 1959, and those words became a matter of principle.

Monka was always one for carelessly cursing, swearing, vowing, and
promising to give something up. This time, however, she remained true to
her word: I never again saw a book in her hands.

But the last time before that was when I looked through a crack in the
wall. It was the two-volume *Nuremburg Trial*. Monka and her girlfriend
had locked themselves in the barn and, sniggering obscenely, were
studying the indecent pictures of the naked men and women in this
book. I caught them at it. They scared me and begged me not to tattle to
the grown-ups, and I didn't—what would have been the use?

She was always surrounded by noise and scandal. Her absences were
accompanied by a general commotion, not a bit less intense in passion
and volume than her morning arrivals. Arnold Aaronovich would yell at
Gertruda Borisovna that she was bringing up a whore and a freeloader;
Gertruda Borisovna with the regal air of a queen in exile was mending a
cigarette burn in Monka's dirty skirt ("Why do you do everything for
her? For that filthy cow?" "Arnold, I'll strangle you." "To sit with her
legs apart like that—she's already grown-up, and to mend her skirt ..."
"Arnold, if you don't shut up right now, those will be your last words!");
with his policeman's straightforwardness, Nelik put in that you could get
syphilis; grandpa, who used to happen upon Monka's panties, all brittle
from ancient menstrual blood, in the most unexpected places, would
shout that it attracted mice.

That summer they decided to lock Monka in the kitchen for the night.
It was a humane plan. They had taken into account her weakness for having a snack, especially at night, and out of despair consoled themselves
with the hope that this would compensate, at least partially, for the pro-
hibition on something tastier. Under the window, in the grass, they fixed
up her brother Nelik, whose policeman's passion for law and order was
most easily satisfied at home.

Next morning the kitchen was empty. For a moment Kornely even allowed that he had gone mad. But after applying the requisite talents of
his calling, he ascertained that Monka had leapt into the cellar—and
more than likely had done the same through the cellar window. There
was one thing the policeman couldn't understand: If she was clever
enough to climb through the hole, that meant that she had gone head

first, but Monka's head couldn't have made it through, because it wasn't small in the least on account of her unbelievably thick black hair, which they had once shaved along with the lice eggs, and had then smeared with kerosene—all this resulted in an even more luxuriant new mane. He courageously hurled himself into the opening—and, of course, got stuck. Grandpa came running at his cries for help. Cursing up a storm, they hammered up the hole tightly, and for good measure they reinforced the patch job with a thick, blood-stained beam on which grandpa, after spreading with his boots the wings beating in the dust, used to chop off the chickens' heads.

So the next time Kornely got the urge in the middle of the night to have a drink of water, and not wanting to risk absenting himself to go to the well, he went to the kitchen, and Raymonda was lying on her mattress on the floor like a good little girl. Next to her a big, athletic fellow, wearing nothing but his tattoos, was diligently trying to have his way. A sailor's striped shirt and a pack of Belomor cigarettes had been tossed onto a stool.

"This is Yurik," Monka said as an invitation to share her happiness. "What, you don't recognize Yurik? It's Yurik!"

Kornely found that he had so much to say and that the words were so ponderous that they formed a cold lead stopper in his throat. Rolling his eyes, white and round, like buttons, and with uniform buckle drawn, he dashed around the house after the screaming and, incidentally, completely naked Raymonda, which woke up the parents' sole comfort, Patrick the standard poodle, who joined the marathon with loud barking, particularly loud in the enchanted emptiness of the white night. Rushing to the window like a whirlwind, Gertruda Borisovna spewed forth her voice, "Patrick, don't run like that, Patrick! You'll give yourself a heart attack, Patrick!"

A policeman showed up—at that very instant Monka scrambled through a hole in the fence and, already a bit more slowly, given her free-and-easy lazy ways, her buttocks retreated, twinkling, on the other side of the road.

Gertruda Borisovna majestically froze by the window shade, imparting to it the significance of a curtain in a theater. The nylon flounces and ruffles turned a magnificent pink on the green nightshirt that she called a peignoir, which couldn't have better suited the pale violet smoke of her hair. The smoke fluttered ghostly in the wind. Gertruda Borisovna was filled with sorrow and a sovereign's gravity. She resembled a widowed queen mother. And she told Kornely what she always did in such cases: "Leave her alone. She's not long for this world anyway."

Then, acutely sensing the incompleteness of the scene, she added, "Believe me, I know what I'm saying. I just had a dream ... oh, my heart's acting up." She winced, very precisely drawing out the pause, and stoically continued, "Not a pleasant dream, believe me."

Gertruda Borisovna's unpleasant dream portrayed the ominous interplay of a white dove, our late great-grandmother dressed in black—and Raymonda, naked, completely naked, which, as everyone knows, represents illness; what's more, Raymonda was eating raven's flesh, and that signifies the very ... thing itself.

"I don't know where I'm going to get the strength to endure it," Gertruda Borisovna ended with a flourish. "And after what I've endured already—who would've guessed?" The Biblical pathos was slightly marred by the fishwife delivery.

If you were to translate Gertruda Borisovna's monologue into the strict language of facts, then it turns out that Monka recently had a bout of rheumatic fever complicated by severe heart trouble. The doctors listened to the irregular knocking, shook their heads, and talked about a sensible regimen and fortifying measures. Precisely from that time on Monka's heart began clamorously to take in the devil only knows what kind of men; each found a special place, each had a special spot, because all the spots were special; with inexhaustible readiness this crippled heart accepted, accommodated, and warmed anybody in the slightest degree endowed with the attributes of male characteristics, and thankful in advance for these dizzyingly beautiful attributes, it forcefully pumped the energized blood—through the veins, through the arteries, and once again gathered in the chest—where the heart warmed it, and warmed itself, and burned. Evidently, this was the sensible regimen for her body and the primary, fortifying measure upon which she had stumbled intuitively. Disease and cure were united. They manifested this interrelationship with alarming regularity. And Gertruda Borisovna justifiably supposed that Monka couldn't continue like this for long.

Due to their exaggerated notion of the role of the work ethic, her parents got her a job as a dishwasher in an ice cream parlor on Obvodny Canal, not far from home. Gertruda Borisovna thought that Monka would come home for lunch so that she could eat right.

Meanwhile, a little work was really just the thing: The broad-shouldered men ordered champagne, the ladies broke off pieces of chocolate, the radio played loudly, and Monka, standing at the sink all day long with her shining blue eye at a hole, watched this never-ending festival of life, and her buttocks, as if they had a life of their own, independent of the rest of her body, swayed back and forth, twitched, and rotated as they were seized by the passionate urge to dance.

She didn't do anything on her own. She couldn't exist alone for a second.

*   *   *

Monka is toiling away under a bush at grandmother's dacha, painting her chewed fingernails with a red pencil. Bring me this, she says to me as I run past, bring me that. The little mirror, you know the one, in my purse ... fingernail clippers ... the thing to curl my eyelashes. But do you know what I want now? Guess. She dreamily rolls her heavenly eyes and affectedly sighs. You don't know? Her plucked eyebrows, which resembled mice tails, rise in deliberate surprise. Come on! It's nothing! She squints her eyes in disbelief (you've obviously gone soft in the head!), she capriciously wrinkles her little duck's nose. Well, have you finally understood? No? Her patience is at the breaking point. Her soft, freckled lips form an offended Cupid's bow. Well! This is too much! She sits down and starts to beat time with her foot, but it's more like she's wagging her tail. I stand with a sympathetic, vacant look on my face.

Then she parts her lips—and utters her very favorite word: "Tr-r-r-eat ..."

Monka, as usual, says it as if she were mimicking someone who resembles herself a great deal, someone whom everybody, herself included, of course knows is being a pest. She twists her mouth like a clown, and her nose—with the little flat area at the tip—crinkles into a fist, as if she were blowing her nose. There's a nasal quality. "Tr-r-r-eat." In general, it's all rather sickening.

Should I bring it this second? On a little tray?

A treat is some herring, an apple. Sugar. Bread and a lightly salted cucumber. "What's with her, she doesn't have legs of her own?" her relatives rage. But Monka is already pestering me about a glass of water or juice. Fruit punch. Sunflower seeds!

This was nothing more than her clever little tricks. In actual fact Monka simply needed company—for any routine undertaking. Her blood circulation, it would appear, functioned only in conjunction with the indispensable condition of the uninterrupted involvement of everybody, or at least somebody, in the process of the activity at hand. Without company she couldn't breathe, she grew dull and withered. Evidently her body from the beginning had been intended solely for the joint realization of specified rituals.

*   *   *

She's watching me with a look that promises some wonderful adventure. Once again I'm standing sympathetically and vacantly. She's losing her patience. Again she quickly winds up all of her pantomimic contortions. Finally, she grumblingly drawls, "Let's go you know where."

Sometimes she designates this differently: "Come with me to the potty!"

Or like this: "Should we go to the trust?"

Or: "Do you want to go to the toilet?"

She had plenty of synonyms! All these names, of course, referred to the wooden, two-roomed little hut behind the barn. As she came out of her side, she would immediately share her interesting impressions.

*   *   *

She had girlfriends everywhere. The exhaustive description Monka supplied for any one of them was confined to the familiar formula: "It's Galka! What, you don't know Galka? It's Galka!"

At first they were all unmarried girls, full of foreboding languor and immodest dreams. Later—divorced, battered women, or married ones, full of foreboding languor and immodest dreams of divorce, a lover, and a new husband. In the interval between these set cycles of their transformations fell—randomly—Raymonda's own marriage.

An alley cat can always guess precisely which grass to chew so it doesn't up and die. Monka's powerful instinct, evidently in very early childhood, luckily recommended that the indispensable *joint activities are more dependably realized with persons of the opposite sex.*

This proved to be the major discovery of her life.

And indeed, it was as if she'd had a premonition that her childhood girlfriends would hardly always be there to keep her company while she looked at pictures. And by its very nature this discovery guaranteed her a firm and, so she dreamed, a sufficiently long-term point of contact with the company of men. In this most natural of associations for two people, she was forever protected from lonely depression, she was saved by her communion with the very essence of life. This exit from the dead end opened up golden, rosy horizons. She was excited, and the peddlers of delicacies at the earthly feast unwittingly poured her a slightly larger drop of peanut oil.

In her wedded state there was no hint of the marriage of a grown woman and everything of adolescent play, or more precisely, of play that had not taken place. Well, the overripe maiden had ventured to play house, and well, she cooked everything: She made plantain soup, pinecone cutlets with a garnish of finely chopped glass for the main course, and little sand cakes with fresh raspberries for dessert; well, she placed the dishes on the tiny table; the dolls—diapered and lulled, were sleeping. What now? Somehow the game's not going well. It's boring ...

But in general, everything was going all right for her.

And so she remained forever dazzled by the unfading Scheherazade-in-the-harem mystery of marriage. This mystery somehow never lost its charm. It bewitchingly twinkled, it invitingly gleamed at the end of the day and helped her bear the mocking, daily whip. Monka patiently fulfilled all the rituals of the game—precisely because this adult, dishonest game called the Institution of Marriage, a game that she had not thought up, and which was exhausting and aggravating with its heaps of insipid and trivial rules, tedious rites, and hourly Draconian fines, a depressing game that guaranteed the hardy victor 100 percent stupefaction—this game possessed a limited nightly ray of light. Crushed by everyday life, these female creatures—those who founder and, in accordance with their ordinary talents for fasting, regularly pay off the nightly quitrent of wedlock (and receive according to their labor), in this ray of light they are able only to extract their temporary allowance of virtual asexuality—a stale cake seized as compensation for a slave's patience, an ox's labor, and a dog's life, but many are deprived of that cake, that final responsibility of a day's labor.

It wasn't like that for Raymonda. With frenzied delight she pushed her way through to the long-awaited, shining chink, as narrow as a needle's eye—and landed in the hypocritically concealed paradise.

A Tree grew in the garden of paradise.

The books that Monka didn't read call it by different names: the Staff of Life, the Root of Passion, the Coral Branch, the Beast, the Devil, the Little Sparrow, the Night Snake, the Viper, and even Dagger, the Maiden Spoiler—depending on the temperament and aesthetic foundations of the author's nationality as well as the local climatic conditions, the calorie content of the food, and the author's personal inclination for exaggeration.

In paradise, and only there, while Monka embraced her Tree of Happiness, her husband, Kolya Rybny, would call her his little mouse, goose, or lamb or even his little ragamuffin (probably an attempt to extol her reckless slovenliness).

Paradise abounded in shameful splendors.

While abiding in paradise, Monka would soundly forget the day's trials. The voice of common sense had long ago convinced her girlfriends that Hymen, like the proletariat, had nothing to her name save fetters. Raymonda didn't believe that. For her the gilded core of wedlock continually beamed with honey and moonlight and bestowed its glimmer upon the dull realities of day, decking out a chicken's tailfeathers with the design of firebirds and peacocks.

In general, Monka knew the school conduct code. No smoking in the open, no putting on lipstick during class, no matter how much you want, even if you really want to, and you're better off not drawing obscene graffiti on the desks. It was the same thing in the Institution of Marriage. One ought to pretend that the main thing were classes, good deeds, and exemplary behavior, but the main thing was something completely different, and, as is the custom among adults, hidden from sight, and Monka was at a loss to understand how those puffed-up A students could so deftly pretend that they were only interested in homework, that they were completely absorbed by these assignments (as if that were the reason for going to the Institute), and they had absolutely nothing to do with that delightful, radiant ... Oh!

Gradually Monka accepted this routine of life, one that she had not instigated. She did the disgusting lessons, when she could she did the minimum, and when she was lucky she loafed, but she didn't grumble at all, since she thought that all this was the usual requirement to get that examination question that was in such short supply. You only had to endure: morning, noon, and night. Just think.

*   *   *

She was living on Obvodny Canal as before, due to the fact that Gertruda Borisovna and her husband had received their own apartment. In the room appeared a homemade couch and a daughter (Kolya Rybny was a skilled craftsman), and the top of the rented piano that was always open was permanently graced by sheet music to the Ukrainian folk song "Oy, the wedding band has cracked" (Monka was sending the child to music lessons). Behind the piano and parallel to it lay a mummy of small proportions—paralyzed from head to toe. Monka's mother-in-law, acquired as a supplement to her out-of-town husband—she just lay and lay there, looking at the ceiling.

Monka would sing resoundingly until she was hoarse the ditty that had been written by somebody else: She gave her neighbors curlers, loaned them a fiver until the next morning, abandoned the child until evening, and, generously covered with bruises, she would explain to Gertruda Borisovna that she had fallen, bumped into a piece of furniture, or even that she had suffered an injury on public transportation. After such explanations she would usually live with mama for several days and everything would go on as before. Yes, Monechka knew by heart absolutely all the little words and all the notes, from beginning to end, of that grown-up ditty.

At this time she was already working in the bar at the Baltic Train Station. A small train car, such as you'd see at the beach, served as the bar. The frivolous appearance didn't fit the exhaust-filled no-man's-land, but the rickety construction was entirely appropriate. On the outside the train car was thickly plastered with American-looking stripes and stars, and inside it offered cognac, toffee, and dried-out cheese, but the main thing was the sinister semidarkness, so delightful after the inhospitable day, a dissolving semidarkness in which a silver ball twinkled as it floated divinely on the waves of imported music.

Monechka shone behind the counter, like the incarnation of a rainbow. Around her the fruits of the Mandragora ripened and became juicy. The impatient flirts were so decked out for love, so lushly bristling with love's arrows, that they looked like porcupines with wings. Monka poured drinks left and right. She winked, giggled, and danced. She even managed to read cards and tell her girlfriends' fortunes.

It's true that the woman doorkeeper had blabbed that Monka and her eight-month pregnant belly had climbed a drain pipe to see her lover. Well, maybe she had climbed it, so what? Nobody else had seen her, okay? And it's true that Kolya Rybny at an inopportune moment had found in Monka's purse an empty envelope, on which instead of the return address was written: "Joke lovingly, but don't love jokingly!" The address was given as general delivery, the handwriting was unfamiliar, and it was postmarked Leningrad. Well, the slut ...

*   *   *

And that's when Gertruda Borisovna enters the scene once again. The fact of the matter is that apart from the two passions already mentioned, she had two other overwhelming ones. You could bet any amount of money, even the Hermitage itself if it were in private hands, that nobody in all his life would guess what these hobbies were. My aunt would simply end up in the *Guinness Book of World Records* with these hobbies of hers if you discovered the interesting aspects of each one.

She exchanged apartments for herself—and wives for her son. There was no direct correlation or logical dependence between these two pursuits (all the more so since her son lived on his own), but they occurred constantly. To be more precise, the start of the game was signaled when my aunt got her first separate apartment. But from that moment on the exchanges occurred constantly, so it was possible to compare their tendencies: Auntie's apartments became better and better, while her son's wives became so bad that they couldn't get any worse. That is, it was as if an inversely proportional metaphysical dependence existed between these two undertakings.

One shouldn't interpret this to mean that my aunt as if in some parable found an ear of corn in a field, exchanged that for a belt, exchanged that for a birch-bark basket, tra-la-la, and finally, say, moved into nothing less than the Yusupov Palace. In her exchanges there was nothing of that despondent advancing movement forward, just as there weren't any monotonously triumphant spiral revolutions; my aunt loved the pure idea and, it seems, she intuitively subscribed to the notion that the goal is nothing, motion is everything.

Each dwelling that arose on Gertruda Borisovna's path possessed a heap of new virtues in comparison to the previous ones, that is, you couldn't even compare them. During this time, Monka was voraciously savoring the honey of domestic bliss and continued, trembling, to crave it insatiably—in other words, during this five-year honeymoon, Gertruda Borisovna managed to move from Karl Marx Street to Barmaleyev Lane, from there to Rasstanaya, from there to Mozhaiskaya, from there to the

Fontanka, and from the Fontanka to Obvodny. The Obvodny apartment was near the Frunzensky Market and, incidentally, not far from Monka, or from the place where my aunt had spent her youth, but then she moved to Pushkin Street, since, in her own words, she had dreamed since childhood of living there: "It's quiet! Culture! The greenery!"—and later she moved to Vosstaniye: "A bay window! The ceilings!"—and later to Vladimirsky Prospect: "The center! The market!"—and later to Tchaikovsky Street: "The Tauridic Gardens! To walk with Patrick!"—and later to Griboyedov Canal: "The subway station Peace Square! The first floor!"—and later to Sofya Perovskaya Street: near the DLT department store.

The one-room apartments became two rooms, the two rooms once again became one room, and then later again two rooms, then later again one room, you couldn't tell the first one and the last one apart.

The ritual of the move always followed the same pattern. Having seen off the moving van, my aunt would hang her favorite pictures and quickly shove the junk out of sight. All that took her half a day. Then she would sit down at the telephone.

"Well? There isn't any comparison!" My aunt summoned her customary pathos and would roll her eyes. "It was stifling there! The ceilings were just under eight feet. But here! You could put in a second floor! Arnold is going to do it ... no, this is definitely the last time. Believe me!"

(One was given to understand: "Could I really survive another move? Believe me!")

But in two weeks' time it turned out that the kitchen was a bit dark, the bedroom a bit noisy, after all, and the stairs a bit of a climb. Then the cycle of looking would begin. It never lasted very long. My aunt was lucky and had a keen eye. And then—sheer coincidence, an apartment out of nowhere: "The kitchen faces south! One room looks out onto the courtyard! And there's an elevator ..."

"No, this is definitely the last time," my aunt would say, with the emphasis on *this*.

A characteristic trait of my aunt's exchanges was that the neighbors on her floor, the ones above and below, in all directions and without exception, turned out to be academics. My aunt simply didn't settle in other places. They might be professors of disciplines that she couldn't even pronounce without stumbling, that wasn't important, and there were even some members of the Academy of Sciences and Ph.D.'s—she didn't know exactly, but that wasn't important.

But it was completely the opposite with the daughters-in-law. My aunt would say on the telephone, "Well? There isn't any comparison!" (One was given to understand: The former one was simply trash, but this one is trash in all respects.)

Had my aunt possessed one atom of common sense, she would not have undertaken to aggravate the process of unmistakable deterioration. But she just couldn't stop herself.

In her raged the soul of desert nomadic peoples. Or to look at it differently, an obsessive fear of death raged, lacerated, and tormented my aunt. She probably couldn't imagine that she was fated to live in that dwelling *until the end,* that it would turn out to be the *final* one, that there she would ... no, I won't say the word. And she couldn't, she didn't wish to imagine that namely this *final* daughter-in-law would give her the *final* glass of water ... and this scum would even poison it, you can rest assured!

And so my aunt was running from death all over the city, while she simultaneously introduced new characters into Nelik's family with a director's powerful hand. The moral overtones of being married so many times kept him from rising higher than sergeant, but my aunt assured everyone that if she hadn't saved him it would have been even worse.

And then the conflict with her son-in-law came to a head.

Kolya Rybny, in the opinion of Gertruda Borisovna, was a country bumpkin (of the highest order), it was precisely he, in the opinion of Gertruda Borisovna, who started Monka drinking and smoking (and with her health!), and besides that he was clearly guilty for dragging along the mummy who lay parallel to the rented piano ("You can't breathe in the room! That's deadly for the child!"), and because of him Monka stopped looking after herself, and didn't eat a thing, so that Gertruda Borisovna had to phone every day and check on her. "Have you touched any food today?"

For all this Kolya Rybny called Gertruda Borisovna a people's artist of the Soviet Union.

And my aunt realized that it was time to shuffle the deck.

She set out to deal Monechka kings, that is, for example, naturally, the manager of a vegetable warehouse or the director of a dietetic cafeteria.

In bed, sated, they would say to Monka confidentially, "Tomorrow I'm taking my Volga in for a tune-up." Or, "Could your brother arrange an appointment in Kresty prison? With my assistant?"

And Monechka gladly shared with every Tom, Dick, and Harry the impressions she carried away from the kings' apartments. She didn't particularly accentuate what exactly she had been doing there. It turned out that she had been invited on an excursion—to examine the color television and all those wonders from across the ocean. And so, one had a special machine for cleaning shoes: You just press a button and—one!—out comes a squiggle of polish, you press another button—two!—please be so kind!—and the brushes clean them—I don't believe it! Another had a bottle: You pour, say, vodka, or wine, say, or cognac, whatever, into it and you reach to pick up your glass and there inside the bottle (Oh, at first I was even scared!) somebody with a Georgian accent says, "I drink to you not because I love you. I drink to you because I love you very much." A third had liquid soap, a fourth some different-colored little balls that you use to chill cocktails, and he gave Monka one to remember him by—so! By the way, how do you think he feels about me? No, just a minute, I understand that he has a family, his wife is in the hospital and all of that, but, for example, he says to me, "I could spend eternity looking into your eyes!" What do you think, does he like me?

Maybe Gertruda Borisovna would have made a successful madam if she had been operating in a civilized world. But here the material she had to work with was defective, good for nothing, and the most disappointing thing was that it came in the shape of her own child: a cloud of dust—and nothing will come of it, you can't fight genes. But she tried! First, she thrust upon Monka her almost new nylon blouse (she's walking around naked!), then her almost new dyed fur hat that looked like a neutered cat (she's going to catch meningitis!), then a pair of almost new sheets with Romantika Sanatorium stamped in black letters—everything disappeared into a yawning abyss, into a black hole. And once again rumors would reach the newly settled parental nest about Monka's reckless, muddleheaded adventures. And again she would run off to mama "to spend the night"—all covered in the bruises of lawful wedlock—babbling about the furniture and public transportation. The cyclops, Arnold Aaronovich, didn't thrash her anymore, but without fail and with the same ardor would conduct an educational hour, where he spoke about his daughter, who was sitting right there with a vacant look on her face, in the third person.

"If only she knew how to take something from a man! Just something, why even something eensy-weensy." He would stick out his stump, trying to illustrate the smallest trifle—and did the same with his voice. "Even just a ruble, well, I don't know. Mama is forever giving you things—this and that! But we aren't going to live forever! Others know what to do when they're with a man—this way! And that! They're women and they know how. But this one! She even pays for everything herself! She'll give away the last thing she has—to anybody! What's wrong with her?" To flesh out his illustration, the invalid would start to tear at the shirt on his chest. "Here! Take it! People like our Raymonda should be donated to a museum, to that, what's it called, yes, the Kunst-kammer!"

"She needs to be taken to a lunatic asylum, to a clinic!" interjected Gertruda Borisovna. "Look at what's become of you! You're not eating at all! You're going to collapse soon—and that'll be that! It'll be too late to do anything, mark my words!"

"No, I know what needs to be done!" Arnold Aaronovich burned with anger. "Just once you listen to me! She needs to be taken to have those, what do you call them, to be sewn up like they do with cats!"

"Arnold, if you don't shut up right now, those will be your last words!" proffered Gertruda Borisovna as her final rejoinder.

And when Monka was already choking on her tears in the spacious parental bed (under the portrait of the writer Hemingway), Gertruda Borisovna would perform her encore in the kitchen. "Ah! (Clutching her heart.) I've always said that she should be left in peace. Let her do what she wants. She's not long for this world anyway." (A sorrowful contraction of her features.)

But they didn't leave her in peace.

Not being completely out of her mind, Gertruda Borisovna, of course, wasn't hoping that the kings would turn Raymonda into a queen. (Who needs her!) But it wasn't so she could run her lips over other people's cocktail balls. Ancient as the desert, the exchange itch egged her on to begin first with breaking up the Raymonda-Rybny union.

"And then it will be obvious," she would say significantly, but nothing stood behind that significance, just as a guardian angel doesn't stand behind a suicide.

If Kolya Rybny had decided to fashion a chastity belt for his dear, good-for-nothing wife, it would have been most effective to execute it in the shape of a muzzle to close the jaws of the gloomy suitors his mother-in-law was palming off—not overly expeditious in terms of the flames of passion, generally speaking, the old fellows were inclined to laziness. Without exception they were family men, big-bellied, flabby, and deadly boring, but (out of laziness) they suffered from incontinence when it came to holding back the compliments they had once invented, compliments that each time, as if it were the first time, brought Monechka closer to that blue color of the dark blue sky. And so, by forcefully closing the mouths of his mother-in-law's agents, who bleat their driveling ambiguities, it would be possible—at least from that side—to avert completely the adulteries. Because (and one should pay particular attention to this) the cavaliers that Monka's mother threw her way, all those tired economic planners who saw in Monka such a refreshing little rose from the garbage dump, the magnetically sinful miasmas that gave them a fleeting respite from the virtuous fumes of the family kitchen—all those possessors of hemorrhoids, briefcases, and money belts elicited only childish delight on Monka's part and nothing more. The old fellows' homes were so interesting and clean that to get in was an honor, just like getting on the battleship *Aurora*. And of course the senile talkativeness of mama's protégés was not the dazzling, reserved laconicism of the objects of Monka's own choosing—the beaten-down workers from the Baltic Factory and, in their own way, the striking fellows who had a sense of fashion in no way inferior to that of sailors and pilots, the drivers and truckers that streamed in after their shifts to Monka's bar. Monka, who valued the secondary characteristics in a man much more than the tertiary and following ones, never—and one must give her credit (and, incidentally, in contrast to the "respectable" ladies)—discussed and never compared in a confidential conversation the manly capabilities of her admirers, be they talkative or quiet.

Mature women, so full of their own virtue and sensibility—all those exemplary, model wives, and bashful housewives, and the rapaciously chaste ones, especially the ones with brains, keepers of the hearth who conduct themselves in intimate relations in just as business-like a manner, tenaciously and soberly as when they stand in front of the meat counter, all those meek, patient darlings, selflessly loving their little rich impotents, or the ones that weren't very rich but comfortable nevertheless, or not impotent, but not loved—they fulfilled their social and civic duty with genteel laziness (besides vigilantly watching so as not to be cheated in weight or cut)—of course, all those women made a show of holding their noses as they turned away from the depraved Monechka.

The skilled craftsman Kolya Rybny meanwhile continued to decorate Monka with a flourishing design of bruises that depicted a garden of eternal flowering; behind the rented piano, the Red October model, the mummy of small proportions was yellowing as before; Gertruda Borisovna moved from Sofya Perovskaya to First Soviet Street. God forbid that during all this time Monka should confess to her husband that the tree of paradise bore fruit beyond the confines of the conjugal bed. She still couldn't explain, after all, that she wanted to stay a bit longer at the festival where they were handing out prizes and presents, and she so loved festivals, presents, prizes, and the main thing—to dance, and it's still an absolute mystery what prizes, presents, and dances will be handed out tomorrow—

maybe they'll be one hundred times better than today's, and maybe the rose-colored roosters will be replaced by sugary *matryoshkas* wrapped up in lightly crinkling foil and tied with a shiny blue ribbon.

If the truth be told, Monka cried a lot of stormy tears at this festival. She solemnly believed every new sideshow magician, she'd hop in the sack race ever so merrily, but the magician would disappear, and the sack would end up on her head every time.

Of course, it was a different matter that Kolya Rybny was also tempted to dance at this children's matinee, but his dancing was lumbering and forced, as if he were counting time in the army, and no matter how much you tried to get his feet in line with the others, everything still looked sack-like. He frequently bumped into the door in the winding and dark bowels of the communal apartment, but Monka was proud of the fact that she continued to be on friendly terms with the neighbors, went out with them to have a beer, got involved in all their troubles, and finally, that she prevailed over them on account of her expansive nature.

And all this in no way hindered her from poisoning herself with iodine, and later, after being discharged from the hospital, it didn't in the least hinder her from washing down a whole handful of sewing needles with a glass of water. After traversing the expected path, the needles exited in a single, tidy bunch, and Monka was wheeled out from that very same hospital to another where the needle-marked are strapped to their beds with belts and are pierced by transparent tubes filled with strange, gurgling liquids; the trusting suicides arrived hoping that they had ended up in the terminal ward. During the brief visits with her girlfriends Monka would pull ever so hard at the waist of her ratty nightgown, and, eyes shining with embarrassment, she would laugh up her sleeve. There were a lot of good-looking young doctors in this hospital, some of them wore glasses and even had beards, and while making the appropriate notation in the medical chart, they carried on such sincere conversations with Monka and—best of all!—told such funny stories (appropriate to the notations), the like of which nobody had ever before carried on and told her. To make a long story short, Monka liked it there.

For the first time the return to the former stage setting stifled her and gave her a pinched look. But fortunately, that passed. More precisely, it continued until she showed up at my place the day after she was discharged from the hospital. In keeping with her inexcusable habit, she flung open my wardrobe without so much as a pause. Do you still wear this skirt? And where did you get this darling thing? I'll try it on, okay? It's my color. Oh, I'm going to be sick. Let me wear it for a while!

I still remember that threadbare dark-blue dress that was shorter than would be decent by three hands ("Look how it shows off my waist, what do you think?"). That dress reanimated Monka instantly and completely. The next day, shining, she was already dancing in her new dress behind the counter at the bar.

During this time Auntie Gertruda Borisovna had managed to live for a while on the Moika, moved to Turgenev Square, and from there to Moscow Prospect; her daughters-in-law had sharply declined from the position of nurse in the narcotics ward to patient in the aforesaid ward; the wedding goblets that Raymonda and Kolya Rybny had shattered for happiness on the day of their wedding turned out to be only the beginning of the end of those countless glasses, plates, bottles, decanters, lampshades, and even mirrors and windowpanes; in vain had they paid with their own lives to pave the road to domestic prosperity, which was as distant as the horizons of gentle utopias.

Translated by Ronald Meyer

YEKATERINA SADUR

KOZLOV'S NIGHTS

Kozlov did not like spring. He particularly disliked the first flowering of the season, when pollen settled in the warm air, and the air became sweet to the taste. The winter rains subsided gradually, and in the mornings Kozlov began to notice drops of moisture trembling on the leaves of the grape vines. It must have rained in the night, he thought to himself, anxiously. The sea warmed through after the long winter, and became clear so you could see right to the bottom; right down to the soft, yellow sand, seaweed, and other mysterious substances, unknown to human beings. Each morning young girls would pass Kozlov's house on their way down to the beach. The wind blew up the hems of their cotton dresses, transforming them into colorful, dappled sails. The girls' laughter rang out and Kozlov's heart would ache with pain. His neighbor, Vanya, would call out: "Hey! Hey!" from behind the vine branches, unable to think of anything else to say, and Kozlov could see how red Vanya's face had become, even his ears were aflame.

There was a particular pungent herb that blossomed in the spring, its flowers like hot, yellow flames on slender green stalks. "My ruin," Kozlov would say to himself, each time he inhaled its sweet fragrance, his pale face suffused with a delicate pink rash.

The transparent spring air seemed to flow like liquid. The outlines of houses and the vineyards behind their fences also turned to liquid, and so did the flushed faces of passers-by. Gradually the earth became warm, and Kozlov felt its heat in the hollows left by his own footsteps.

In the evenings, Vanya played his pipe beside the wattle fence, and Kozlov's heart would once more ache with pain. Old Zina would come out onto her porch to shell sunflower seeds, and sigh to the sad strains of Vanya's music. For a long time she sat and sighed, and by nightfall the steps would be covered with the shining black shells of sunflower seeds.

"If only he'd play something cheerful," old Zina once said. "It's depressing enough here on Malaya Mamayskaya Street."

But Vanya didn't hear her. He simply stretched himself out in the long grass, played his pipe, and watched as the stars came out one after another in the crowded sky. The young girls returning from the sea, tired and subdued, stopped to listen to the music, and hidden behind the vine leaves, Kozlov stood close to them, his eyes downcast so he could only see their bare feet, coated with gray dust. Once he looked up and glimpsed a braid of hair, tossed by the wind from a pair of shoulders, a delicate patch of suntanned skin. But he didn't manage to examine her face. "This will be my ruin," he thought as he hurried into the house. Kozlov languished in the spring.

The spring nights were dark and damp, like a bottle of ink. The rain fell quietly, almost imperceptibly, as if afraid of waking people from their slumbers, and, just as imperceptibly, toward morning, would stop, its only trace the cold dew drops left on leaves and grass.

Looking in from Malaya Mamayskaya Street at night, the windows of Kozlov's house were a strange sight. His curtains, dark blue during the day, shone pale azure, lit up by the bright light of a candle, and it seemed as if the room was thronged with guests, all frozen in immobility. Among the motionless guests moved a single figure with a candle in his hand. He looked exactly like Kozlov. He gazed into the faces of his visitors, passed his hand across their hair, but he was neither stroking them, nor wiping off dust.

Kozlov would wake up at night and lie in the dark with his eyes open for a long time, listening for street sounds. But outside all was quiet. Kozlov got out of bed and lit a candle. He disliked electric light. It hurts my eyes, he thought. The walls of his room glowed pink in the candlelight, a special kind of pink veiled in a layer of darkness. The wax figures loomed up out of the darkness, the shadows performing weird dances on the walls in the dim candlelight. Kozlov's shadow danced too. He enjoyed this: He would take a step, and his shadow on the wall would tremble and stretch, then the other shadows would do the same, like a group of circling folk dancers or a retinue of soldiers; if he turned his head, the shadow on the wall would obediently turn too. "I am your master," said Kozlov to the wax figures, but they did not reply. "Me, I'm your master," he repeated, looking at the dancing shadows.

Kozlov spent every night melting and molding wax, and gradually, his room became populated by strange wax visitors. He painted their faces, and they almost seemed alive. There was a red-haired girl with a mongrel dog. Kozlov had wanted the girl to smile, but when he painted her face, his hand had trembled and her smile slipped sideways, turning out more like a smirk. Next to her sat an old man selling apples. Kozlov had sculpted him so he was slightly stooped, with broad, gnarled hands. He had the faded blue eyes of old age. The apples neatly stacked in pyramids in front of him. They were fiery red, sprinkled with yellow around the stems, and looked exactly like real apples. One of them—and Kozlov was rather proud of this—had tooth marks on it. The little boy from next door had assumed the apples were real and had tried to bite into one, only to find his teeth sliding over hardened wax. Beside the old man sat Zina, flanked by two sunflowers on thin stalks and a little sheep. When she first saw herself sculpted in wax, Zina gave a loud cry and slapped her knee in joy. There were also a number of unfinished figures, some with only one arm, others without a head. For some reason Kozlov felt afraid of them and moved them away into the corner of the room.

Once, as Kozlov slept, he thought he heard weeping; the thin, rending cry of a baby. It must be coming from the corner, he thought in terror and opened his eyes. Before his sleepy eyes, the darkness seemed to flow in inky blue-black strips. Could I have dreamed it? Kozlov wondered and crossed himself. But immediately the weeping started again, this time a liquid, watery wailing coming from outside the window. Oh it's just cats in heat, he decided, relieved. He lit a candle. The light of the yellow flame played across the faces of the wax cripples, illuminating a missing eye or a smooth, wax chin deprived of a mouth. In the mirror on the wall, Kozlov was reflected pinkish-yellow, candle in hand. From one side he was watched by a number of painted, slightly glossy faces, from the other by a group of deformed figures. Suddenly Kozlov thought he could hear them sighing and moaning. Slowly, step by step, they seemed to be moving toward him, those without legs clinging to the ones who could walk. As they walked they gave incoherent cries, shouting into his face; Kozlov could not make out what they were saying, but he knew they must be words of reproach. And suddenly, all the figures began to melt. First their features started to run, as if melting in the heat of a fire, and then warm drops of wax splattered onto the floor. Before long the figures standing before Kozlov were replaced by a cluster of candle ends, and the floor was awash with hot wax.

"A flood!" he cried, frightened by the sound of his own voice and afraid his shouting might open up cracks in the ceiling.

Nighttime drowned Malaya Mamayskaya Street in a violet haze, darkening the green grape vines and turning the white walls of the houses blue. The rain-soaked ground sobbed wetly beneath the feet of people returning home late at night.

"A flood!" repeated Kozlov, but this time he whispered. A chalky dust whitened his arms, like the arms of plaster statues at railway stations. The curtains at the windows wafted up, as if someone had breathed on them.

"Is someone there?" called Kozlov into the darkness. His candle revealed nothing but slightly crushed flowers.

"Yes, there is," replied a soft voice, and a small face like a wrinkled rennet apple appeared in the dark space of the window. Two eyes shone like black drops of liquid. Kozlov examined the face. It was a girl, small and supple, and somehow shrunken.

"What do you want?" Kozlov almost mimed the words, afraid that if he raised his voice the ceiling would again be covered with cracks.

"I'm Alyonka," said the girl. Her lips curved as she spoke, but the rest of her face remained immobile.

"I see ..."

The face outside the window smiled—the little yellow apple was covered with a mesh of wrinkles.

"Over there, in the corner," and she pointed with a short, sharp finger into the depths of the room. Kozlov turned to confront the empty faces of the crippled figures. "No, higher up," she whispered. "Can't you see the icon hanging in the corner?" Kozlov nodded. "Turn its face to the wall, it's bothering me," and she gave a yelp of laughter, her delicate lips leaped into a smile, the corners turned up revealing small, even teeth. The walls of Kozlov's room trembled and the floorboards hummed beneath his feet. The whole room was transformed into a deep sigh. Kozlov turned the icon's face to the wall. He felt as if his strength was at an end, as if there was not enough air in the room.

*   *   *

Old Zina lay dreaming of a hot August noon and a sweet watermelon. A swarm of sleepy flies hovered over the watermelon, and Zina could clearly see that they were as black and shiny as the seeds in the fruit's red flesh. A drop of pink juice dripped onto the tablecloth. For a moment it trembled on the white linen, and the black flies trembled above it. Then it soaked into the cloth and became a pink blot. Zina's spectacles slid down her nose, and immediately her vision blurred. The flies were now just black spots in the warm air, and the watermelon a big red patch with a green rim. She looked out of the window, still without adjusting her glasses—where the August sky streamed like blue silk. But suddenly a thick and dark storm cloud appeared and floated across the radiant, gilded sky. Standing on the storm cloud was none other than Elijah the Thundermaker, his mighty arms crossed on his chest. Beside his large pink feet, a pile of brilliant lightning bolts were drying out.

"Are you just sitting there, Zina?" Elijah inquired, frowning sternly.

"Just sitting here, sir," Zina replied, crossing herself and bowing over and over again. "Would you like a piece of melon?"

Elijah nodded portentously. Old Zina plunged a knife into the melon's tough, stripey skin and hacked off a pink triangle. "There you are!" Elijah ate the watermelon, heaped praise upon Zina, and she saw a transparent ribbon of juice running along his arm and into his sleeve. Elijah floated away into the distance, still holding his piece of watermelon, and old Zina sat and watched him vanish, gazing at his lilac-colored coat and the lilac storm cloud beneath him, and his pink feet sticking out.

The next morning when old Zina went out into the garden she still remembered her dream. I wonder what it meant? she mused, stroking her sheep, white as a cloud, who looked up at her with dull, loving eyes, and continued its leisurely chewing. The air was still morning-moist and the storm clouds of the night before had not yet dispersed. It seemed as if the grass and the vines and apple trees had been sprinkled with milk. Zina sat down to drink her morning cup of tea.

"Petrovna!" she called across the fence.

"Eh?"

"Come over here a minute!"

Petrovna came. She was a short, shriveled old woman, her head permanently stretched forward on its long neck, as if she was gazing into the distance. Old Zina, on the other hand, was large and plump. She wore a white cotton head scarf, as she had in her youth, and glasses with thick, swirling lenses and black frames.

They sat in the garden at a round, wooden table covered with an oil-cloth. They poured their tea from the teapot straight into saucers and blew on it for a long time. The saucers were of delicate, translucent china,

and when they were full of tea, they reflected the sky. Zina coughed loudly. It sounded like gunshots.

"Last night," said old Zina, "I dreamed of clouds floating in the sky. All
soft, just like your featherbed. White ... and then this blue one appeared.
Well, I thought to myself, There must be a reason for that. And sure
enough, who should be riding on the cloud, but the prophet Elijah!"

"You're putting me on!" screeched Petrovna.

"I'm not! It's true! So you see, there's the Prophet Elijah, riding along
all golden. And he's got a pile of glittering golden lightning bolts by his
feet, so bright they make your eyes water. And Elijah comes up to my
window and says: 'How do you do, Zina!'"

"You're making it up!"

"No! It's true! He comes up to my window. So then Elijah ..."

A dull, aluminium teapot with a wooden handle stood on the round
table. A rusty pool of liquid spread out on the oilcloth, and in it floated a
dried vine leaf. The red and white diamond design of the cloth was refracted through the trembling water. The air was heavy and sweet with
the scent of the lilacs flowering in Zina's garden. China saucers and empty
teacups stood on the table. There was a deep dish rimmed with a lilac
band, as if it had absorbed the color of the three-petaled florets. The dish
was full of round, pinkish-golden pancakes. Each time Zina took a pancake she examined it closely and then looked up at the sky, as if to see
how closely the pancake resembled the sun. And they really did look like
the sun.

On the table there was also a simple cut-glass vase, containing a single
branch of white apple blossom. Spring, and the length of time it had
stood in the glass of water had encouraged the branch to grow thin root
filaments, which trembled in the water, like living creatures.

"You were quite right to offer him the watermelon," said Petrovna,
after she'd heard the rest of Zina's dream.

"That was what I thought too, but where would I have got my hands
on a watermelon? After all, it's spring now, not August."

"That's true," Petrovna drawled. Suddenly leaning across the table, she
whispered, "Have you heard about Alyonka?"

"What about her?" said Zina.

"They say she's woken up again after the winter," Petrovna whispered
furtively. "And she's taken to walking the streets again, searching for
young lads. I only hope none of them fall in love with her! We're going to
have no peace, I can tell!"

"You don't say!" said Zina, crossing herself. "Lord save us!"

"It's true!" Petrovna went on. "Do you remember young Pashka Niki-forov who disappeared last spring?"

"I remember," replied Zina, frozen motionless with her saucer raised to her lips. "They searched for him for a long time, but he was nowhere to be found. He'd run away from town, they said."

"No," whispered Petrovna. "That's not what they said at all! I heard that Alyonka lured him down to the sea at night. He swam out after her, then suddenly he felt tired and wanted to swim back. But Alyonka had put a spell on him and he didn't know which way to swim. He thought he was swimming toward the shore, but all the time he was swimming far-ther and farther out to sea."

"It can't be true!" shrieked old Zina.

"Oh yes it is. He sank right down to the bottom, and Alyonka dived after him and began to caress his dead body. It's easy for her to go under water. Her legs turn into fishes' tails at the ends."

"That's true," Zina agreed. "I once met her on my way to the market and she was walking barefoot through the dust. 'What do you think you're doing, miss?' I said to her. 'Walking about with bare feet.' She just laughed and said nothing. And then suddenly I noticed that her feet were all covered in scales."

"And you can be sure Pashka's not the only one she's gone for," Petrov-na went on, her eyes flicking nervously from side to side. "She's dragged many down to the seabed. And they say that once they're down there she kisses them and turns into a fish. Then she comes out onto the beach as a girl again, weeping. They say she will kill any young man she falls in love with."

Old Zina nibbled little pieces off her pancake. From time to time she ex-claimed loudly at Petrovna's words.

"She only calms down in winter, when she's just like anyone else. She kind of falls asleep. And in spring she seems to come into flower. Only it's a poisonous flower. ..."

"You're quite right," Zina nodded. The sheep gave a frightened bleat.

*   *   *

Meanwhile Kozlov was waking up. All night he had dreamed about the ginger-haired girl with her crooked red mouth. She had suddenly come to life and run shrieking around the room, screwing up her eyes to look at things and poking out the narrow, fiery-red ribbon of her tongue. How can I have fallen asleep holding a candle end? Kozlov wondered, staring down at his blistered fingers. The window was firmly closed, its latch down, and the flowers outside were pressed right against the glass. The morning had already warmed the air in the room, making it unbearably stale and stuffy. What strange dreams I've been having, Kozlov thought, recalling his anxious night. But the wax figures now stood peacefully along the wall, brightly painted and showing no signs of having melted. "Asya," said Kozlov, and went up to the little figure standing at the head of the bed. He loved this particular doll. Everything about her must be lifelike, he had thought, when he had molded her out of wax. And the figure was exactly like a reflection in a mirror, a twin sister. Kozlov was not even certain which of the two he preferred—the living girl or her motionless double. Each morning he would talk to her, lightly holding her waxen wrists (not pressing too hard with his fingers for fear of melting the wax). He would gaze into the dilated pupils of her gray-blue eyes, and the painted doll's face would look back at him.

"Listen to me," Kozlov would say to her. "You've been breaking my heart for more than a year now. This is the second spring. And you don't even know it. You're so delicate and transparent, you don't even get brown in the sun. We live in the same town but I've no idea how to approach you!"

And suddenly before Kozlov's eyes, Asya's milky-white face became swarthier, and the eyes that looked back at him were no longer gray-blue, but the beady black eyes of a predatory animal.

"Alyonka ..." he whispered, horrified, and suddenly noticed that the icon of the Virgin Mary was turned to face the wall. "So it wasn't a dream," he whispered. He felt as if he had been struck in the chest, somewhere in the region of his heart.

"Alyonka!"

Kozlov went out into the garden, and was struck by its beauty. Only it was not a joyful beauty, but a beauty born of tears. The milky mist and dampness of morning still hung in the air. The mist was so densely white that it seemed almost blue. The conical lilac blossoms, made up of tiny three-petaled florets, assaulted him with their heavy, stupefying scent. The wilting apple blossoms seemed like flakes of white paper on something large and green. I'm standing on a living creature, he thought, looking down at the ground. The earth was not yet warm after the night, and it reached out to his feet with a cold, delicate touch, as if bidding him farewell. This spring the Chinese rennet apple tree was covered with paper-white blossoms too. The dwarf tree slept all through the winter, but now in spring it had awakened, filled with palpitating, seething life, and in the cracks of its bark, Kozlov could see dark sap. The sound of sighs and a rustling whisper issued from behind the curly fronds hiding old Zina's garden. Again Kozlov heard the word *"Alyonka,"* again he heard, "She will kill any young man she falls in love with!" And in anguish he thought, Has she fallen in love with me?

* * *

Alyonka lay on the rocks, her high-cheekboned face turned toward the sun. Her eyes were closed against the burning rays, and the air looked pink through her lowered eyelids. At first the color was translucent, but then it thickened and became crimson, pouring over the upturned palms of her hands and flooding over her whole body, from her feet to the crown of her head. The top of her head felt pleasantly heavy. But when the heaviness stopped being pleasant and started to become painful, Alyonka stood up and walked into the sea. "How clean you are," she whispered, sliding her feet across a pebble darkened by the water. Alyonka was small and supple, her body was evenly tanned, a golden color. And where the water touched her skin she looked even darker. Alyonka scooped up a handful of sea, and the lines on her hand showed up clearly through the water. The reflection of the sun was a glinting half moon in the cupped handful of water; the pink thread of Alyonka's lifeline trembled.

In the winter Alyonka spent her time peacefully, looking out of the window watching the snow falling on the sea, and the raging December storms. Sometimes, instead of snow there was pouring rain, forming rings on the water. But when spring came she knew that the winter melancholy would pass, and a strange power would awaken in her, making her want to sob and run, no matter where, and then even running wasn't enough, she wanted to fly high above the earth, higher than the angels, and then ...

The sky merged with the sea. Alyonka gazed intently into the distance. White horses were forming on the surface of the water, the first sign of a storm, but Alyonka stayed where she was, and a scarcely perceptible smile played about her lips. Squinting into the distance she could see someone swimming strongly toward the shore. She could make out the swimmer's bronzed shoulders and the birdlike strokes of his muscular arms, only his face was not yet visible. Then all of a sudden he stretched his light body out full length in the water, and hung motionless, resting. It was then that Alyonka first saw his face. He's handsome, she thought, smiling strangely. He's going to drown in a minute. ... The swimmer disappeared beneath the waves.

*   *   *

Kozlov took off along the street with a heavy sense of foreboding. He was going for a perfectly ordinary walk, but the morning made him feel weary. It was cool and damp in the shade of the grapevines. But as he headed toward the railway station, he emerged onto a dusty street and a jumble of sounds floated toward him. Uncle Sasha was sitting in the shade playing his accordion. The medals on his black jacket clinked. Pinpoints of light danced on the medals.

Kozlov felt he was walking through a thick fog, bewitched. He felt as if all eyes were turned on him, as if people were jostling him and then laughing quietly behind his back. But the passers-by, wearied by the heat of the morning, didn't even notice him: a fairly short, narrow-shouldered man who wore his hair parted in the middle. His face was narrow, sharp-chinned, and his eyes were a pale green, as if diluted in water. Only occasionally they would spark into life and appear greener than grass. Kozlov's face habitually wore a rather unpleasant expression—"sneerious," as old Zina said. His body would have appeared fragile, were it not for his hands. Kozlov's hands were powerful, with fine, tapering fingers, and if he touched you, you could feel a burning strength vibrating in them. He walked slowly toward the station. His cotton shirt, patterned blue and green, clung to his sweaty back. He longed for a cool breeze.

*   *   *

The station was a small, insignificant building. The patch of porous asphalt, strewn with trampled yellowish-white cigarette butts and frothy blobs of spit, was burning hot. Kozlov noticed shy blades of grass huddled deep in cracks in the asphalt. Dear God, I've got to get away, he thought. Two plaster statues languishing in the sunshine watched him wearily. One—with a tender, virginal gaze and a smile on her stone lips—leaned on an oar and a rusty puddle of rainwater had gathered in the crook of her elbow. The second statue was of a young boy.

Kozlov stopped by the plaster maiden and looked at the prudish swimming costume straps that crossed her antique shoulders.

The train arrived, and from it emerged a tall, pale woman from the north with her small, pale daughter. She carried a tartan suitcase tied up with string, and Kozlov noticed how her soft fingers were swollen and reddened.

"Is this the south, mommy?" the little girl asked in a clear voice, her fingers spread wide. Her hands were small and childishly plump. Kozlov could see the layer of gray grime from the train journey on her pale skin. But he also saw the latticed shade of the leaves falling across her face, and the length of the shadow from her own eyelashes, trembling on her cheeks. Our town is unworthy of such marvelous creatures, he thought. A sudden gust of wind lifted the hem of her heavy skirt, revealing pale knees, which had never known the sea. The wind turned the air bitter. A dry dust settled on the roof of his mouth. Kozlov asked, "Can I h-h-help?" looking at the tartan suitcase. The wind whisked a rustling newspaper up off the asphalt around the plaster maiden. The woman's blue eyes, screwed up against the sun, chanced upon Kozlov, but his words were lost in the sound of the wind. She inspected the statue concealed by the newspaper and read the inscription on the pedestal: "... irl with an oar." Nearby, glistening on the asphalt like a gilded horseshoe, lay the letter *G*.

*   *   *

From her window Asya could see the metal roof of Kozlov's house, its brick chimney spotted with soot. In the afternoons the roof became burning hot. But when the iron glowed orange, she knew evening had come. Asya thought about Kozlov. This spring is the second year I've been walking past his house, and he burns me up with his eyes. Why does he stand there and say nothing? Why doesn't he speak to me?

*   *   *

Kozlov languished in the sticky air. He could breathe only with great effort, and each breath he took made his chest ache. The day broiled on.

Even the shade offered no salvation. The woman from the north wandered around the town, anticipating her first glimpse of the sea. In one hand she carried the tartan suitcase, with the other she clasped her daughter's plump hand. Their fingers became swollen. The little girl looked around brightly. Two black pigtails tied with colored elastic bands poked out through narrow slits in her panama hat. "When will the day be over?" whispered Kozlov, eager for nightfall. "When will the day be over? Oh when?" He could already see just how he would mold the beautiful neck of the woman from the north—white, overlaid with a light layer of grime from the train. The narrow back of the woman from the north swayed through the crowd, child mincing along behind. Kozlov sniffed the air, smelling the sourish smell of the market. In the spring people sold off the remains of their winter stores and the first flowers of May. Lilac twigs stood in glass jars full of yellowing water. A few branches would fall to the ground, where they were quickly transformed into a slippery pulp beneath the feet of passers-by.

"Buy some, Mommy!" the little girl from the north demanded in ringing tones. And her mother obediently did so. There were Ukrainians selling wrinkled figs. Yellow apples veined with red, left over from last winter, were set out neatly and polished with vegetable oil. The faces of the Ukrainians shone. The woman from the north held a multicolored fan of banknotes in one hand, and Kozlov saw how fine her fingers were, and grew weary longing for night.

There was a Tartar trying to sell a donkey. The donkey brayed. A cherry plum tree swayed in response. The Tartar lashed the donkey with a whip. The donkey lashed the Tartar with his tail.

"Buy him, Mommy!" said the little girl from the north. Her mother, lost in thought, said nothing.

Wasps clad in stripey, turn-of-the-century bathing costumes hovered over the honey.

"Get away ... ge-e-et awa-a-a-ay." The Ukrainian waved his hands at them.

Old Zina was selling her triangular sunflower seeds. They looked like beetles with their wings folded. Bunches of herbs were laid out in front of her: shaggy bouquets of mint, tiny golden, heart-shaped leaves of sage, purple and green oregano. They gave off an acrid smell. Kozlov went up to the stall.

"You do look pale!" said old Zina. "Didn't you get any sleep last night? You've got black rings under your eyes."

"I need some herbs, something for my heart," groaned Kozlov.

"Your heart's troubling you?" She looked closely at Kozlov. "Herbs won't be any good for you. There are no herbs to cure melancholy. Why don't you come and see me tomorrow, and I'll read your cards for you!"

The meat stalls stretched out before him. Flabby, shuddering pieces of meat. They had gone soft in the sun. Kozlov was afraid …

The sour smell of kumiss tantalized his nostrils. The fermented mare's milk—smooth and white, like the skin of a child—stood in tin milk churns. The woman from the north had loaded her tartan suitcase onto the donkey. She asked for some and as she began to drink, it seemed to Kozlov that her bright mouth was covered with a delicate white film.

Kozlov marveled at the fish. There was one that particularly caught his attention. It had green eyes and fins like fingers. It lay on an iron tray, gasping greedily with the last of its strength. Kozlov wanted to buy it. He began to bargain for it. All the other fish were dead, covered with silver scales, their little bellies split open to reveal pink insides.

Kozlov's neighbor Vanya was sitting by the market gates, selling shiny iron jewelry. There were earrings shaped like doves with little black eyes, and twisted rings set with red glass stones, and yellow and black beads made out of shells from the seashore, and glass beads like fishes' eyes.

"Buy some, Mommy!" commanded the little girl, pointing with a plump finger. The woman from the north stopped the donkey and obediently held out some money. All at once a pair of iron hearts were sparkling in the child's delicate ears.

"Night, I want it to be nighttime," whispered Kozlov, watching the blazing day. He laid a hand on his chest. He felt as if his heart had turned into a bird, and the bird was struggling to escape.

Kozlov walked down Malaya Mamayskaya Street toward the sea, passing blue wicket gates, and counting the "Rooms to Let" signs. The woman from the north and her daughter walked ahead of him. She was sneezing from the dust. The donkey followed. The child kept pulling leaves off the vines till she had gathered a whole bouquet. The pale little girl from the north cried out in a clear voice:

"Oh Mommy, look at that funny dog!"

The dog was a sheep. Kozlov laughed.

But when she caught sight of the sea, she just said, "Oh Mommy!" because she could find no other words. And Kozlov laughed again.

The sea was truly bewitching. Deep blue overlaid with yellow. The woman stopped the donkey and took her shoes off. She had narrow, white feet with curved, pink nails. She lifted her daughter onto the donkey's back and undid her tight, lace-up shoes. The woman from the north walked into the sea. The water darkened the hem of her skirt. The donkey followed. The little girl sat squarely on his back, her pink feet digging into his sweaty sides. They moved farther and farther from the shore. The donkey began to swim. The panama hat with slits cut in it became a hazy blob in the distance.

A crowd of people gathered on the shore. Some of them were shouting and waving their arms. Kozlov went up to them. The body of a drowned man lay on the hot shingle. He looked as though he were still alive, his eyes wide open. His eyes were blue, as if they had soaked up the color of the sea. And the imprints of the stones were visible on his tanned skin. His mouth was slightly open, as if asking for something, or anticipating a kiss, but white bubbles were already foaming on his lips, and everyone knew he was dead. Kozlov caught sight of Alyonka in the crowd. She was staring intently at the face of the drowned man, and her lips were slightly parted, as if responding to his kiss.

"So young!" sighed a woman in the crowd. "The body's not even swollen. He must have just drowned."

"Handsome too!" another exclaimed.

"I know whose work this is!" said a third, and looked at Alyonka. At this the girl's lips pressed together and curved into a smile; a strange, burning smile, as if her mouth was being pulled upward at the corners. She surveyed the crowd, and her eyes rested on Kozlov. At once, Kozlov realized the smile was meant for him, and his whole body began to ache. He completely forgot about his desire to spend the night molding a figure of the white-bodied woman from the north and her little daughter with the damp forehead.

"Alyonka," whispered Kozlov in horror. But at that moment he caught sight of Asya in the crowd. All at once a tide of tenderness flooded over him, a tenderness that almost made him weep. He wanted to tell people about his yearning, so they would understand and weep with him, but his lips would not obey him, they went on uttering the name "Alyonka."

"What's the matter with me?" he whispered. Alyonka disappeared into the crowd.

*　　*　　*

Kozlov wandered through the town in a state of anguish. Weary with the heat, the town was half asleep. Mongrels lay in the dust, their short legs stretched out and their eyes rolling. Sweaty bodies flashed past Kozlov. Their expressions were incomprehensible. Kozlov did not recognize anyone. He walked close beside the fences, and the branches of apple trees covered in blossom whipped him in the face. "Alyonka, Alyonka," he whispered over and over again. "She shouldn't have gone off ..." His heart ached with yearning, a yearning that drained away all his strength. Kozlov laid a hand on his chest, as if trying to restrain something. His hair was clammy with sweat and stuck up in clumps. He came to the marble stand of a drinking fountain. He leaned over to drink and found himself looking at a blue plastic mermaid, her head leaning on her own tail. The mermaid held a little jug, from the mouth of which issued a stream of warm water. I wonder what it's like under the water? he thought. It must be all green on the seabed. He could see Alyonka's face quite clearly. Uncle Sasha walked past. He was playing a march tune, pumping the red, pleated bellows of his accordion.

Kozlov stopped by the canteen. The greasy smell of unwashed dishes and the sound of rattling crockery drifted out of the window. The cooks had rolled up their sleeves and were emptying the reddish remains of rissoles and pale lumps of pasta out of the saucepans. Kozlov saw their shining dimpled elbows, and the muscles flexing beneath the surface of their pudgy flesh. I'm going to build up my strength, he thought, looking at his own arms. A small flock of flowery frocks hurried past, laughing loudly. They're alive, he thought. They're laughing. Suddenly he felt frightened by his own thoughts. I'm alive as well, aren't I? I can laugh too. A suntanned body moved lazily through the crowd toward Kozlov, and once again he glimpsed the patch of suntanned skin beneath the braid of hair. Once again he dared not look at the face. He heard her say: "Come to the castle tomorrow evening!" He heard the passionate sound of the word *come,* and he knew it was Alyonka. "Why are you torturing me like this?" he asked. But she had already disappeared into the crowd.

Kozlov wandered through the town until evening. The people awoke from their midday slumbers and looked at him in surprise. He was muttering incomprehensibly to himself. "What's up with you?" they said to him as he walked away. "Alyonka." Kozlov whispered the name over and over again.

As dusk fell Vanya began to play his pipe. If only he'd stop that whistling, Kozlov thought. When it was completely dark and stars began to appear in the sky, he gazed for a long time at their pale glimmering and felt calmer. Suddenly one of the stars plunged downward. "Please let me be all right!" he cried, bidding the star farewell.

*   *   *

Alyonka stood on the seashore and watched the falling star. Please let me be all right! she thought, and grinned.

*   *   *

Kozlov passed an agitated night. He dreamed that Alyonka had stretched out her fingers to unbutton his collar and then pulled out his heart, red and moist. Kozlov felt a pain in his empty chest and Alyonka threw his heart down on the pebbles and stamped on it. Clots of wet shingle clung to Kozlov's big heart and to Alyonka's legs, hiding the scales on her ankles. "Let's go for a swim," said Alyonka. Kozlov knew that he must not go into the sea with her. First the water came up to his knees, then up to his waist, then it reached his empty chest. Alyonka placed a hand on the nape of his neck and forced his head under water. Kozlov opened his eyes and saw the hazy outlines of a scaly tail and a pair of translucent fins; a school of grayish fish swam past him wriggling; down among the greenness at the bottom were suspended heavy clusters of mussels. Some of the purple shells were open, like eyelids, revealing flaccid, trembling bodies inside. A row of drowned men lay on the seabed, their arms folded on their chests. Some were blue and amorphous. Others, the more recent ones, perfectly smooth, not even slightly bloated. "You are their master," said Alyonka, and the drowned figures stretched out their arms to Kozlov. The water began to heave and the green fronds of seaweed trembled, and Kozlov saw that each of the drowned men had an open wound in his chest, charred around the edges. "You are our lord," they said. "No!" shouted Kozlov, and woke up.

*   *   *

The night was black and empty. It sucked away his soul and lurked outside the window smacking its lips. Kozlov put his hand to his chest and felt a weak knocking, like a fledgling pecking at the inside of an eggshell. "It's still beating," he rejoiced and burst into tears. The darkness shuddered with his loud sobs. It seemed to Kozlov that the crippled figures in the corner were groaning and clasping their hands to their chests, covering up gaping wounds. The plump buds of a night violet burst open with a tiny flicking sound, revealing pale petal edges. The petals forced their way out, their color changing from pale mauve to a poisonous blue. A forked, red string could be seen in the center of each flower. They breathed heavily, watching Kozlov. A moth flew above his head. As he fell asleep, he watched its body and hairy little legs.

* * *

Alyonka was tearing off a broken branch of an apple tree. She was surrounded by unfamiliar figures dressed in white. Kozlov couldn't see their faces. "Where am I?" asked Kozlov, looking down at the stars. "You are standing on top of life itself," replied Alyonka, stretching out a twig covered in delicate brown bark. "You've flown up higher than the angels." "But those aren't angels," said Kozlov, pointing at the unknown figures. "Yes, they are," Alyonka nodded. "And you are their master!" Kozlov waved a twig. It bent in the dense air, and whipped one of the unknown figures. He was delighted. He thrashed the angels and they moaned. The louder they moaned, the more delighted he was. Kozlov looked at their faces, but could see only blurred, pink shapes. Suddenly he heard someone begin to laugh quietly. "I am your master," cried Kozlov. "You are," Alyonka agreed, licking her sticky fingers. The angels moaned, but Kozlov could still hear laughter. "Your faces, I want to see your faces!" he shouted, waving his switch. But the angels laughed all the more, and wouldn't show him their faces.

* * *

Petrovna had a little grandson, Vasya. His hands were still baby-plump. His parents brought him from the north for three months in the summer. Vasya did not like the south. The heat made him sweat. The freckles on the pink-veined skin of his eyelids were magnified by the lenses of his glasses. "Why don't you go down to the seaside, Vasya?" Petrovna would say. "The sea will still be there another day," Vasya would reply. He had a red toy car with only one wheel. Its paint was chipped and kept peeling off in star shapes. You could see the rusty metal underneath. A flowering lilac bush stood outside the window. Vasya breathed in, his nostrils flaring. Through the window he could see Kozlov's wax figures. He remembered how he had once taken a bite out of one of the apples.

Vasya and Petrovna sat in the garden. The air was blue with lilac flowers. On the table stood a jar of honey, with a wasp suspended in it, as if
petrified in amber. Petrovna gazed tenderly at her grandson. She watched
the lilac swaying above his downy head; a thread of honey trickled from
the wide-mouthed jar onto the oilcloth, and Vasya smeared it with his finger. But suddenly the color of the lilac darkened. It began to shed its
flowers, and Vasya stared fixedly ahead of him through the thick lenses of
his glasses. Petrovna looked around and saw Alyonka. Alyonka looked at
the lilac flowers and they turned black and began to fall from the tree,
and when she looked at Vasya, he froze.

                    *   *   *

Kozlov woke up. Dust hung in the slanting beams of light. He flung
open the stuffy window and made up his mind. I'll go and see Asya.
Maybe she'll put me out of my misery! On the way he met Vasya who was
holding a sulphur yellow butterfly by the tips of its wings.

"Hey!"

Kozlov stopped. Vasya, his brow wrinkled, looked up at Kozlov, wondering whether to speak or remain silent. "Someone was looking for you,"
he said finally. "A ti-i-iny little girl. And all the lilac in our garden wilted."
He pulled the wings off the sulphur yellow butterfly and the whiskery
body fell onto the dusty ground. "She makes everything go still."

"Alyonka," whispered Kozlov.

"That's her," Vasya agreed, stamping on the wormlike body of the butterfly.

"She wants to suck the soul out of my body," said Kozlov. "She promises me all kinds of riches in return."

"I expect she's lying," said Vasya.

                    *   *   *

Kozlov went to Zina's house. In the garden stood an empty table, its
sticky oilcloth marked with tea stains. An apple tree branch with live roots
was stuck in a jar. A sheep stood bleating beneath the canopy of the porch.

Kozlov went inside. The walls of old Zina's house were decorated with
postcards: two doves holding a heart with the words *Love me as I love you!*

written in red letters. There was another one of a pink man kissing a woman with ebulliently curly hair. On one wall hung a plush carpet, its pile worn bald in patches. The carpet depicted a Circassian mounted on a horse, with a white-skinned, screaming girl flung across the saddle. The Circassian was urging his steed on toward the Caucasus mountains, which could be seen in the misty green distance. A dark wooden cupboard had sprays of lilac thrust into the crack between its doors. On the dressing table stood a gold-rimmed dish with black hairpins, sunflower seed shells, and a toothless comb. There was also a glass vase filled with lilacs of various colors, the reflection of the lilacs in the mirror turned the small bouquet into a large bush. A life full of joy, thought Kozlov, and he longed for his own former existence. There was a smell of warmth in the room. Zina came in.

"I've come," said Kozlov. "You promised you'd help me."

Zina looked at Kozlov and sighed. Streaks of gray showed in his thinning hair. Kozlov's mouth felt dry and cracked.

"It's bad, very bad," whispered old Zina. "Your heart's only just beating."

She opened the doors of the cupboard and the sprays of lilac fell to the floor. She disappeared inside the cupboard and emerged with a bunch of gray, unrecognizable herbs and a greasy pack of cards.

"You make sure you shut your window at night," said old Zina, sitting Kozlov down at the table. "Otherwise the fog will come creeping in—and there's no knowing what kind of perfidious power it can bring."

"I dreamed of angels," said Kozlov.

"Angels don't fly in the fog."

She spread the cards out on the table in groups of three, searching for Kozlov among the kings.

"That will be you," she said, pointing to a king with a red heart in the corner. Kozlov stared attentively at the card. The king looked exactly like him: the narrow-chinned face, the same green eyes, only the crown on his head and the round, red cheeks were different.

"Why does he have hooves?" Kozlov asked.

"For heaven's sake!" Zina exclaimed. "Those aren't hooves, he's holding a scepter."

Kozlov and the king exchanged glances.

Zina placed the king in the middle of the table and selected a card at random from the pack. She left it face down.

"That's what lies under your heart," she said. Kozlov examined the back of the card: There were two red lions, spattered with blood, fighting.

"These are your thoughts," Zina continued. "And this is what you crush underfoot."

Kozlov was surrounded by a ring of snarling lions.

"When are you going to turn the cards over?" He was frightened.

Zina turned the greasy cards face up. Beneath Kozlov's heart lay the queen of diamonds. It's Asya! he thought. On top of his heart was an angry, black queen. She was marked with the same little heart as Kozlov's king, only it was black, and above it protruded the hilt of a dagger. The queen had the round, red cheeks of all playing card characters. Her skin was baby white, but covered in wrinkles. Kozlov did not like her. What's she doing on top of my heart? he thought. Her hair was black and shiny like tar and hung down in tresses.

"Beneath your heart, there is love," Zina began to explain. "And on top of your heart—anguish. You're being tempted by visions that are trying to make you forget your love." Reflections of the little black hearts and the dagger hilts sticking out of them flickered in Kozlov's eyes. "If you give in to temptation, you will perish."

"I'll go and see Asya," said Kozlov.

On the blue-flowered pink wallpaper of Zina's room someone had drawn a shaggy devil. He was covered with long hair and had a long, naked tail. It was one of Vasya's efforts. The devil held the end of his tail in one of his hands and waved it like a whip or a branch of an apple tree. Kozlov happened to look out of the window. He thought he glimpsed Alyonka, shimmering in the green light, her braided hair hanging over her sunburned shoulders. The lilac on the dressing table withered and turned black.

"I'm going to go and see Asya anyway," he said. Suddenly he began to sob loudly.

Zina was frightened. "What is it?" She caught sight of the charred lilac in the mirror. "Oh, you poor boy, you poor lad." She placed a bunch of gray herbs in Kozlov's feeble hand. "Make them into tea and drink it before you go to bed. It'll help you sleep."

Kozlov walked slowly out of the house. Zina discreetly made a sign of the cross over his departing figure, and the back of his head prickled. The curtains at the window lifted slightly, as if someone was breathing on them.

*   *   *

Petrovna held out her hand to Vasya. He ignored her. He dropped his toy car in the grass and clung to the apple tree with one hand.

"Come along now, Vasya!" Petrovna pleaded.

Vasya refused to move and continued to cling to the apple tree. It swayed and creaked and dry petals, brown around the edges, sprinkled down. Some of the petals fell behind his glasses, and suddenly he could no longer see his car lying in the grass. "Wait, Granny!" Vasya cried. He rubbed his glasses with his fingers, stamped the petals into the grass, and picked up his car. His hand was red and swollen.

"Aren't you going to come with me, eh?" Petrovna asked tenderly.

"All right then, I'm coming," Vasya agreed, rubbing his puffy hands together.

* * *

"Oh Zina, it's dreadful! Dreadful!" Petrovna called through the open door. Zina was sweeping up the crushed herbs and thinking about Kozlov. Petrovna pulled Vasya into the room after her. He stood in the bright square where the light from the window fell on the floor, puffing and panting.

"Alyonka came by," cried Petrovna. "All the flowers withered! Vasya was turned to stone! What's going to happen next?"

Vasya's glance fell upon the devil on the pink wallpaper. "Why did I make such a mess of his tail?" He retrieved a blue pencil from the pocket of his leggings and began to cover the tail with long hair until it began to resemble a palm frond.

Petrovna noticed the charred lilac on the dressing table. "Did that wither too?" she asked eagerly.

Zina nodded. "Don't worry, she wasn't looking for Vasya." Zina pointed to Kozlov's window. "He's as good as done for."

* * *

Kozlov walked along sobbing. He felt as if he was looking at the world through water, nothing was clear. With his fish's eyes he walked past his neighbor Vanya, who stood holding a handful of glass beads. "One ruble each, come and buy!" he shouted. Kozlov could discern tall-stemmed, yellow flowers growing in the grass. Their heads were bowed, as if in confession of guilt. Kozlov saw clearly that a viscous, red liquid was dripping down the stems. The tranquil vine leaves draped over the fence outside

Asya's house cast irregular polygons of shade. Kozlov noticed a stirring beneath the leaves. Something blue was struggling to break out into the open. Then from under the leaves, there emerged pale blue petal edges. The petals opened out, curled at the edges, revealing a reddish, forked sting.

"Asya!" he shouted. Asya appeared from among the foliage. There was something strange about her.

"What do you want?" asked the girl.

"I've been searching for you for such a long time," said Kozlov. "You should pull off those flowers growing on your fence, they're creeping closer and closer toward you."

Asya turned to look at the tranquil vine leaves. They shivered in the wind.

"There! Look!" shouted Kozlov, and he hurled himself toward the fence. "They're flowering, and it means I'm going to die!"

He tore at the tendrils of vine, threw them down, and stamped on them. Asya looked at him in fear.

"Don't you understand?" Kozlov shouted. "She's bewitched me! She's everywhere! She made me turn my icon to face the wall! She even looked out at me from the playing cards."

"Well, there's nothing here!" said Asya. "You've probably got a fever. Your forehead's perspiring."

"She comes to me in my dreams. She's torturing me!" And suddenly Kozlov looked at Asya and saw that her pale little face was turning swarthy, that her cheekbones stood out clearly, and her mouth was burning red.

"Alyonka!" he cried. "I hate you!"

"Oh, this is terrible!" whispered Asya, running into the house.

When she was calm again, she saw that the lilac bushes in the garden were all broken, the grass by the fence trampled, and most of the leaves had been blown off the vine. Beneath the leaves on the ground, Asya thought she could see something dark blue, sighing.

*   *   *

"It isn't summer yet!" said Vasya, snapping off a branch of lilac. "Nothing's growing properly ... apart from those stinking flowers."

He was looking around Kozlov's garden. The branches of the trees were densely woven, but through gaps in the foliage Vasya could see Kozlov's window, and in it the reflection of the sky. Yellow-headed arrows glinted in the grass, and instead of sticky sap, a viscous, red liquid trickled down their stems.

"I want it to be summer!" said Vasya, and stamped his feet.

*   *   *

Kozlov walked down to the sea along the embankment. The station platform was lined with old women selling bunches of lilac, paper cones of sunflower seeds, and boiled potatoes garnished with brown curls of onion. The moment the trains stopped, hands holding rubles would stretch out of the murky windows. The old women seized the rubles with nimble, swarthy fingers, and the pale hands would withdraw again, clutching blue bunches of lilac, paper twists of sunflower seeds, candy in the shape of cockerels on thin wooden sticks. Some of the hands that stretched out held no money. They just wanted to touch the southern air.

Kozlov walked down to the sea. Brown cores of last year's apples lay among the gray pebbles. Spilled sunflower seeds shone like tears. The air was sweet and heavy. Kozlov threw off his sweaty shirt, letting the sun beat down on his skinny back. I'm not afraid, he thought, looking at the sea. But he couldn't bring himself to go into the water. First the sun warmed him, then it began to burn. His scorched body begged for mercy. Kozlov dragged himself across the burning shingle into the shade.

*   *   *

Rays of sunlight slanted through the open windows. Dust hung gray in the beams of light. Dear God! Bring him to his senses! thought Asya. She felt sorry for Kozlov. She dreamed that someone warm and white was wrapping her in something warm and white, whispering softly in her ear, "Don't be afraid ... don't be afraid." When she woke up, the words "Don't be afraid" still seemed to hover in the midday air.

*   *   *

A cloud wafted in the sky like a feather.

The evening sky flamed blue and yellow. An orange moon rose above the knotted juniper bushes. Kozlov's burned body ached, but the cool of night soothed the pain. He was overjoyed that night had come. Only one thing disturbed him: in the sky, among the liquid, feathery clouds, rode an old man. He waved to Kozlov and pointed toward the castle. "Go, Kozlov!" he said. "You are expected."

Slowly Kozlov climbed the hill. A cemetery stretched along both sides of the road. Its fence shone white. A gateway rose up in an arch. Vines covered the ruined castle. Its gray stone walls were interspersed with red bricks. Kozlov's sunburned skin was sore and peeling. The skin revealed underneath was pink and childlike. I'm like a snake, thought Kozlov.

Alyonka appeared through the castle gates. She wore a rough, yellow shirt, open at the neck, and Kozlov could see the pale hollow between her collarbones. At night Alyonka's face was milky-pale and smelled sourish, like kumiss. Blue, branching veins shone through her delicate skin and one of her cheeks was marked with a thin scratch. She reached out and touched Kozlov and a strange sensation of warmth ran through him.

"Mine," said Alyonka, unbuttoning her coarse blouse. Kozlov was transfixed by the fluttering movement of her collarbone.

"People say your legs are covered in scales," he whispered. "They say you come to us from out of the water."

"That's what they say," Alyonka agreed, leaning toward Kozlov and kissing him on the dimple of his cleft chin. Kozlov could see Alyonka's narrow feet and her rounded toes.

"I'm going to die," he whispered.

"Yes, you're going to die," she agreed.

With the tip of his tongue, Kozlov licked the pink nails on her white toes, the arch of her foot; he kissed the dried-out mussel scratches on her slim knees. "My ruin," Kozlov was still whispering.

"I'm your ruin … your ruin," Alyonka repeated. Alyonka was like kumiss.

"I love you," she whispered, pressing her lips to the tanned skin of Kozlov's shoulders. Kozlov moaned with pain, but it was a pain filled with joy. Kozlov looked at Alyonka, and Alyonka looked like a scream so intense that it pierces your ears.

"I am dead," whispered Kozlov as he collapsed onto the grass. Out of the corner of his eye he could see Alyonka's yellow shirt and a bright shred of sky. He saw how, in a split second, Alyonka's black hair tumbled down above the grass, and how the tips of the grass brushed against her ankles.

"You are dead," said Alyonka, as she walked away through the castle gates. And Kozlov could hear the sea sobbing below the castle.

*   *   *

Alyonka flung open the garden gate. The night was almost over. As she went into the house a moth brushed against her face. It blundered about in the yellow circle of the lamp. The triangular patch of light bleached the dark blue walls and shone on the edge of the table, where rock-hard peas—yellow, white, and watery green—were scattered. A mirror with a broken corner hung on the wall reflecting half of Alyonka's face: a black eye, the curve of a cheekbone, and a pink, long-lobed ear. The reflection hinted at a cleft chin. Alyonka poured water into a basin, into which she tossed three dried peas. The water turned red. Alyonka saw Kozlov lying helplessly at the gates of the castle.

"When morning comes he will awake."

Into the room, through the wide open window flew Asya: a tiny, transparent figure, scarcely bigger than a matchbox. She stood on the table and appeared to be asleep.

"Wake up," said Alyonka. The spirit opened her eyes. "In the morning you will remember nothing of what you have seen."

A vision of the stifling town floated in the red water. Kozlov languished in the stifling heat. And then she saw the sea, and angels, and the road stretching away to the castle, and then Kozlov, lying in the grass. The spirit struggled sobbing above the dish. She wanted to fly away, but could not tear herself free.

"You will die too," said Alyonka, and very gently she blew. At this Asya's spirit trembled and flew out of the window like an autumn leaf.

"I can't live without you," said Alyonka, looking through the water at the motionless Kozlov. "But I can't live with you either!"

Suddenly she flung herself sobbing onto the bed, but as quickly her sobs subsided and she became calm.

*   *   *

The following morning a goatherd wearing trousers rolled up to his knees and rubber flip-flops leaned over Kozlov. The goats, with ropes around their necks, gazed yearningly at their master. Kozlov lay prone, his face buried in the grass. His skin was cracked and covered in blisters. He's given himself a nasty dose of sunburn, thought the goatherd. His skin's all split! Just then Kozlov gave a moan.

"Are you alive?" The goatherd was astonished.

"No," Kozlov croaked. "I'm dead."

*   *   *

A one-legged old man stood at the door of the church, holding a cap in his outstretched hand. A number of copper coins shone in the cap. The old man squinted in the sunlight, turning his eyes into a single deep wrinkle. "Please give." The old women who passed reached out daintily and looked into the cap.

A red-cheeked old priest with a rosy bald head swung a censer in the half-empty church. The candles crackled faintly as they burned. The wax melted into curling snakes. The priest intoned, "Eloi, Eloi, Christ cried out. Lama sabachthani?"—which is, being interpreted: "My God! My God! Why hast thou forsaken me?"

Kozlov arrived at the church gates.

"Please give?" asked the old man and Kozlov pulled out a handful of change. The old man was squinting at the bright sunlight. "Infidels and witches, in the church porch."

*　　*　　*

The sound of singing wafted out of an open window:
"I slept, and then I had a dream ..."
A woman was singing in a high, cracked voice. Uncle Sasha, the accordionist, walked past, his medals clinking on their red and black ribbons. Cooks in scorched overalls, almost hidden by clouds of smoke, grilled kabobs. A half-grown chicken hurled itself under the wheels of a bicycle. A barefoot porter walked past, carrying a crate of beer.
A storm hung in the air.
Summer was on its way.

*　　*　　*

The sea waves had licked away the sign saying "Do not walk along the waterfront during storms!" Sasha, the accordionist, walked slowly along the breakwater. His medals shone in the sun. It seemed as if the sun's rays were trying to pierce his chest, but were deflected by the metal. White-frilled waves rolled against the breakwater. Uncle Sasha looked around with a glassy stare. He pumped the red pleated accordion. A march tune burst from the bellows. The sea sobbed. Uncle Sasha, the accordionist, walked to the end of the breakwater and stepped into the waves.

*　　*　　*

Kozlov was afraid of summer. He knew that its one aim was to burn him. Winter's all right, he thought to himself. It leaves you in peace, you can get used to the rain, and then all of a sudden it's summer. The heat.

*　　*　　*

Petrovna was putting Vasya to bed. She noticed how loud his breathing was, and his short-sighted pupils were dilated. Outside it was getting dark and Petrovna's eyelids were drooping, but Vasya was still awake.

"Why aren't you asleep?" Petrovna asked.

"I'm thinking," Vasya replied, spinning the rubber tire of his toy car.

Finally Vasya fell asleep. He dreamed he saw a green meadow with a peg standing in the middle of it to which a shaggy, black goat was tethered. The black goat looked at Vasya with red eyes.

"Bearded billy goat!" shouted Vasya. "You're not going to chase me!"

The goat strained at the rope, but the peg was driven deep into the ground. Vasya tore a switch from a tree, beat the goat, and jumped onto his back. At that moment a goat-catcher and a goatherd emerged from the bushes. The former carried a whip, the latter a bunch of grass. The goatherd held out his bunch of grass to the goat but just as the animal stretched out to reach it, the goat-catcher lashed at him with his whip. The goat jumped into the air. Vasya laughed. He dug his heels into the goat's sides and the goat ran around the peg on the end of his rope. Behind him ran the goat-catcher and the goatherd.

*   *   *

Old Zina awoke. The night was stifling. She had dreamed that someone was knocking on her roof. She went out into the yard and saw Kozlov, sitting by her brick chimney stack. "Why are you making that kicking noise on the roof?" Zina inquired. "It's because I've got such heavy shoes on," Kozlov replied. "Well, just take them off, and pipe down a bit." Kozlov undid the laces of his shoes and threw them down onto the grass. Zina saw that his feet ended in white hooves.

*   *   *

Kozlov bent over Asya. "I would like to remember you," he whispered, as if in farewell. "But you're already quite transparent."

"I haven't got much strength left," Asya replied. "Only a little flicker of life."

"So she's killed you too," said Kozlov. "You as well as me."

*   *   *

Kozlov flung open the door of his stuffy room. The wax figures were covered in a fine layer of dust, but Kozlov did not even glance at them. He melted some wax and began to mold a body, a tiny figure hardly bigger than a matchbox.

"Alyonka ... Alyonka," he whispered again and again.

The body was small and lithe and smelled faintly of kumiss. Kozlov picked up a long, metal needle. The body shrank and looked at him beseechingly; he pierced it right through the heart. The point of the needle stuck out through the wax back.

*   *   *

Old Zina awoke to find herself thinking about Alyonka. What's she up to now? Sending me dreadful dreams like this! I'm going to go and see her, even if I am scared. But when she opened Alyonka's door, she saw that the room was empty. All that remained were some multicolored peas and a little heap of ash lying on the floor.

Summer came.

The sun burned Kozlov's skin.

Translated by Rachel Osorio

About the Authors and Editors

Ludmilla Ulitskaya, b. 1943 in Bashkiria. A geneticist by training, Ulitskaya graduated from Moscow State University in 1967 and briefly worked in her specialty while also raising a family. Left jobless after her research laboratory ran afoul of Soviet authorities, Ulitskaya eventually joined the Moscow Jewish Theater in an advisory capacity and began writing fiction. She came to the public's attention only during glasnost, however, when her stories and novellas began appearing in Russia and abroad.

Permeated with a tolerant, humorous warmth, Ulitskaya's stories exemplify that strand of the humanist tradition that neither denounces nor deifies, but attempts to understand human psychology in its infinitely varied manifestations. Reconciliation to and acceptance of what cannot be fathomed or altered take on the status of a philosophical position in Ulitskaya's fictional universe. Although anti-Semitism, violence, and extreme or "anomalous" acts of intimacy occur frequently in that universe, they never serve a sensationalist function. Instead, they provide shadowy passages into characters' troubled psyches and invaluable opportunities for self-transcendence.

Ulitskaya's novella *Sonia* was shortlisted for the Russian Booker Prize in 1993; collections of her prose have appeared in French and German translation; and a volume of her selected fiction is slated for publication by the New Press in the United States. The surprising fact that a Russian publisher only recently (1994) brought out a similar collection in the original Russian affords a dispiriting insight into Russia's current publishing practices.

Svetlana Vasilenko, b. 1956 in Kapustin Yar—the Russian equivalent of Cape Canaveral. Raised in the security zone of the Soviets' chief military site for launching rockets, Vasilenko early sensed her existentialist identity as a child of the atomic age. She likewise aligned herself from childhood with the female half of the world. Vasilenko, significantly, is her mother's surname, and one of her strongest emotional supports during childhood and adolescence was her paternal grandmother, whom she visited annually in Petersburg.

After moving to Moscow, Vasilenko held a variety of jobs, including those of fruit hauler and postwoman, before completing the creative writing program at the Gorky Literature Institute (1983) and a series of courses in film directing (1989). By then she had acquired a modest fame through the publication of her first piece of fiction, "Going after Goat Antelopes," which received a prize as the best story of 1982. Since glasnost, Vasilenko's fiction has appeared primarily in collections of women's prose, and the modesty of her output may be partly explained by her increasing professional involvement in video and film.

A finely tuned sense of the poetic and associative powers of language, as well as an aura of suspended fatality, marks Vasilenko's prose, which frequently records familial and "romantic" relations at a moment of epiphany or decisive choice.

Lydia Ginzburg, b. 1902 in Odessa, d. 1990 in St. Petersburg. A literary scholar, art historian, essayist, and author of a synthetic genre of prose that straddles the boundaries of essay and fiction, Ginzburg witnessed and participated in the major historical and political upheavals that have wracked her country in the twentieth century. During her studies at the Petersburg Institute of the History of Fine Arts, she maintained close contacts with those Formalist critics who were her classmates: Tynianov, Tomashevsky, and Eikhenbaum, and virtually all of her work has close connections with their influential approach to genres and their evolution.

Debuting as a critic in 1926, Ginzburg throughout her long life produced such theoretico-critical studies as *On Lyric Poetry* (1964), *On Psychological Prose* (1971), and *On the Old and the New* (1982), as well as historico-philosophical recollections (*Notes of a Siege Survivor*) and works that defy classification, such as the narrative contained in this collection. A profound sense of history and concrete detail, along with a rather convoluted style that simultaneously seeks precision and comprehensiveness, characterize her writing.

The moral and cultural weight of Ginzburg's biography and persona elevated her to the status of a cultural guru in the last decade of her life. During the 1980s, in fact, she acted as mentor to several younger generations of writers (including the poet Elena Shvarts) and critics in St. Petersburg. From the perspective of gender, Ginzburg's lesbianism and her experience of regularly being the sole woman in the all-male company of renowned intellectuals present a fascinating sociopsychological case.

Galina Scherbakova, b. 1932 in Dzerzhinsk. After teaching and traveling all over the Soviet Union as a journalist, in the 1970s Scherbakova began devoting herself full time to fiction. Financial need prompted her to supplement her family income during the 1980s by writing film scenarios.

Her first publication, the novella titled *You Wouldn't Dream of It* (1979), won her instant popularity and later was transformed into a wildly successful film. Since then, her narratives have appeared in a broad range of mainstream journals. Although moral choices in personal and professional life, the psychology of love, and the effects of time's passage continue to remain the focal concerns of Scherbakova's fiction, since glasnost the humor, outspokenness, and sexual explicitness of her writing have increased. Especially in the last few years she has spotlighted tensions between generations that have undergone dramatically different formative experiences and emerged with conflicting values. Translations of her prose in France,

Germany, Finland, the United States, Hungary, and Bulgaria suggest that readers across national boundaries appreciate her irony, skill in economically delineating character and situation, and eye for eloquent detail.

Irina Polyanskaya, b. 1952 in Kasli, the Urals. Born at a research facility for educated prisoners to which her chemist-parents were sent after serving out their terms in the Kolyma labor camps under Stalin, Polyanskaya had a peripatetic childhood on account of her parents' inability to find permanent jobs once their exile ended. Doubtless as a consequence of this unsettled way of life, domestic settings in Polyanskaya's fiction project a mood of emotional instability.

While publishing items in local papers from the age of fourteen, Polyanskaya studied drama, then briefly worked as a journalist, before enrolling in the Gorky Institute of World Literature (IMLI) in Moscow as a poetry student. Like countless other Russian writers, she accepted a series of menial jobs to eke out a living, including those of hospital orderly and watchwoman.

Polyanskaya's prose started appearing in mainstream journals in 1983, her most ambitious and longest work to date being her novella *Mitigating Circumstances* (1989). Psychological insight and lyrical nuance characterize her narratives, the majority of which trace familial relationships and examine the isolation of individuals who yearn for yet cannot forge fulfilling or meaningful human ties.

Nina Sadur, b. 1950 in Novosibirsk. Born to a family of intellectuals in a Siberian working-class neighborhood, Sadur early knew the pain of alienation and the excitement of the unknown. An insatiable reader from an early age, she wrote poetry and prose for her own pleasure before enrolling in Moscow's Gorky Literary Institute, where she studied drama.

Postgraduate (1983) efforts to publish her prose and drama proved unsuccessful, even after she was accepted into the Writers' Union in 1989. Sadur's talent started receiving recognition only in the 1990s.

Sadur's fiction and plays draw on folklore to convey an existential vision of a world beyond our control. Indebted to Gogol and the tradition of the grotesque, Sadur manages to synthesize humor, terror, and a palpable sense of complex psychology, whether it be in such absurdist plays as *Red Paradise* (1988), which has affinities with the Theater of Cruelty, or in the cycle of stories titled *Percipient*, reminiscent of Poe and the tradition of Gothic horror, to which the selections in this volume belong.

Not only works steeped in fantasy and enigma but more transparently accessible narratives, such as the novella *South* (1989), which traces the subtle shifts in its protagonist's mental and psychological processes, have earned Sadur a following among the urban reading public. Her stage adaptations from other authors, including *Panochka,* which reworks Gogol's tale "Viy," tend to emphasize the dark, incalculable powers that guide our actions and perceptions. Indeed, Sadur claims that the world as we know it lies in thrall to the devil.

Ksenia Klimova, b. 1958 in Moscow. A journalist currently on the regular staff of the weekly *Capital* (Stolitsa), Klimova is known less for fiction than for her articles and essays. Indeed, the two pieces included in this collection more properly belong to sketches than fictional narratives. They document contemporary social mores, particularly Klimova's preoccupation with persons with disabilities, who remain largely unacknowledged and marginalized in Russia.

Herself a member of the Society for Disabled Athletes, Klimova has indefatigably agitated for changes in Russia's attitude toward people with disabilities. These efforts are part of her general commitment to combating social inequities in a system that has little regard for individual needs.

Marina Palei, b. 1955 in St. Petersburg. Palei's professional training in medicine ill prepared her for the horrors at various levels of the medical profession, including those of orderly and nurse. She abandoned hospitals for a succession of primitive jobs as a cleaner, stoker, watchwoman, and—anomalously—model, before joining the Gorky Literature Institute in Moscow, from which she graduated with honors in 1990.

Since then Palei has earned a reputation as an original prosaist who fully exploits the Russian language's rich potential in stories that combine minutely observed realia with vivid imaginative flights. Her love of film, fantasy, circuses, and bizarre costumery both spring from and draw her to the cinema of Fellini, one of her cultural icons. His *Nights of Cabiria* (1956) serves as the chief source of reference for her major narrative, the novella *Cabiria from the Bypass* (1992), from which the selection in this volume is extracted.

As a representative of New Women's Prose—stylistically experimental fiction by the younger, post-Stalin generation of writers—Palei employs irony and verbal play in her exploration of women's physical, spiritual, and emotional experiences. *Cabiria* offers an unusual portrait of a sexually insatiable female whose libidinous energy ultimately proves to be synonymous with the life force itself.

Yekaterina Sadur, b. 1973 in Novosibirsk. Daughter of Nina Sadur, with whom she left Siberia for Moscow in 1985, Yekaterina Sadur started writing and translating from French while still an adolescent. Fascinated by the forbidden, deformed, and mysterious, as well as compassionate toward the old, disabled, and victimized, she captures extreme or borderline physical and psychological states in a manner reminiscent of Gogol, Dostoyevsky, and Sologub.

She reportedly has just completed a full-length novel titled *Shifting from Shadow into Light.*

The Editors. **Ayesha Kagal** is Moscow correspondent for the *Times of India.* **Natasha Perova** is editor of the acclaimed Slavic literary journal *Glas* and lives in Moscow. **Helena Goscilo** is professor of Slavic languages, literatures, and cultures at the University of Pittsburgh.

About the Book

THE SELECTIONS IN THIS ANTHOLOGY overturn Soviet-era taboos with a vengeance. First published in the aftermath of Mikhail Gorbachev's liberalizing reforms, these stories revel in the basic commonalities of human experience even as they reassert a peculiarly Russian belief in the spiritual, mystical, and supernatural. They satirize Soviet literary canons while exploring a full gamut of styles, from neorealism to magico-folkloric fantasy.

Included in the volume are works by well-known pioneers of the "new women's prose" as well as by less familiar talents. Bold in thematic conception and stylistic experimentation, their stories are socially engaged—in the classic Russian literary tradition—and yet at the same time intensely personal.

While many of these writers share a feminist outlook, their perspectives are vastly disparate and often steeped in a peculiarly post-Soviet irony: In one story, for example, a girl with no money and no prospects of earning any turns to prostitution—and fails because of her lack of entrepreneurial talent.

Yet common to all are recurrent and interwoven motifs of self-discovery, sexual power, emotional attachment, social alienation, and vulnerability to uncontrollable forces. The ambiguous ways in which these themes are played out reveal much about what has changed and what remains at the core of a complex culture in transition.